CASSY ROOP

VOID

Cassy Roop is a fitness goddess by day and romance author by night. When she isn't writing furiously on her next novel, she's making books look beautiful inside and out as a graphic designer. She has an unhealthy obsession with peanut butter, pedicures, and all things Les Mills group fitness, and has on occasion been seen purchasing clothes that aren't athletic apparel (although rare). She is also the author of *The Price of Love, Ashley's Bend, Figure Eight, Triquetra,* and *Axel Hitch.*

Books by Cassy Roop

The Price of Love
Ashley's Bend
Figure Eight
Triquetra
Axel Hitch
Void

VOID

VOID

Claire,
Love will always win ;)
♡ Cassy Roop

CASSY ROOP

First published by Cassy Roop, United States, 2015

VOID FIRST EDITION, FEBRUARY 2015
Copyright © 2015 by Cassy Roop

Without limiting the rights under copyright reserved above, no part of this publication may be reproduced, stored in or introduced into a retrieval system, or transmitted, in any form, or by any means (electronic, mechanical, photocopying, recording, or otherwise) without the prior written permission of both the copyright owner and the above publisher of this book.

This is a work of fiction. Names, characters, places, brands, media, and incidents are either the product of the author's imagination or are used fictitiously. The author acknowledges the trademarked status and trademark owners of various products, bands, and/or restaurants referenced in this work of fiction, which have been used without permission. The publication/use of these trademarks is not authorized, associated with, or sponsored by the trademark owners.

ISBN: 978-1508443360

Editing by Emma Mack and Desiree DeOrto
Cover design by Cassy Roop of Pink Ink Designs
Formatting by Pink Ink Designs
Front Cover Photo by Mandy Hollis Photography
Front cover model: Rainey Wilson

To Emma
Thank you for your *sparkle*.
And for believing in me.

ACKNOWLEDGEMENTS

Thank you to my mom for always having my back and helping me to believe I can do anything.

To my husband for the countless times he has took on the responsibility of watching our 3 spawn so that I can write or design. For always telling me I can do this when I want to quit sometimes.

To my street team, Cassy's Lassies for being rock solid. You are a very special group of ladies and I love you all wholeheartedly!

To my betas, Emma and Desi, Judi, Aleatha Romig, Harper Sloan, and my IndiePendent girls. This book wouldn't have been possible without you.

To my readers. It has been one hell of a year. Thank you from the bottom of my heart for your love and support.

CHAPTER ONE

Jericho/Nicola

I SAT IN A CHAIR THAT was four times bigger than I was. The man across from me pushed the glasses he wore back up the crooked bridge of his nose as we sat staring at each other. Mom and Dad sat in chairs right next to me, yet no one said anything. The old man, whose hair was parted over the side of his head to hide the balding, shiny flesh of his skin, never took his eyes off me as if expecting me to say something.

From the time I could remember, I was told I was different. My parents bragged about how I never cried as a baby, nor did I throw temper tantrums like a majority of children my age did. I never got angry or upset, and often wondered why people did cry or got upset.

When I was three and a half, my goldfish died. I remember the housekeeper, someone who often spent more time with me than my own mother, sat me on a chair to try to explain what had happened to Freddie. I shrugged her off and simply said "okay." When I was four, I fell off my bike and got a nasty gash on my right knee, but not once did I shed a tear. Sure, it hurt like crazy, but the pain wasn't unbearable.

This was the fourth time my parents had brought me to see this old man, who only seemed to ask me way too many questions, ones mainly about how I was feeling. Truth be told, I was often bored. I felt no connection to this man or any of the questions that he asked me.

"Nicola, do you ever feel sad?" The doctor asked as he scribbled something down on a piece of paper in front of him. I looked around the office noticing books that took up the entirety of one wall. A large window was adjacent to the books and on the two other remaining walls, were certificates or awards of some kind.

"Nicola? Do you understand what it means to be sad?" He asked me again when he noticed my attention had turned elsewhere. I nodded my head as I stroked the blonde yarn hair on the doll that sat in my lap.

"Have you ever been sad before? Have you ever been angry? Maybe at your mom or dad?" I looked over to my parents who were both looking at me as if they were anticipating my answer.

"No," I replied, telling them the truth.

The old man blew out a breath and removed his glasses from his face before wiping them and putting them back on.

"Nicola, you can go over to the table in the corner of the room and play with the blocks if you wish." I scooted off the chair and made my way over to the corner and proceeded to stack the blocks one on top of the other. I was thankful to be away from the old man's scrutinous stare, but I could still hear the conversation he was having with my parents, like I wasn't even in the room.

"Senator and Mrs. Forbes, obviously you know that Nicola is...*different*. That much is obvious because you chose to seek treatment for her."

"What do you think we could do to get her to...I don't know," I heard my father ask.

"Experience emotions? Because that is what seems to be lacking here. I will admit to you that she is the first case I have seen of this condition."

"What condition would that be?" Asked my mother in her sweet, poised, and well-practiced voice.

"Mrs. Forbes, we believe that Nicola has Alexithymia. It is where a person doesn't experience emotions like you and I do. You said yourself she didn't cry as an infant. She didn't react to some of the questions I have asked of her. She doesn't show any emotion. The only time I have seen her attempt to feel anything is when she is in physical contact with either one of you. Like when you hugged her before walking into my office, or when Mr. Forbes put his arm around her. It seems that she seeks physical contact in order to experience some feelings."

"You are saying she has no emotions?" My father asked as he leaned in towards the old man.

"I'm not saying she doesn't have *any*. I've watched her become a bit irritated at my questions. I've also seen hints of anger, but nothing that would cause a reaction out of her. She's just..."

"Void?" My father chimed in.

"I wouldn't say that necessarily, Senator. She just doesn't have the ability to process them as you and I do."

"What can we do to help her? I love my daughter, but it's like she's a complete stranger to me, Doctor. I want to experience all the things that a mother normally gets to with her daughter."

I didn't understand much of anything that my mother was

feeling at that moment, but I could hear the thickness in her voice and saw the tears in her eyes as I glanced up and saw my father take hold of her hand

"I understand that, Mrs. Forbes, but someone with her condition isn't treated easily. It could take weeks, or even years, for us to find her trigger."

"Trigger?" My parents both asked in unison.

"We need to do something that will set off a sort of chain reaction within her. Shock her into feeling something. Dig deep within her mind to find whatever it is that is keeping her from processing her emotions."

"What do you suggest?"

"Therapy. Hypnosis. It may take a while, but we will find your daughter hidden inside this shell of a person that you see before you. We just have to find the catalyst to bring her out."

My mother and father shook hands with the old man whom I knew now to be a doctor. I tried to read people's faces to better understand what they were feeling. My mother's eyes held a sense of vacancy within them. Almost like the fight she had been putting forth all my life suddenly left her. The relationship between my parents and me was never the same after the appointment. Hearing that you are void when you are only five years old wasn't something that someone my age really understood. I'm not sure I understood it, even as I grew up.

That visit turned into several sessions a week and another doctor later in the span of nearly twenty-four years. It was near the end of that twenty-fourth year in therapy that I found what, or should I say whom, my trigger was.

CHAPTER ONE

JERICHO/NICOLA

I SWEAR TO GOD if I had to fake one more orgasm today, my fucking head was going to explode. The heavy-set older man's sweat dripped onto my back as he tried ferociously to pound into me from behind. He was breathing so hard I feared that he would have a heart attack if he didn't lose his fucking load soon.

"Oh baby. Yeah, like that," I said in my well-practiced, seductive voice as I stared down at my nails while thinking about how I needed to schedule an appointment for a manicure. I needed to call my agent as well and tell her that if she scheduled me with anymore older men who had issues keeping it up long enough to even penetrate me, then I would throttle her.

This wasn't the way I envisioned my life playing out when I was younger. I never had the thoughts of "Hey, I'm going to be an escort when I grow up". I know what you are thinking. Escort, call girl, prostitute, whore. What's the difference? The difference is I don't care. I don't care about the men I fuck on a daily basis. I don't care that they might have families at home.

I don't care if they are some of the most powerful men in the news or the movies. The difference is I *just don't care.*

I don't experience many of the emotions or feelings that normal people do. I don't feel remorse. I don't feel emotional pain. I occasionally experience happiness, anger, and agitation, but I sure as hell don't feel love. It is something that I have always dealt with. I don't have the ability to identify or describe most of the everyday feelings that people experience. It is a condition I was born with. Gifted by the grace of God to live almost emotionless in this world of fucked up shit.

What is the one thing I do experience? Pleasure. Having sex is the only time that my mind and my body get to truly... *feel.* I guess you could say that is the reason behind my chosen profession. Having sex with men gives me a sense of tipping the hat at normalcy. Having someone buried deep within the walls of me is the only occurrence in which I don't feel like a stagnant, vacant person.

"Oh Jericho, your pussy is tighter than I remember," the man behind me said as he pounded into me with as much force as he could before he choked out his release. I tried to clench my inner muscles as tight as I could, willing for even a hint of an orgasm to follow.

Nope.

Nothing.

Fuck.

I hung my head in frustration as the man pulled out of me. Pressing my palms into the mattress, I lifted my chest and scooted to the side of the bed to put my clothes back on as the man walked to the bathroom to discard the used condom. I watched as his wrinkled, sagging ass jiggled with each step he took. I would have laughed if I felt some amusement. I would have shuddered in disgust if I knew what that felt like. Instead, I reached for the brown envelope on the side table and slipped it into my bag. Mr. Patterson was probably the easiest grand I made. It took him all of about five minutes when he could have had a whole hour. My policy though is once you cum, we're finished and the session was over. My clients know this. It kept shit from being personal and gave me a reason to high tail it the fuck out of there without having to actually engage in conversations I couldn't care less about.

"Always a pleasure, Jericho. I put a little something in your envelope this month. I will call and schedule another session with Alexandra soon."

"Thank you, Mr. Patterson," I said as I put my coat back on and slung my purse over my shoulder and exited the hotel room.

The frigid air of New York hit me in the face as I finally made my way outside. Walking to the curb, I threw my hand up in the air and allowed my leg to stick out a little from my coat. Sure it was cold enough to freeze my pussy lips shut, but I'd do anything to be able to get into a cab faster.

One of the familiar yellow cabs with the stereotypical Middle Eastern man pulled up to the curb, and I hurried my freezing ass into the car. After barking orders to the cabbie to take me to my downtown Manhattan apartment, my phone rang from inside my bag.

"Lexie," I said, addressing my agent.

"Are you done with Mr. Patterson already? Wow, that is a record, even for him," her throaty, cigarette smoke produced voice said through the speaker.

"Why the fuck do you keep scheduling him with me, Alexandra? It is a waste of a good orgasm that some other man could have given me. If I'm going to fuck someone, I should at least get the benefits of it."

"So I'm Alexandra now. Are you pissed? Wait. Never mind, forget I asked. Stupid question."

"Why are you calling if you knew I was with Mr. Patterson?"

"Because I know Mr. Patterson," she chuckled again while I stayed silent. "Ugh, you are such a hard ass, Jericho."

"I don't feel like playing games, Lex. I have nasty old man sweat on me, and all I want to do is curl up in my tub and give myself the much needed and deserved orgasm that your Mr. Patterson deprived me of tonight. Shit, it's been like four times in a row now. I think you should give him to one of the other girls."

"I tried, he wants you."

"Everyone wants me."

"Conceited much?"

"Get to the point."

"I need a favor. Kiki sprained her ankle or some shit and her client is refusing to cancel. He said to provide someone else, or he wouldn't require our services anymore."

"Not my problem, Lexie. I'm done. As I said, old man sweaty, wrinkled balls is reeking off of my body."

"Jericho, when do I ever ask you for a favor?"

"All the time."

"Point well made. But, please. He is one of our biggest clients. He pays well. Cash. Four grand."

I paused from our conversation to try and process what Lexie was saying. Four grand? That would cover my living expenses for the month plus have plenty left over to go shopping. But who the hell would pay that much money to be with a woman one time? The thought had me a little turned off. What if he was old like Mr. Patterson? What if he wanted some kinky animal shit going on?

"He isn't some sick motherfucker who is into bestiality and shit like that either, is he?"

"Oh my God, no. I would never send any of my girls to a client like that. You know very well that we screen all of our clients thoroughly. It is my job to protect you girls while you make money for yourselves as well as for me."

"Fine, but I want next weekend off, Lexie. I'm due for it."

"Deal. But there are a few stipulations."

"Why doesn't that surprise me?"

"The client requires complete anonymity. You have to wear a blindfold the entire time you are in session and will not be allowed to remove it until after he leaves."

"That I can do, Lex. At least that way I don't have to look at his wrinkles or his hairy ass and can imagine it's someone like Brad Pitt fucking the hell out of me."

"Good. I'll send his driver to your apartment in the next hour. Jer, this one is important. He is one of our highest paying clients. Do your best."

After hanging up, I wondered what kind of man I would have to deal with tonight. I was tired, even after my lack of orgasm with Mr. Patterson, but maybe I could get my much-needed release after all.

The cabbie pulled up in front of my apartment building, and I handed him a twenty through the slot in the glass that separated us. After telling him to keep the change, I made my way through the frigid New York air and into my building. The Camarades was a small set of 'for sale' condos housed just minutes from downtown Manhattan. They leaned more towards the luxury side of life and I found solace in knowing that I worked my ass off, literally, for the amenities of them. After a short elevator ride to the top floor, I produced the key from my purse and opened the door to my apartment. Sitting in the corner of the building, my apartment produced a beautiful view of the Manhattan skyline. Lights twinkled in through my windows, casting illuminating shadows across the dark, stained wood floors.

Flipping on the light, I sat my purse down on the bar and noticed the blinking red light on my answering machine. I didn't have time to listen to whoever was trying to reach me because I needed to get ready to meet Mr. Mystery Client. Padding into my bathroom, I turned the shower onto a temperature that wasn't quite scalding but would be hot enough for me to stand while I washed the remnants of Mr. Patterson from my body.

I did a double check to make sure my body was smooth everywhere, something that most of my clients preferred, I lathered up my preferred honeysuckle body wash onto a loofah and began scrubbing my skin. Using the same scented shampoo, I paid special attention to the long strands of my pin straight, blonde hair that contained highlights that only the expensive salons in town were able to produce.

I came from a very prestigious family. My father was a New Jersey senator, and my mother ran in the highest of social circles. From memory, they were good parents, but they weren't around much of my childhood, which was spent mostly in dormitories at a boarding school. Little did I know that not only were my parents broke, but they left me with absolutely nothing the day I was told my freshman year that they were both killed in a plane crash. Now, if I experienced emotions like normal people, I would have broken down and cried that day, but instead I felt nothing. My heart didn't ache, nor did I cry a single tear. Not even when they were placed in their coffins and lowered into the ground.

People take me for a hard ass. Someone who has no empathy for the things that would affect others. It isn't that I am doing it on purpose; I just have no control over what I do and don't feel, except when it comes to pleasure. When my parents left me with nothing, I mean they left me with *nothing*. The house, that I lived in, was foreclosed on. The boarding school that I went to kicked me out because my parents had failed to pay the tuition for several semesters. I was left with only the clothes on my back and the ability to not let my circumstances affect me.

That is why I became what I was today. I had to find a means of survival—a way to put food in my belly and a roof over my head. I had no family, my grandparents all having died before I was born. I had no siblings, no close relatives. I was completely and utterly alone. When I was approached in a dark alley, in a less than desirable neighborhood of somewhere in New York, by a man willing to give me fifty dollars for a few moments of time in my pussy, I said what the hell. When he gave me seventy because I was quote "the best pussy he had ever had", my profession was born. I worked for several years on my own and then I met Alexandra, my agent. She started booking me with clients instead of me finding them on my own. I got paid more money, she got her cut, and we were both happy.

I saved enough money for a down payment on my condo, and everything I have furnished it with since. So to me the little luxuries, like my favorite honeysuckle bath products, weren't taken for granted because they were a reminder of the struggle I went through to get to where I was today.

After rinsing off, I made my way down the hall to my bedroom. A normal person's closet might contain things like dress suits, several pairs of jeans and some cute tops. My closet was full of lingerie, and not just any lingerie, but the high-quality shit that I had to fuck five men for in order to afford. I picked my favorite red lace bra and garter from the hanger where they hung pristinely in my closet, made my way over to my bed and laid it down before I padded over to my dresser and produced a pair of red silk stockings that matched. Using a towel, I dried my hair and sat on my bed with my honeysuckle lotion and began to smooth the creamy concoction on my tanned skin.

The scent was soothing to me—giving me a sexy feel when I had to perform some not-so-sexy acts with some not-so-sexy clients. When the lotion was absorbed into my skin, I rolled the stockings up my legs to where they came to rest mid-thigh. Reaching over, I grabbed the lingerie and got dressed, adjusting my breasts in the cup of my bra to where they looked their perkiest. Alexandra said this client was important, and I had never been one to disappoint, but I was also intrigued by the anonymity he required. Was he some dirty rich man who tried to hide his extra-marital activities from his wife? Or was he some lonely old widow looking for a one-night companion?

Who gives a shit? It's four grand.

My phone beeped in my purse, and I retrieved it to find a text from my agent.

Lexie: Car will be there in 15. Don't be late. This client is big on promptness.

I rolled my eyes and threw the phone back into my purse. If this guy wanted an escort so badly, he could wait. I proceeded back down the hall to the bathroom where I blew out my towel-dried hair until it settled softly down to my mid-back. After applying a few finishing touches with the flat iron, I went to work creating a dark smoky eye and paired it off with a dark red lip that matched the color of my lingerie.

There was a knock on my condo door just as I slipped the black form fitting dress I chose into place and grabbed my purse from the kitchen island. Opening the door as I grabbed my dark trench coat, I was greeted by a gorgeous looking man dressed in a solid black suit with matching solid black tie and chauffeur hat. My eyes raked over the late twenty-something man and knew he couldn't be any older than I was. His broad shoulders and narrow waist made the black suit he wore fit his body perfectly. Dark, soft curls fell just above his brows and matched the small amount of scruff that graced his face. He was tall, possibly well over six feet as he towered over me even in my Louboutin heels. I admired his pert nose and strong jaw and smiled in appreciative delight at the deliciousness of the man that stood in front of me.

"Miss Lane?" He questioned as he bowed slightly in my direction.

"Ah, uh, yes. That's me," I stammered.

What the fuck? That has never happened before. Of course, it wasn't every day that a sexy as fuck man showed up at my door to pick me up either.

"I'm here to escort you to your destination," he extended an arm to me and I nodded, looping my arm through his and followed him out of the door. We turned so I could secure the lock with my key and then I proceeded to follow him down the corridor to the elevators. Heat from his body radiated through the suit he wore, causing a rise in my own body temperature. That was what I craved. Feelings. Pleasure being one of the only things that I was able to experience on a normal, everyday basis, quickly became my addiction.

We exited the elevator and made our way outside into the

freezing night air. I hugged my coat tighter around my body, and the man led me to the sleek, black car that waited at the curb. Releasing my arm to open the door, he guided me in, making sure I was comfortable before rounding it to get into the driver's seat.

"Where are we going?" I asked as I removed my purse from my shoulder and sat it on the seat next to me. It was then that I noticed the blindfold sitting there. I picked it up, letting the silky material slide across one hand.

"I'm not allowed to tell you, Miss Lane. I'm afraid that is a matter of discretion. Also, if you could place the blindfold over your eyes, I can begin to proceed to your intended destination."

"Of course," I replied, obeying his request as I put the blindfold in place. Securing it with a knot at the back of my head, I informed the driver it was okay to leave.

Someone was going through a lot of trouble to not let anyone know what he was about to do. He must be someone important, someone in the public eye, or someone very, very rich. I shrugged my shoulders. I didn't care who the fuck he was. The only thing I cared about was the four grand I was going to walk away with tonight.

CHAPTER TWO

ANDRIS

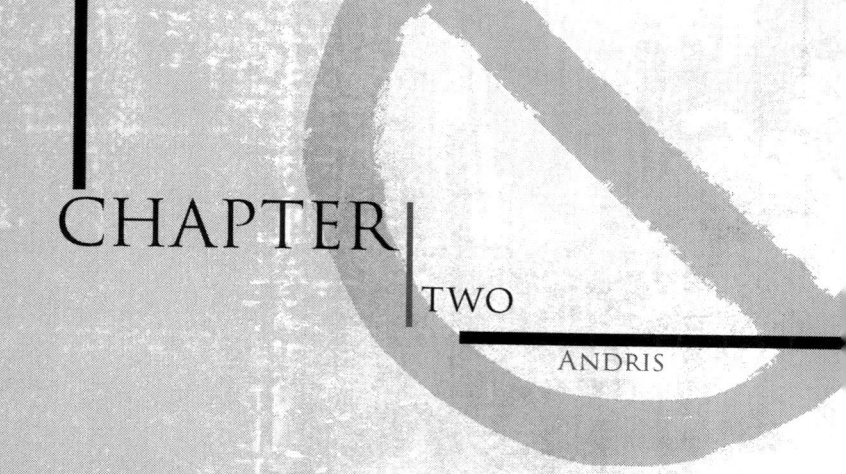

"ANDRIS, I NEED YOU to be sure that you are completely prepared to take over the task of running the clinic," my uncle told me for the tenth time in the last half hour. Gunn and Associates was one of the most prestigious and desired therapy clinics in Manhattan. Built by my grandfather from the ground up after he graduated from medical school, it quickly became one of the most sought out therapy clinics in greater New York. Our clients ranged from New York socialites to celebrities and real estate moguls. My uncle took over the practice when my grandfather retired over fifteen years ago, after nearly thirty years as a practicing psychiatrist. My uncle, Robert Gunn, had been running it since. That is, until next week when I would be taking over.

I graduated medical school four years ago and didn't think twice about going to work at Gunn and Associates. In fact, it was damn near expected of me from the time I was in diapers. My own father would have been the predecessor had he not died of a heart attack more than eight years prior, leaving me the next in line to control the Gunn throne. We had a few other practicing psychologists and psychiatrists employed at the clinic that weren't family, yet they were equally qualified for the job, but it was a family tradition that was not wavered from. A Gunn must be in control.

Most days my job was very rewarding, being able to help people who struggled with real mental disabilities, but there were times I wanted to throw my hands up and say *what the fuck* to those rich housewives who only saw me to get a refill on their Xanax prescriptions.

"Bobbie, we have been over this countless times. I'm ready. I've been bred to do this since birth. You of all people should know that."

"Yes, well, this isn't just a fucking walk in the park, Andris."

I rolled my eyes in frustration. My uncle was the demanding and controlling type, very much like my father and my grandfather. They often stayed at the clinic for hours after closing to pour over cases and required all the other associates and staff to do so as well, stating they weren't asking them to do anymore than what they were doing themselves. That is how I became a workaholic, never able to leave work at work when I got home. I would stay up for hours upon hours letting case situations run through my mind to the point that I probably needed therapy for myself.

"I understand that, Bobbie. I won't let you, grandfather, or my own father down."

"You also understand the consequences if this clinic fails, correct?" He asked, boring his nearly seventy-year-old eyes at me. I had looked up to this man at one time in my life, but after discovering the "secret involvement" that he had gotten not only our clinic, but our family into as well, I no longer viewed him as the once hero of my childhood. I wanted it to be my mission to get out from this involvement and rectify the situation that we were in, but I had no clue how to get there. It wasn't something I could do overnight, but instead needed to proceed into with caution, if I wanted to get out of it alive.

He nodded his silver, combed-over head at me and clapped me on one shoulder with the cup of his hand.

"Good. I have worked hard to provide for the lifestyle of this family, and I expect, *they* expect, for you to carry on with it."

My uncle walked out of my office, shutting the door behind him. This time next week, the clinic would officially and legally be signed over to me. There was nothing they could do to stop me from getting out of our 'situation'.

"Dr. Gunn? Your three-thirty is here," the receptionist said through the speaker on my phone.

"Thank you, Laura Lee. I'll be right out."

I picked up the file on my desk and looked at it to study my next patient.

Female.

Thirty-four.

Chronic depression.

Great. Another fucking socialite looking for her fix with nothing better to do than toss back a few downers in order to not have to experience her own reality. She was a former patient of my uncle's. He insisted that I take the case and not give it to one of the other doctors or therapists in the practice.

I closed the folder and rested my head on my fists momentarily as I allowed my doctoral mask to fall into place. I was nothing if not professional in my practice of therapy and medicine. My personal life was a different story, but here, I was respected. It was a high like no other, not being looked down upon by your peers, but admired for your hard work and your achievements. I could blame my asshole father for that desire. With him, I never felt like I was good enough. Bringing home all A's in high school and college didn't count unless I did the extra credit to get over the one hundred percent mark. My father pushed me to strive for excellence, to be the best of the best, and I found that I was constantly trying to earn his praise or approval.

Getting up from the chair, I walked to my office door and down the corridor to the waiting room. When I opened the door, I noticed that there were several patients waiting, but only one of them matched the description of my next appointment. She sat with one of her elegant legs crossed over the other, enough that her pencil skirt rose up to meet her mid-thigh. She was tanned, not one of the natural varieties, but the spa bought version. Her dark brunette hair was perfectly coifed into a chignon at the back of her head that left the creamy flesh of her neck exposed to admire.

I watched her for several moments as she flipped through the pages of a fashion magazine that she held in her hands. I tried to imagine what she was thinking about as she looked at the glossy pictures of perfectly thin and airbrushed women. She probably wanted to know how much it would set her husband back to do the procedure, so that she could look like those fake women.

I focused in on her face and noticed that her makeup was immaculate, not a lash or color out of place. The contours of her cheekbones were perfectly manicured by high dollar beauty products as she continued to stare at the pages.

As if some unspoken words had passed between us, she turned her head, and her striking gray eyes settled on mine. Smiling at me with perfect teeth, she closed the magazine and reached for the familiar Louis Vuitton bag nestled in the chair beside her.

"Mrs. Cardinelli?" I asked as she rose to her feet, long legs peeking out from the black skirt that accentuated her limbs, all the way down to the also familiar black and red high priced shoes.

"Yes," she replied with the elegant grace of a debutant.

"Right this way, please," I said, gesturing for her to come through the door and pointing down the hallway towards my office.

"Third office on the right," I directed, allowing her to walk in front of me. I got the full view of her perfectly rounded, and probably liposucked, ass as she swayed her hips seductively with each step. The violet blouse she wore was sheer enough to provide a small preview of the black lace bra that lay beneath the soft fabric.

Once we entered my office, I instructed her to have a seat in one of the plush chairs that faced my desk as I rounded it to take a seat in my familiar leather chair. Flipping open her folder once more, I reached for my pad of paper and a pen to take notes of the session.

"You are younger than I had originally pictured," she stated nonchalantly as she placed her purse on the floor at her feet. As she bent over, I couldn't help but notice the soft mounds of her cleavage that peeked out from the unbuttoned top of her shirt. A gold charm graced her slender neck, held on by a small gold chain. It was a crest of sorts, possibly familial or of something of significance towards her judging by the way she placed a small, delicate hand to her chest and played with the metal trinket at the base of her throat.

"Your uncle never told me."

"Is that a problem for you, Mrs. Cardinelli? I assure you that I am just as qualified, if not more so, than my uncle to provide your care. But if you prefer to see one of the other practitioners in the clinic, I can make arrangements."

She seemed a bit put off by the small amount of sternness in my voice, but quickly recovered with a sweet smile that could have brought any normal person to their knees.

"No, there is no issue. Just a little bit surprising."

I cleared my throat, clicking the tip of my pen over and over thinking about what my first move with this woman would be. She was obviously born and bred in the limelight, or she was trained to be the perfect embodiment of what a perfect housewife would entail. She had a hint of intelligence about her, as she sat up straight and placed her hands in her lap, ever the Stepford model of perfection. I wasn't going to lie, the woman was fucking sexy as hell, walking sin, and possibly more trouble than she was worth.

"So, Mrs. Cardinelli, I have read your file and it says here that you suffer from depression. What makes you feel that way?"

She tapped a perfectly manicured nail against the full, pouty, ruby red seam of her lips, contemplating my question. Her top teeth came out to bite the flesh of her lower one, letting the skin roll between them and then letting it go. It was a seductive move, something that made my cock twitch in my pants. My eyes darkened as I continued to watch her; the knowledge that she knew what she was doing didn't pass far from my mind.

"Well, Dr. Gunn,"

"Andris. Call me Andris."

"Well, Andris..." she started, letting my name roll along the tip of her tongue like warm liquid as she drew out each letter in a soft purr of her vocal chords, "My husband is a very demanded man. He often works very long hours. We have no children. I live in a fully staffed fourteen bedroom mansion, but I have never felt more alone in my life. There are only so many charity functions and galas I can attend before I start to lose my fucking mind. Having to put on a fake smile before all of the catty, gossip spreading women that run in my circles becomes tiresome and downright undesirable."

"So you are falling into bits of depression because you feel like you are alone?"

She stared at me out of the corner of her eye, watching my reaction and assessing her next choice of words.

"It is my husband's requirement that I come here, Andris. He doesn't like me to be unhappy, and in return, he gets what he wants."

I looked down at her file once more.

Spouse: Antonio Cardinelli.

Now it fucking clicked, I sighed in frustration. No wonder my uncle insisted that I take this specific client on personally.

"I take it you just put two and two together, Doctor."

Fucking great. The Stepford housewife in front of me was the wife of the man that my uncle got the family and the clinic involved with. He was also the man that I was determined to get away from.

"I guess you could say that."

She rose from her seat and walked over to the shelf that aligned one wall of my office and housed a majority of books, novels, and research intended documents. Brushing her hands on the leather bound rows of printed work, she paused when she pulled one out and opened up the binding.

"And you also must know that there are certain...*arrangements* between our families?" She asked, pausing to look over at me before snapping the book shut and not batting an eyelash.

"I'm well aware of the arrangements, yes."

She walked over, the stealthiness of a jaguar in her pristine steps as she rounded my desk and sat her perfectly rounded ass on the edge, and crossed her legs in front of me. Her black skirt slid up the creamy space of her thighs as she settled one hand on the hard, smooth wood of my antique desk and lifted the other to adjust the tie at the base of my neck. Picking up the silk fabric, she allowed it to slide trough her fingers before letting it come to rest on my chest once more.

"So, you realize all this psychobabble bullshit is unnecessary? I don't need you to analyze me, Doctor. I just need you to give me what I came for."

She brought a delicate hand up to hold my chin as she pulled at my lip with the pad of her thumb and allowed her nail to lightly scratch the skin. She smiled, grinning slyly from ear to ear before she turned my head sideways and leaned in to whisper into my ear.

"I'm glad you understand the circumstances between us. I think I am really going to enjoy our *sessions* together."

Her warm breath passed my ear, causing a small shiver to course through my body. My dick sprang to life as she used the very tip of her tongue to trace the sensitive flesh of my earlobe.

"Mmm. I am so very glad you are replacing your uncle. Fucking him was becoming a bore, but you? I think I will rather enjoy this. Now write me what I need, get me the package, and I'll be on my way."

She pulled away from me and rounded the desk to retrieve her purse. I once again clicked open my pen and wrote out her demand on the prescription pad sitting in front of me. It went against every moral bone in my body to do what I was about to do, but I had no choice. Antonio Cardinelli was not a man to fuck with, and apparently neither was his young wife.

After slapping my signature on the dedicated line, I tore the page from the pad and handed it to her. She once again rounded the desk and placed her hands on either side of the arms on my chair, leaning in so her tits were directly in my face. The smell of her expensive perfume filtered through my nostrils as she brought her face close to mine.

"Thank you, Andris. Help me make my husband happy, and I promise to help make you...*happy*," she said, reaching down to palm my dick and balls, stroking me through the dark fabric of my suit pants. An involuntary hiss passed my lips. I'm a man and, morals or not, a fucking sexy as hell woman was cupping my fucking package. Any normal male would have had the same reaction that my traitorous dick had.

She kissed me on the corner of my mouth, the sweet smell of cinnamon coming from her breath, before she let go of my cock and pushed instantly away from me and turned around to walk out of the office. Pausing at the door, she turned around and winked at me.

"Until next time, Doctor." Then she walked out.

I don't remember how long I sat there staring at the door after she left. What the fuck just happened? My dick was so hard, it pressed against the seam of my pants in a painful protest to break forth from its confines.

I picked up the phone, dialing the same number I had called for several years whenever I needed a release without the dreaded complications of commitment. She was fabulous and always gave me what I needed, whenever I needed it.

And right now, I needed her.

CHAPTER THREE

Jericho/Nicola

I SAT SILENTLY IN the back of the car as the world around me passed by. My driver had long gone silent, leaving me to stew in the backseat with wonder and curiosity as to where I could be going. Five, ten, maybe twenty minutes passed by before the car finally came to a stop. Honestly, I didn't care where the fuck I was, as long as that four grand was in my pocket when I left wherever the fuck it is that I was.

My door opened, and the cold air from outside filled the cab and caused a chill to come to my body.

"Miss Lane, take my hand, please," my driver instructed. I reached through the darkness of the blindfold to find my purse lying on the seat next to me. I extended my hand to him and felt the warmth of his engulf mine as he assisted me out of the car. Looping my arm through his, he guided me alongside of him into the coolness of the night before opening the door to a building and entering. I tried to pay attention to the noise of my surroundings, but was met with nothing but silence.

We walked quietly through the building, the clicking of

my heels and the pitch of our breaths the only sounds I could hear. When I heard the familiar ding of an elevator, my driver guided me into the waiting car and my stomach ticked as the car began to ascend floors.

"I know I'm not supposed to ask questions, but may I ask your name?"

He thought quietly to himself for a few moments as the elevator continued to rise. Just when I didn't think he would answer me, he leaned in and whispered into my ear.

"You can call me Sinclaire."

I let out a slow breath, praying that he didn't feel my body tremble when his warm breath brushed my ear. Being with old man Patterson earlier had left me wanting an orgasm so badly I could taste it on the tip of my tongue, and for some reason, this dark haired stranger's close proximity was sending confusing signals straight to my clit that was now buzzing with anticipation for what was to come. At least with the blindfold in place, I wouldn't have to see the asshole who was about to fuck me for four thousand dollars, and that was perfectly okay with me.

"Okay, Sinclaire. How long will I be here, and how will I get home?"

"I will be driving you home after the session has ended."

The elevator dinged and I heard the car doors open. I was greeted with the smell of rich leather and dark wood. It had a pleasant effect on my senses. Maybe tonight wouldn't turn out to be such a bust after all.

"Wait here," Sinclaire instructed me as I heard him walk away. Even through the blackness of the blindfold, I could tell that the lights in the room I was standing in had just dimmed. I couldn't tell if there were any windows or anything that would connect me to the outside world.

A soft stream of classical music began to play through speakers that seemed to be placed throughout the room. Judging by the sound filtering through, the room must have been pretty large. I heard footsteps as they slowly approached me, and I wondered who it would be. The client, or Sinclaire?

"There are a few rules I need to discuss with you, Miss Lane. Again I must stress the importance of leaving the blindfold on. You will not hear the client, nor will you hear him speak. The only voice you will hear will be mine as I feed you the client's instructions. Now, before we begin, are there any limits that we need to go over?"

Limits? I had none. That is what happens when you become a professional whore. You don't worry about what it is that you will or won't do, you just concentrate on what it is the client wants so you can earn your pay.

"I have no limits, Sinclaire, although I do require at least fifty percent of the fee to be placed in my bag and the other fifty to follow after the completion of my services."

"Fair enough, Miss Lane. The client will be pleased with your positive attitude of limits as well."

I noticed a hint of darkness cloud his voice, but shrugged it off. If the client got his rocks off from another person being in the room to guide and watch, them more power to him. It wasn't like I hadn't had to please a client before by performing with another participant. There were some sick and fucked up people in this world, but I did what I had to do in order to survive. The benefit of not giving a shit about any of the stuff I did was a wonderful perk for my profession.

"Will you be joining in on the session, Sinclaire?" I asked inquisitively.

"Er, um, no," he stuttered and I arched my brow from under the blindfold wondering why he seemed to trip over the answer he provided me.

"Shall we begin? Your client is waiting."

"Lead the way."

I was led to what I believed could be the center of the room. The rich smell of leather became more potent as I got closer to the source of the aroma.

"There is a bed behind you, Miss Lane. Please remove your coat and dress, then have a seat. I peeled the fabric from my shoulders and felt around to find the bed, placing my coat next to me as my ass came into contact with soft, silky satin sheets. I let the coolness absorb into my skin as my body began to flush with excitement. This was what I craved more than anything in the world. Pleasure was something I needed like a heroin addict needed a fix. It was one of the rare emotions that I got to feel, the physical concept of someone driving into me making my body and nerve endings come to life as euphoria filtered through me with each thrust. Being an escort, I had a good reason to practice the only thing that could really make me feel. Sex wasn't just sex for me, it was a way of making me feel normal—making the emptiness and emotional blindness that was inside of me come to life, if only for a moment of time.

A warm, strong hand caressed my cheekbone, sending a shiver of delight through me. An electric charge of lust and desire for what was to come. The tips of his fingers were rough, toughened with time and I wondered what it was that he did to make them that way. I closed my eyes from behind the blindfold, even though I couldn't see anything to begin with, and allowed my body to absorb his touch as he ran his finger across my jaw and down the curvature of my neck. My breathing became shorter as I tried to concentrate of the sensations I felt just from the touch of my client.

His finger traced down my shoulder and to the tops of my breasts not covered by the red lingerie that I wore. Suddenly it was gone, and I felt cold from the lack of touch.

"Your client is very pleased with what he sees, Miss Lane. In fact, so much so, he is willing to up the price of your fee to five thousand if you agree to let him bind you."

Bind me? Why not. I've done it many times before.

"I have no issues being bound."

"Good. He would also like for me to place these headphones over your ears. You will still be able to hear me, but nothing else."

"Okay…" I said curiously. Why would he want the headphones over my ears when the only person speaking to me was Sinclaire anyway?

My client returned, gently placing the headphones over my ears and what little rustling noises I did hear, soon melted away into nothing.

Noise canceling headphones. It was almost like wearing ear plugs. A small amount of crackling came through and then Sinclaire's voice followed.

"Can you hear me, Miss Lane? Nod if so."

I complied with a small shake of my head.

"Lie back on the bed and push yourself up towards the top."

My body glided almost effortlessly across the smooth silk of the sheets and I laid my head down on very plush pillows, allowing them to absorb the weight of my head. The soft material at my back made me feel sexy in a luxurious kind of way. Although I couldn't see them, I imagined them a dark color, maybe navy blue, or even black, making sharp contrast with the crimson color of my lingerie. I imagined the tan color of my skin becoming paler against the inky linens.

A large, warm hand circled my wrist and my heart beat could no doubt be felt through the pulse point of the thin layer of skin there. I felt my client's fingers gently brush against my flesh as he expertly worked what felt like buckles to leather cuffs and secured them around my wrists. His warm hand skirted across my body as he rubbed against the surface of my skin, tracing the small, invisible hairs until he reached my ankle. With the same expert practice, my ankle was secured to the bed and he quickly followed up with the same task on the other side of my body.

"Are you okay, Miss Lane?" I heard Sinclaire whisper through the headphones.

"Yes," I managed to reply with a swallow, as anticipation began to build to the point where my breathing became even more labored.

I had been with some strange clients in the past. Some who requested things of me that I never, in my wildest dreams, would have imagined. The positive part about my job was that, with my inability to care, I had no hesitations about saying yes to their requests.

As I laid on the bed in front of not only one, but two men, one who was instructing me, and the other who was touching me, I felt...*excitement*. I smiled slyly to myself. This was the reason why I did what I did. I hated that I was empty inside. Not only did I have the issue of not being able to process my own emotions, but I couldn't understand those of others a majority of the time. It was painful to walk around every day of your life and watch others experience things that you didn't understand because you had a hard time feeling the things they did.

With sex, I was able to feel. I was able to process what was going on inside of me, no longer feeling void; no longer feeling like I was broken or ineffective.

I jumped when my client's nails scraped against the soles of both of my feet, sending a charge of electricity rippling as it climbed my thighs and hit that sweet spot in my body that was the only thing that existed to allow me to feel normal. I felt my clit stiffen, throb with a need to be touched as I laid spread eagle on the bed.

Something soft tickled the inside of my thigh. *Was it a feather? A scarf?* I couldn't tell, but the sensations it was transposing within me were extraordinary. I could feel the small bumps rise on my skin as my body cooled and heated at the same time. The soft object traced the lines of my stomach, circling my navel before ascending upward towards my breasts.

As soon as the object appeared, it was gone. I had no choice but to lay there as my mind raced and my body buzzed. I couldn't see. I couldn't hear, and it made every one of my senses heightened to extraordinary levels. Each time he touched me, it felt stronger. Each time he walked past me and I imagined him admiring my body, I could smell the woodsy scent of his skin, mixed with perspiration and arousal.

After several moments, and me wondering if he was going to continue, I felt a gentle brush across my cheekbone before his finger traced over towards my lips and pulling it away from where I was chewing on my lower lip with my teeth. I felt his warm breath as he placed a gentle kiss on the corner of my mouth before ascending his lips down my throat and into the curve of my neck. I turned my head away from him, giving him better access to one of the most erogenous zones in my body. The soft, but scruffy hairs on his face caused friction with my skin and only added to my rapidly building pleasure.

I felt a buzzing in my chest and realized it was my own noises and I sighed and nearly growled in satisfaction as he found the spot just below my ear that turned me on more than any other place on my body. A slow swipe of his tongue against my flesh had my hips bucking off the bed, begging for something, anything to put pressure against my clit.

As if he heard my internal conversation with myself, his warm hand came down to cup my pussy, his thumb circling my clit with just enough pressure to ease the ache.

"Your client is very pleased by the response you are giving him, Miss Lane."

"Well, please tell my client that he pleases me as well. I just...oh God..." I tried to say, but the words stopped just short of my lips as his hand slipped inside of my panties and traced the seam of my folds. The wetness, already deeply present, coated his fingers as he teased and taunted me with slow, sensual strokes. I clenched my fists, my nails finding the soft leather of the cuffs that bound my wrists and digging in.

"Please...please whoever you are..." I begged. My eyes opened from behind the blindfold. I've never begged a client before. Never asked a client to do anything to me unless they asked me too.

What the fuck? How the hell did that just happen?

My client must have felt my stillness and the internal battle with myself because instantly his thumb made contact with my clit as not one, but two of his long, thick fingers slipped inside of me. My back arched and the muscles in my thighs clenched. It didn't take long before I felt the familiar build up from deep within my lower belly. Elation and bliss began to progress in my body.

Yes.

This is what I wanted. This is what I needed. It was the only thing I didn't have to try to force my head or my body to feel. It came to me, without any effort or any coaxing on my part. When a man was inside of me, it was then that I felt whole. I got to feel the things that normally ran null in my everyday life.

I felt open, fully engaged with what he was doing with my body. I didn't care who this man was. I didn't care where he came from, or what he did for a living. The only thing I cared about was reaching that point where my body exploded, that the resulting subjective orgasm sent my body skyrocketing so hard, that I felt like I would pass out for a few seconds.

Within the space of a breath, my panties were ripped from my body, and the front of my corset torn away from my breasts. Cool air hit my skin as I felt him move away from me.

No!

Then suddenly, my ankles were released from their restraints and I was flipped over to where I was facing down on the bed. The movement nearly knocked the breath from my body. My wrists, now crisscrossed over my head, left me with little to hold onto as I felt his warm hands on my ass, lifting my hips to where they were now poised in the air and my cheek rested on the bed. Gentle caresses on my ass made the ache worse and I shook it, silently indicating for him to drive into me.

Heat, a stinging, but welcomed pain hit my right side as his hand collided with my skin, resulting in a deeper warmth that was almost too much to bear. The vibrations in my body quickly turned to throbs and I felt the wetness of my pussy begin to trickle down my thigh as it thirsted for him to fill my body.

His grip on my hips tightened and I stilled, trying to absorb the heat of his body from behind me. I bit my lip in anticipation as he began to rub his dick along the seam of my ass. Through the sensation of his touch, I could tell he was huge. The hardness sliding closer and closer to my entrance. It was instant. A single drive, and my body opened to him, welcoming his presence as he stilled inside of me. A bite of pain seared my core, but it only added to my pleasure. Slowly he began to rock into me, his balls tapping against my clit with each thrust.

One of his hands glided up the smooth surface of my back and I felt him take hold of the strands of my hair and give it a gentle, but firm tug. My chest rose from the bed and the cuffs at my wrists tightened just enough for me to use them as leverage to help keep my chest up.

I had never felt pleasure that intense before. I had never had the courtesy of another man watch me in the throes of passion while another man pounded into me from behind. It was new, it was different, it was…incredible. My body began to experience sensations I had never felt before. I didn't know whether to laugh or sob as I began to become overwhelmed by the new experience. I remember crying a few times in my life, and of course I could understand humor, but empathy? Love? Complete happiness? None of those things I have ever experienced before. I couldn't see this man's face, or hear his voice, but I have experienced more sensations with him than I had in all of my existence upon this earth.

His thrusts were coming quicker now, his hips colliding with my ass as his rhythm was timed precisely.

"Oh my God, Yes!" I yelled into the room. I could only hear the sound of my own breathing and the muffled tone of my voice as it vibrated through me. I had no way of telling if my client was enjoying the experience as much as I was, but I didn't give a shit. I was teetering on the edge of bliss and oblivion as he continued to drive into me, my body jolting forward with each thrust. My chest and arms burned, but the feelings I was having were almost too agonizing to sustain and I only begged for him to continue so that my body could feel the release and surrender to the incredible amount of pleasure I was experiencing.

It only took a few more thrusts of his cock and I lost control of my body, stilling as I cried out into the room as my senses were electrocuted over and over again. It was only several more for him and I felt him also surrender as he emptied into me and I felt the warmth of his ejaculation through the condom. My body, having felt like it had just ingested one too many cocktails, became drunk on the surge of pleasure, finally collapsed and shook into the sheets below me.

I felt his warm lips press into the curve at my back, and I stilled. Then suddenly he withdrew from me and instantly I wanted to beg him for more. I let my knees give out from underneath me as I came to rest fully on my front, absorbing the coolness of the sheets and allowed them to cool my overheated body. I felt a tear fall from the corner of my eye and absorb into the soft material of the scarf. Whatever the hell just happened scared me.

What the hell was I feeling? My body quaked to the point I felt like I was seizing. I wasn't cold, but the complete opposite. I felt my chest tighten as if a vice grip were around my ribcage. So many feelings that I hadn't ever felt before began to force their way out of my body and I began to feel something else that I had only ever read about.

Panic.

Fear.

I began to thrash against the restraints, feeling the leather bite into my skin as I tugged.

"Miss Lane! Please calm down. Are you okay?"

"No!" I yelled continuing to fight against the restraints. I felt him return, removing the cuffs from my hands and as soon as I was free, I scrambled off the bed, my body falling to the floor with a heavy thud. I quickly removed the headphones from my head and then reached for the blindfold, but was stopped by a warm pair of hands.

"No. Do not remove the blindfold. Breathe, Miss Lane. Breathe." Sinclaire said in a soothing voice as he cupped my chin in his hands and stroked my cheeks with the pad of his thumbs. Slowly, I felt the panic begin to subside and my breathing begin to even out.

"Stay right here while I get you something to wear home." Sinclaire instructed. I stayed like he had asked me because for some strange reason, he seemed to be soothing to me. I felt like I could trust him as ironic as it sounded seeing that he was just as much a stranger as my client was.

"Stand up, please." I heard him ask, and I rose to my feet to stand in front of him. I heard him let out a puff of air before he placed a soft piece of fabric over my head and I slipped my arms through the holes. It felt as luxurious as cashmere as the material came to rest mid-thigh, just long enough to cover the stockings I still wore.

"That should keep you warm until I get you home. Please leave the blindfold on until then." I nodded as he told me to slip the arms into my jacket and took my arm in his to lead me from the room. I looked behind me, stupid I know, seeing as I couldn't see anything, as if trying to say goodbye to whoever it was that gave me not only the best orgasm of my life, but also so many other things I've never felt before, no matter how much it scared me.

All I felt was blackness, as if he were no longer in the room. It made me wonder who he was. Something that was also new to me. And for the first time in my life, as Sinclaire led me from the room and out of the building, I realized something.

I cared.

THE ANNOYING SOUND of my phone buzzing on the table beside my bed woke me up from one of the best sleeps of my life. I yawned, stretching and noticed the delicious soreness of my body that reminded me that last night really did happen. Squinting, I looked over at the alarm clock.

Ten a.m.

Only one person would be calling me at this time in the morning. I picked up my phone to confirm the person on the other end. I groaned.

"Lexie, seriously. You better have a good reason for calling me this early."

I rubbed the sleep from my eyes. It felt like I had barely gone to sleep after being up half of the night replaying the events with "mystery client" over and over in my mind. I also thought about the strange way in which he conducted business and how nice and soothing Sinclaire was to me. How many women had he brought to—wherever the hell it was that I was taken—and fucked them into a near oblivion?

"I need you to get dressed and get over here, *now*."

She sounded stern. Lexie was usually a pretty happy-go-lucky type of person until you fucked with her business. She became a rabid bear in heat whenever one of her girls was threatened, or a client didn't comply with the rules of the agency.

"What the hell is going on, Lexie?" I asked, sitting up in the bed and removing the comforter from my legs. I still had on the red silk stockings underneath my cotton nightgown. I stared at them, once again remembering the night before.

"You know I don't like discussing business over the phone, Nicola."

"I told you not to call me that."

"Well, then listen to me, *Jericho*, and get your ass over here. You have twenty minutes."

She hung up on me. I stared at my phone for several minutes after the screen had gone black. Lexie had never hung up on me before, so whatever was going on must have been serious.

After brushing my teeth and hair, I slipped on a pair of black leggings and looked for a sweater to wear in my closet when I came across the cashmere sweater dress that Sinclaire put me in last night. I ran my hand down the soft material all the way to the sleeve and massaged it between my fingers. I pulled it from my hanger and lifted it up to my nose, inhaling deeply. If I tried really hard, I could still make out the woodsy smell of my "mystery client" and the pleasure I instantly felt shocked me. Usually I had to have the heavy petting and at least a small amount of foreplay to get into the mood, but one whiff of the man's scent and my body came alive.

I slipped the dress over my head and let the hem come to rest at my mid-thigh just as it had the night before. I reached for a belt in my closet and adjusted it to sit at the top of my waist and paired it with my black knee-high leather boots. As I pulled the zipper up, they reminded me of the leather that bound my wrists last night and I pulled the sleeves of the sweater back to see the faint red marks that were still present. A surge of electricity swam through me, sending currents to each of my limbs and a tingle to my scalp.

No man had ever affected me the way my mystery client had before. Hell, no *person* had ever affected me that way before. I never even felt those kind of strong emotions the night my parents died in the plane crash. When they died, I felt hurt, but not enough to send me into a downward spiral that most people would fall into after they lost loved ones. Truth be told, I barely knew my parents.

Paula and Michael Forbes were practically strangers to me. I was born Nicola Marie Forbes, but after their death and I got into my current profession, I started going by Jericho Lane. I still used my given name for legal matters, but used Jericho as a means to avoid my past life. My father, I soon learned after his death, was involved with some rather shady people. People who apparently wanted to take out their frustrations on me when he died and tried to pry their money out of me. The surprise was on them when I told them there wasn't any money, not even anything for me to survive on. It didn't stop their relentless pursuit, though.

I grabbed my purse from the counter and made sure to secure the lock on my condo. It was another freezing New York day. I ventured outside and slipped my sunglasses over my eyes before hailing a cab. The good thing about living in New York was the cabs and the subway. I didn't have the need for a car, and therefore didn't have to pay the ridiculous amount of money it would cost to garage the damn thing.

It took a little over fifteen minutes to get through traffic to Alexandra's "office" downtown. It was a small store disguised as a flower shop just on the outskirts of Manhattan. Sure, it was a legitimate business in the front of the store, having several employees who worked there during the few short hours it was open, but the real money maker was in the back. That is where the conference room was, as well as several rooms made up for clients to use if they preferred to conduct their sessions there as opposed to a hotel or their home.

I waved at the two young women putting together arrangements as I walked in and proceeded to the back in search of Lexie. I found her pouring over paperwork, her nose buried in the forms in front of her as her glasses hung from the tip of her nose. She was older than me, by several years in fact. I thought she was at least a decade older than me, but when I tried to ask her, she told me to shut up. She was sweet, in the domineering motherly sort of way, but also a fucking snake if you pissed her off.

"What is so damn important that you insist I high-tail my ass over here in person?" I asked as I plopped down in the chair across from her desk, and let my purse fall to the floor with a thud. She looked at me, pushing her glasses up the bridge of her nose and tossed her long blonde hair over her shoulder. Without saying a word, she rose from the chair and walked to the office door and closed it before returning to her seat.

"This must be serious?" I asked as I watched her steeple her fingers under her chin.

"This is for your ears only, and I don't need any of the other girls hearing it. It doesn't leave this office and the only person you are to discuss it with is me, understood?"

"Um, okay…" I said, drawing out the last word. My brow arched in curiosity and I watched as she straightened some papers and placed a paperclip to hold them together and then tossed them over to me.

"What the fuck is this?" I asked as I picked up the paperwork and looked at her expectantly. She reached for her coffee cup and took a long sip before setting it back down and licking her lips. Sitting back in her chair, she nodded her head in the direction of the papers in my hand.

"That, my dear, is a contract."

"A contract?" I questioned repeating what she just said.

"Yep."

"Okay, Lexie. I give. A fucking contract for what?"

"Well, it seems you impressed a certain high paying client of ours last night and he wants to schedule your next twelve sessions with him. Once a week for the next twelve weeks."

"What?" I asked in disbelief as I started to rapidly flick through the papers.

"You heard me, don't act stupid, Jericho, it's beneath you. He had some rules and stipulations about the contract though. You can't 'service' anyone but him in the next twelve weeks. You are to remain blindfolded during each session, and be on call if he were to require an extra session during the week."

Even though I felt excited about the fact that my "mystery client" wanted a contract with me, it also angered me a little to be so demanding of my time.

Excitement.

Anger.

Two things I rarely experienced. What the fuck was this man doing to me? I felt awkward being nearly thirty years old and have never gotten angry enough to want to punch someone, or feel that nervous excitement I felt as I looked through the contract.

"Lexie, I can't afford to limit myself to one client a week for the next twelve weeks. I have a condo to finish paying for, living expenses, and other things.

"Oh, I think you will. He is offering ten grand per session."

My jaw hit the floor.

CHAPTER FOUR

ANDRIS

THERE WERE A MOUNTAIN of case files sitting on my desk when I arrived at the clinic the next morning. My uncle took it upon himself to have his secretary bring all of the important files to me first thing so that I had the opportunity to go through them. His words, not mine.

I sat my briefcase at the foot of my desk and settled myself into the comfort of my chair. My secretary came in carrying a cup in her hand and sat it down in front of me. The warm vapor and aroma of the particular gourmet French roast coffee that helped me get my day going, filtered through my nose, giving me a surge of energy from just the scent alone.

"Thank you, Laura Lee. You know just how to start my day out right," I said, smiling up at her and reaching for my cup to take a sip of the hot, fragrant liquid.

"Well, I better. I've been working for you for nearly four years, Mr. Gunn. I should know by now," she replied chuckling.

Laura Lee was a forty-four year old divorcee with a soft voice and sweet smile. She was petite and slightly on the rotund side, but her personality made her very attractive. She was constantly turning down passes from the patients that walked in through our door, saying that one husband was enough for a lifetime. She always wore her dark gray, peppered hair in a bun at the nape of her neck and some sort of blouse with a long flowing skirt. Her make-up was kept clean, giving her a fresh look.

"How many times have I asked you to call me Andris?"

She tapped one of her unpolished nails to her lips and looked up at the ceiling as if she were contemplating my question.

"Probably for about as long as I've been working for you, Mr. Gunn," she smiled.

"So that's how it's going to be?" I asked, joining in on her laughter.

"Your uncle has you biting at the bit already, doesn't he?" She asked as she nodded towards the stack of folders on my desk.

"No rest for the weary."

"Well," she said, leaning in and placing her palms on the desk and looking over her shoulder before turning back to me, "when you are the chief in charge next week, hopefully you will not be as bull-headed or…"

"An asshole?" I interrupted.

"I guess you could say that."

"Don't worry, Laura Lee. When I am in charge there will be a lot of changes. But for now," I said, pausing to look at the folders once more and sighing, "I have to be good and get through all of these. Then I can decide which ones are the important ones for me to keep and which ones I can give to Daryn and Bruce."

"Don't take this the wrong way, but I am so very pleased that you are nothing like your uncle."

I smiled at her and she winked before turning to walk out of my office.

I reached for the stack, separating them in half and started on the pile closest to me.

A famous NBA player who had a sex addiction.

A young female who had been sexually abused.

There was a patient who suffered from panic attacks and had a great fear of bridges. Another who thought Santa Clause was his brother and that his mother was the Tooth Fairy.

I paused when I got to the last file in the stack because it looked different from the others. It was thick with notes that not only had my grandfather made, but also my uncle. Flipping it open I noticed that the client had been attending our practice since she was five years old.

Alexithymia. The inability to recognize emotions and their subtleties. According to my uncle's notes, the nearly thirty-year-old female had a limited understanding of what caused feelings, had a constricted style of thinking, was hypersensitive to physical sensations, and she was detached or tentative with others. This was probably one of the first cases of that condition that I had to deal with. I continued to flip through the pages and pages of notes consisting of conversations with my grandfather and father, intrigued by this woman.

When I got to the back, I saw a session in which my uncle talked with her about the death of her parents. Daughter of Senator Michael Forbes who was killed in a plane crash along with his young wife, when the woman, Nicola, was just in high school.

Nicola Forbes was informed of her parents passing

today. Her teachers thought it best that she was told in the presence of her psychiatrist just in case this incident was the start of a chain reaction that would set her off. I sat her in the same chair that she sat in when she first started coming to our clinic and had sessions with my father. I watched her as her eyes wandered around the room, the surroundings familiar to her, but still seeming new. She was older now at fourteen years old; growing up in front of our eyes, but yet, not changing in too many ways. She had a plethora of support surrounding her, including two of her instructors from school as well as the counselor and principal. They all stood around her as she sat in the chair in front of me like she had so many times before.

"Nicola?"

"Yes, Doctor Gunn?"

"We have brought you here today because we have some news we need to tell you. Your teachers are all here for support, as well as Principal Masters."

She nodded her head and looked at the three women standing behind her before turning her piercing blue eyes back to me.

"Your mother and father were killed in a plane crash today on their way to Washington D.C. The plane went down somewhere in Pennsylvania. We don't know what happened, or what could have caused the crash, but we do know that no one survived."

I waited for the moment when the switch would flip on in her brain; the moment that we all thought would trigger some sort of reaction out of her.

But nothing came.

She sat stoically staring at me, not a tear to her eyes

nor a change in her breathing. She sat poised, ladylike, and stiff like a socialite would be expected to present themselves.

"Do you understand what I just told you?"

"Yes, Sir. I do. My parents were killed in a plane crash."

"And how does that make you feel?

"How is it supposed to make me feel?"

That was the same response I got out of her every time I questioned what she was feeling. I took a deep breath, frustrated that after nine years there was absolutely no progress made with this patient. I have waited and watched this girl grow up. The emptiness inside of her becomes more prevalent as time goes by.

"Well, in your situation, most people would feel sad. They would probably cry and mourn for their loved ones."

"Well, Doctor Gunn, I don't know what love is. I don't know what love feels like. I would cry, only I don't know what would cause me to do that. My parents, if you didn't notice, didn't have much to do with me. I've been thrown away into boarding schools and left to myself while they would gallivant around the country. I'm sorry that my lack of sadness seems to upset you."

The last bit of her statement caught my attention. Not only had Nicola had difficulties recognizing her own emotions, but also recognizing emotions in others.

"You understood that I was upset by your lack of response?"

"Well, I have been coming to see you and Senior Mr. Gunn for the last nine years. I have learnt your facial expressions and have caught on to what seems to upset or *frustrate you. I just don't feel anything."*

Progress.

She recognized my emotions through repetition. Maybe this was something that we needed to progress with further in order to find our breakthrough.

I finished reading the notes my uncle had taken. I could hear the excitement in his writing after discovering her recognition of certain emotions. Even though he had made an ass out of himself and the family name by becoming involved with the Cardinelli family, he was a very good doctor. He was very intuitive, smart, and could often have found a solution to his patient's problems after one session, but the man lacked common sense. I lifted the page I just finished reading to find another note written just three days after.

Nicola missed her appointment today. Called to leave messages at her home, but the phone was disconnected. I called her school, but they said she had been removed due to circumstances they weren't allowed to disclose.

I looked over at the chart on the inside flap of the folder, where we kept an attendance of when the patients came to their sessions. I noticed that Nicola didn't return for nearly seven months after the session she found out about her parents. My brows furrowed together as I wondered what it was that could have kept her away from her therapy for so long. Nine years was quite a long time, and probably one of only a few constants in her life.

I looked at the gold Rolex watch on my left wrist, a present from my grandfather when I graduated. My first appointment wasn't due for another twenty minutes, so I decided to run out to the lobby to refill my coffee cup and stretch my legs before I was stuck behind my desk all day.

I motioned for Laura Lee to sit back down when she saw me pass by her desk.

"I got it," I smiled and she smiled back quickly before going back to work with preparing the patient files that were to be seen in the clinic today. Picking up one of the little coffee cups that we kept on a neat little stand, that housed several different flavors and brews, I inserted it into the machine and closed the lid, pressing the button. I watched as the steaming liquid poured into the cup and the great aroma filtered into the waiting area. Dumping in my required amount of six sugars and four creamers into the steaming liquid, I gave it a quick stir before taking a long draw. I didn't care that it singed the tip of my tongue. The only thing I needed was the jolt of the caffeine as it fired into my system due to my late night.

I vaguely remembered the bell of the lobby room door ringing, signaling the arrival of the day's first patient. A middle aged man wearing plaid golfer's pants and a pastel salmon colored shirt, approached Laura Lee at her desk. I was getting such a kick out of how someone could walk out into public wearing such attire, that I didn't register the bell ringing again. I began to walk towards the door, that would lead me to my office, and had my hand poised on the knob when I heard a familiar voice. One that haunted my dreams all night long as I tossed and turned in my oversized luxurious bed, alone. I had memorized every shape of her body, every line and curve that made up the beauty that invaded my thoughts. I could still smell the soft scent of her skin and the way that her arm burned into mine as she walked beside me.

"Nicola Forbes to see Dr. Gunn please."

I turned around, not quite sure if I had heard her correctly. My mouth went instantly dry and I had to mentally coerce my cock not to stand at attention from the electricity of her beauty shocking my system.

She signed a clipboard and then handed it back to Laura Lee, smiling politely. I was jealous of her teeth. The way that her lips framed them, just barely touching the rims of the plump redness. I noticed the way her ruby lipstick made her teeth beautifully white, and how her high cheekbones made her eyes squint slightly as she smiled. The coffee cup in my hands nearly plummeted to the floor as my hands began to slightly tremble from the nearness of her.

In an instant, she looked up, as if sensing me, the smile still present on her face. It only faltered for a fraction of a second before she scanned me from head to toe.

"Sinclaire?"

CHAPTER FIVE

Jericho/Nicola

"MISS LANE," Sinclaire nodded at me. The lady sitting in the reception chair flicked her eyes rapidly back and forth between me and him as we all said nothing for several long seconds. I wished I could explain what happened when I saw him standing there. It was almost like someone had taken a car battery, hooked it to cables and touched every single place on my body. I could feel every tiny, nearly invisible hair on my body stand on its ends, as tingles ran unobstructedly throughout.

"Well, *Sinclaire*," the lady behind the reception desk stated with a hint of humor in her voice as she said his name, "Your first appointment is here."

"Right this way, Miss Lane," he said as he pushed open the door leading back to a set of offices, all in which I was familiar with.

"Forbes."

He stopped, turning around as his dark eyebrow arched in question.

"My name is Nicola Forbes. Jericho is something I use for…"

"I understand, Miss Forbes. Follow me please." His short, clipped tone caught me slightly off guard.

Was he new to the clinic? But more importantly, why was he the one who led me to my client last night? A plethora of questions circumnavigated their way through my brain on our short walk to his office. He paused at the door, gesturing with his hand for me to enter. The smell of his cologne overtook my senses as I walked past him. I walked in, familiar with the same bookshelf, and nearly the same table of blocks that sat in the corner from the time I was five years old.

"This was old man Gunn's office," I stated as I removed my purse from my shoulder and sat down in a chair in front of the desk. I crossed my legs, sitting tall with my chin held high—a move that I had perfected over the years.

"It was," he replied as he undid the buttons on his jacket before sitting down in the overly large leather chair behind the desk. I may not have been able to feel or have a solid understanding of those feelings, but I had learned to read facial expressions and to be able to label emotions through them. As I watched Sinclaire, I noticed the dark blue rim of his eyes blended in with the darkening blue of his irises, making them look like pools of navy ink, or a starless sky. His jaw was firm as he chewed on the inner side of his lip, debating with himself over what to say next. I sat there, not breaking eye contact, partly because it was how I had been bred, and partly because I didn't want to. His eyes were something I could stare into all day. They were beautiful, something to appreciate, a masterful work of God. I watched his Adam's apple move as he swallowed, following it down the line of his jaw to rest on his perfect lips. I admired the gentle wave in his hair and how a few tendrils seemed to always fall just above his brow.

"Miss Lane," he said in a rush of breath.

"Nicola. My name is Nicola," I corrected him. He closed his eyes only for a brief second and then re-opened them.

"Nicola, my uncle, Robert Gunn whom you are familiar with, is retiring as of next week. I will be taking over the clinic as well as becoming the doctor to oversee your therapy."

Right down to business, like there wasn't a giant elephant in the room.

"Why didn't you tell me that you were a doctor? More importantly, that you were going to be *my* doctor, last night?"

"I had no idea who you were last night. You were introduced as Jericho Lane, I assumed that was your name. I had no knowledge that you were a patient here at the clinic, nor did I know that your name was Nicola Forbes."

"Not even when you read my file?" I asked gesturing with my eyes toward the manila folder on his desk that had my name scrawled across the top.

"No, I didn't put two and two together, until I saw you standing at the reception desk." I believed him, especially if his reaction was any indication.

"I can always turn over your case to one of the other doctors in the clinic if you feel like the situation of *last night* would compromise your care."

His eyes darkened when he spoke about last night and I felt the surface of my skin flush, sending a wave of heat through me. The physicality that I felt while in his presence last night wasn't like any other sexual experience I had ever had. My senses were heightened on so many levels when my mind and body were both taken possession from *him*.

My mystery client.

The fire in his touch. The graze of his fingers along the swell of my breasts. The expert way he made my body come alive as if awakening me from a deep slumber. All of those things encompassed with the sensations I got to feel with intimacy were nearly too much for me. Then there was the fact that Sinclaire was watching the entire time, instructing me on how to move and what to do, and it only made the night that much more intense. I was turned on not only from the man who was physically manipulating my body, but also by the man watching him do so.

"That won't be necessary. We are both adults. What goes on in the privacy of our personal lives doesn't have to affect our professional relationship, Sinclaire. But my question is this, if you have this fabulous job here, why do you work for...whoever it was that sought the services of my agency last night?"

One hand brushed against the small amount of stubble that graced his jaw, while his other tapped a rhythmic cadence against his coffee cup in front of him.

"I help a *friend* who needs my assistance to satiate his desires. A friend who has difficulty when it comes to the opposite sex."

"What kind of issues?" I asked, trying to gain more knowledge about my client. I still hadn't responded to his request for my services over the span of the upcoming twelve weeks. Lexie blew up my phone last night with a thousand text messages telling me how important it was to the agency to remain on this client's good side. She stressed the importance of how I needed the income as well as the guaranteed *release* I would have on a weekly basis. All of those factors worked together in a case that was damn near difficult for me to want to turn down.

"I'm afraid I cannot discuss that with you. Patient-doctor confidentiality."

"So he's a patient of yours?"

"I guess you could say that. Now, how about we talk about you."

Here we go. The same shit. The same conversations that I always have when someone knows about the trait in which I suffer.

"You look like you're aggravated," he noted, arching an eyebrow as if asking a question instead of making a statement. That was something that both the therapists before him did. They would tell me about an emotion or feeling that they "thought" I had to help me try to identify those emotions.

"I guess. It just feels like the same conversation that I have had for the last twenty-four years. *Tell us about you, Nicola. How are you feeling? What does this make you feel?* It is the same thing over and over again, so if aggravated is what it makes me *feel*? Then yes, I guess I am aggravated."

"Then you should know that as your doctors, we try our best to help you recognize those emotions so that you become more familiar with them, in hopes that you will recognize them when you feel them yourself."

He crossed his fingers underneath his chin as he rested his elbows on his desk. I watched the fabric of his coat stretch across the muscles of his broad shoulders. The things I recognized the most were the motions of the body. I could tell if someone was turned on by a look in their eyes, or a way in which they presented themselves. The way Sinclaire kept fidgeting and changing his sitting position, told me he was uncomfortable. The deep smolder of his navy eyes told me that he liked what he saw in front of him. But it was how my body felt at that moment that was different to me. Usually I had to have some sort of physical contact in order for my physical emotions to turn on, but with Sinclaire I was turned on just by the way he looked at me.

It was amazing. Something that I have never had the pleasure to experience before. I looked away, glancing around the familiar room. I tried to look everywhere but directly at him as the wetness between my legs began to form, signaling my growing desire. It was then that I saw the documentation of his doctorate degree.

Andris S. Gunn.

"You told me your name was Sinclaire."

His eyes followed my gaze to the certificate on the wall behind him.

"You told me your name was Jericho. I guess we both have secrets, don't we?" He asked, tilting his head to the side before running his hand through his hair.

"I guess we do. So the "s" stands for Sinclaire?"

"Yes. Why did you choose Jericho Lane?"

"I didn't want to be associated with my mother and father."

The people who left me with nothing. I thought silently. He nodded, as if seeming to understand my reason that no further explanation was warranted.

"I know some of this may be repetitive, Nicola, but instead of focusing on the emotions that you don't feel, how about you tell me the ones that you do recognize in others as well as yourself."

I smoothed out the invisible wrinkles in my dress pants, letting my palms slide across the smooth and perfectly pressed fabric.

"Pleasure. Physical contact."

I looked up to find his eyes upon me, narrowing in assessment. This therapy session was completely different from all of my others. First off, the psychiatrists were old and had no inclination of my profession. Second, they didn't affect me the way the man sitting before me did. It was damn near impossible for me to sit still in his presence, especially when he was moving his dexterous fingers across the flesh of his bottom lip, as he was presently doing. It was hard for me not to stare at his beauty or to control the need for him to fuck me on his large antique desk.

"You saw exactly everything I do feel last night." I pointed out to him. A small surge of energy ran through me as the memories from the night before came flooding back to me. The desire to know more about the man in front of me as well as the mystery man who physically touched me while Andris's voice filtered through my ears was becoming more prominent with each moment.

He rose from his desk, stalking in my direction, quietly assessing me the entire way. It was something I should have been used to by now; being assessed was something that occurred every day in my life. People always wondered why I was broken, why I had no filter, or why I was distant and uncaring. But being under the scrutiny of Andris Gunn was different. It created reactions within me that no other therapist, or acquaintance in my life, had ever brought out in me. It was also quickly becoming my new addiction.

He sat on the edge of his desk with his arms crossed over his chest. My eyes trailed down to the dark leather of his belt before following the lines of his muscular thighs hidden by the expensive material of his pants.

"So I did. But what I want to know is how it made you *feel*." I smiled coyly at him. This is where the no-filter, don't care, Nicola got to come out. He wanted to know how it made me *feel?* Then I would tell him, and maybe feed him with the desire he had created in me.

I licked my lips, coating them in moisture as I looked towards the floor briefly before I batted my eyes up at him. He continued to sit on the edge of his desk in front of me, his position giving him height over where I sat in the chair. His demeanor and posture displayed an air of control or dominance. I brought a hand up towards my neck, letting it rest on the skin exposed from my button down blouse, before trailing two fingers down towards the swell of my breasts.

His reaction didn't go unnoticed. The small hitch in his breath. The way he shifted himself on the desk, and the way the arms crossed over his chest came down to grip the edge of the desk, causing his knuckles to whiten.

"He made the room warmer, just from his presence, creating a static charge. When he touched me, it was like a jolt, a sharp zap that made my stomach feel like it had bottomed out. You know, like the feeling you get when a car goes over a hill too fast? Well, I felt like that car, the incline steadily increasing pressure until it crested over the top and free fell towards the bottom," I replied crossing my legs, trying to suppress the ache I felt between them from the memories.

"I felt hyper-aware of him, focused one hundred percent on the man I couldn't see, yet my brain felt foggy at the same time."

He shifted again as I brought my fingertips to my lips.

"When his lips pressed to mine, it was like I couldn't get enough. My heart was beating wildly in my chest, the pulse felt all the way down…" I said stopping to nibble on the pad of my thumb.

Andris cleared his throat and I opened my eyes to look up

at him, my vision cloudy with desire. I noticed the slight flush to his face and the way he had his jaw tightly clenched.

"Please, continue," he instructed. Taking a deep breath I did.

"My palms began to tingle. I ached to touch him in return; to pull him closer to me when my body sought for some part of him to be between my legs. It was a rush of adrenaline when he bound me to the bed, leaving me open and bare to him. I felt him stake claim in ownership of my body with each caress, each touch."

I was chewing on my lip now, amazed at how turned on I was with my mystery man not even in the room. It was new, welcomed, and completely *euphoric*. My body buzzed to life and it made it hard to sit still in front of Andris. I felt the bite that my teeth made into the flesh of my lip and I licked them, tasting the metallic presence of blood. Instantly, his hand cupped my jaw and the pad of his thumb brushed across my bottom lip.

"You're bleeding."

He got up from the desk and walked out of the office, closing the door behind him. I lifted my hand to my lips and pulled it back to find the pinkish red hue of blood on the tips of my fingers, rubbing it between them. The door to the office opened and Andris reappeared carrying a towel and walked right up to me before lifting the towel and placing it on my lips. Even though he wasn't touching me with his skin, I could feel the heat through the towel making my lips pulse in accordance.

Gently, he patted the warm compress and the red soon became pink and then nothing as the bleeding stopped. I couldn't help but look into the deep blue of his eyes, noticing how vibrant they were up close. From far away, they looked dark and brooding, but up close, I could see the tiniest of gold flecks around his pupils.

"I think it stopped." He said, still standing dangerously close to me. It was the same surge of energy I felt when I was with him and my client last night. How was it that after nearly thirty years of vacancy, my emotions were beginning to open up and all because of two men; one I have seen, the other still mysterious and secret.

"Keep this with you in case it starts again."

I felt drained as if my body had just run a marathon in a sprint. The new things that were taking place inside of me did something that I also wasn't used to.

Being overwhelmed.

I watched Andris take a drink out of the coffee cup that sat on his desk before setting it down and reaching for a pen. He flipped open my folder and jotted down a few notes, all the while I was trying to bring my body back down to a level that wasn't threatening to make me explode from the inside out.

"So pleasure, you feel. Pleasure, you understand," he stated just before leaning in and whispering like we were accompanied by other people in the room.

"Is this why you do what you do? Is that why you are an escort?"

"Yes."

"I see." He seemed taken aback by my answer, an almost angry look in his eyes. "I have homework for you for our next session."

"What? I'm back in high school now?" I asked.

"It is to help you, Nicola. That way you don't have to sell your body in order to feel things."

"There is nothing wrong with what I do."

"Other people beg to differ."

"Well, I don't care what others think."

He took a long breath, running his hands through both sides of his hair, leaving a messy, disheveled look in the wake of his actions.

"I want you to keep a journal. Expressive writing can be beneficial in helping to stretch your ability to detect emotions. You need to do it every day, but write beyond just the events of the day. Include observations, things that you think you are feeling, even if you aren't sure. It may be hard at first, but the overall goal is to broaden your observations within and outside of yourself."

He opened a drawer to his left and pulled out something wrapped in white tissue paper. Peeling it back, he revealed a beautiful leather bound journal. Reaching over, he handed it to me and I ran my hands along the smooth surface of the leather.

"Use this."

I opened the pages to find them stark white, something ironic since on the inside, I was black. Vacant.

"You don't have to be a whore, Nicola. You can do this on your own, and I want to help you do it."

A stabbing pain hit me in the chest and gut and the journal fell from my hands and landed with a thump onto the dark hardwood of the floor. My breath temporarily left me in a rush as if I had been sucker punched, and as quickly as it appeared, it left me. Bending over, I reached for the journal and my purse before standing to my feet.

What the hell was that? My blood felt like it was boiling in my veins, like a caldron sitting upon a fire. I didn't say anything to Andris as I made my way over to his office door, afraid of the things that were happening to me. My legs wobbled slightly as I walked and I just prayed I had made it out the door before they gave way from underneath me.

"Nicola?"

I stopped in my tracks, my hand poised on the door knob, but I didn't turn around to look at him.

"In here, I am Dr. Andris Gunn."

I spun around and looked at him as I clutched the journal to my chest, like I was trying to hide behind it.

"And you are Nicola Forbes. That doesn't change. But out there?" He said, pointing to the window of his office and my gaze followed to where the sun was shining brightly outside.

"Out there, I am Sinclaire and you are Jericho."

I didn't say anything. Instead, I turned around and walked out of his office. I made my way all the way out of the lobby and onto the sidewalk where I hailed a cab. It was moments after I had climbed into the back seat that the realization hit me. I reflected back on the few times I could remember my mother and father fighting. I vividly remembered my mother clenching her chest after my father had said something to her and she lashed back out at him.

What I had just felt up in Andris's office…was *anger*.

ANDRIS

FUCK.

I gripped the sides of my hair hard enough to feel a small, piercing pain in my scalp before letting it go. I was in deep, deep trouble. The pangs of jealousy that swept through me when Nicola described how *he* made her feel as *he* touched and caressed her were surprising. The instant rise in my arousal as I watched her body flush with desire from her memories alone, had me close to wanting to throw her on the floor and give her everything she wanted and needed. But I was her doctor. How fucked up was it that she was my patient? Staying involved with her outside of treatment would be a disaster, but the pull I felt towards her was so strong I didn't think I could break the ties.

I was jealous of her client. Jealous that he could bring out emotions and desires in her that I wanted to do. I had only met her last night by chance. Kiki was our regular escort. She was always available to us whenever we needed her, but now having met Nicola, I knew there was no going back for either of us.

I sat in my chair for several moments, my fingers tapping against her folder, fighting between ethics and desire. My mind was telling me one thing, while my body told me another. I could still smell the faint honeysuckle scent of her skin lingering in my office long after she had left.

Pleasure. She feels pleasure.

That was something that patients with her condition typically felt. Not so much pleasure, but the ability to experience the emotions that they are void to, through physical contact.

The internal battle within me raged in full force, and I was half a heartbeat away from turning her case over to one of the other doctors when I had an epiphany.

I could use our sessions on a client level with our sessions on a therapy level to provoke her. When she spoke about last night, I felt every thought through her words and her actions... and she *felt* them too.

Yes.

I smiled to myself. It was fucked up and morally wrong, but I was willing to risk my license and my life that this would work. I could use sex to throw a wrench in her ability to know her own self-experiences, as well as what others think and feel.

It was a risky experiment, one that I had no control to use to go with it, but it was now a thought that wouldn't leave my mind.

I picked up the phone, dialing the familiar number.

"Alexandra, we need to talk."

CHAPTER SIX

JERICHO/NICOLA

"HE WHAT?" I exclaimed as I sat across from Lexie in her office that afternoon.

"He upped the ante. Twelve and a half grand per session."

I sat back in my chair. How the hell could I turn that down? Especially after my therapy session with Andris. Did he call the client and tell him about me? Is that why he upped the price?

"Why is this guy so dead set on having me? I thought Kiki was his usual reservation. I only filled in one night, and all of a sudden he wants me for twelve weeks?

"I don't know, Jer, but you would seriously be an idiot if you turned it down. That's more money than you make in five months. That's…"

"A hundred and fifty thousand dollars," I said, interrupting her. The shock of just how much money that was had me in disbelief.

"That is in addition to what he is paying me to contract you out. I don't know what you did to this man, but whatever it was, keep doing it."

"What did Kiki say about it when you talked to her?" Lexie waved her hand through the air as she took a long drag from her electronic cigarette.

"She was a little pissed at first, but I gave her some of your regular clients, including old man Patterson, since the contract requires to be with no other clients for the duration of the twelve weeks."

Why did this man have a desire to keep me to himself? The thought though, made me shiver as the familiar electric pulses invaded me, like it did every time I thought about him. I wished I knew his name. I wished I could see his face. He was probably some old ogre who would have me running in the other direction.

Who the fuck was I kidding? The man was probably gorgeous beyond all knowledge. One of those reclusive CEO men, who hid their insecurities behind walls of mansions and millions of dollars. I found myself going over the possibilities, each scenario playing like a silent movie before me, but each one resulting in me coming undone beneath him as Sinclaire guided and watched.

"So?" Lexie asked, interrupting my thoughts.

"So..."

"Are you going to take the job?" She slid the stack of papers over to me. I didn't have to ask her what they were. I already knew.

I picked them up and the pen that Lexie handed me. I glanced over it briefly before I scrolled down to the bottom of the last page and noticed a signature at the bottom, but it was too messy to make out an actual name.

"He already signed it?"

"Yeah," Lexie replied as she slipped her electric cigarette back into the top drawer of her desk. She pulled out an envelope and handed it over to me. I took it, and looked at her with curiosity.

"This is the first session's payment. *In advance.* He said as soon as you sign, it's yours."

I clicked the top of the pen, and without a second thought I signed my name to the bottom of the contract and placed the pen down on top of the stack of papers. Lexie handed me the envelope where I expected to open it and find a check. Instead, it was cash.

"Have you talked to him?"

"The client?" She asked and I nodded. "No. He has his assistant, Sinclaire, call me and negotiate everything."

Sinclaire. Or Andris. I couldn't let Lexie know that he was my new psychiatrist. She would be tearing that contract up in less than two heartbeats. If it was one thing that Lexie was very strict on, it was my therapy. She, like my doctors, believed that I would be cured of my lack of certain emotions. After nearly twenty-five years in therapy, I hated to tell her that it probably wasn't going to happen. I needed this money. It would finish paying off my condo as well as have enough left over for me to start real savings. When you are left with absolutely nothing, you remember every struggle that you faced trying to survive. I remembered being fourteen years old and sleeping on the streets of New York. I remember looking for food in restaurant dumpsters or having to go to the Salvation Army to get a warm meal. No one cared about the poor Senator's daughter and the fact that she was homeless and hungry after her parents died.

"He told me the conditions are just like last night. Sinclaire will be there with you and the client. You know what to do if you ever feel like the situation is unsafe, correct?"

Lexie required us to have her number pre-programed in our phones as speed dial one. That way all we had to do was press "one" and send. She knew we would need her, if, or when she answered and all she heard was background noise. Our clients were required to provide her with the address and location of where our session would be held. There was also a time limit so that the client couldn't keep us over a certain amount of time. We also had Vinny, Lexie's scarily huge husband, who had won national bodybuilding competitions, ready to kick the asses of some clients who decided they wanted to break the rules.

"Yes. I have a feeling that everything will be okay."

"Okay, then. I'll have your schedule cleared for the next twelve weeks. What are you going to do with all your free time?"

Good question. I was usually always sleeping during the day, unless I was attending therapy, because the majority of my clients required their sessions at night. There were a few that would make arrangements for a daytime meeting, but the majority of them were after normal working hours.

I opened the envelope once more, letting my thumb glide through the stacks of hundred dollar bills.

"First things first. I'm going shopping."

I HOPPED INTO A CAB and headed towards lower Manhattan. I held my purse close to me, knowing that I carried twelve and a half grand in there, full of cash. I knew exactly where my first stop was going to me.

Agent Provocateur.

Although expensive, it held some of the world's most beautiful and exquisite lingerie that was designed to reveal or conceal, hug curves, or be flirty, fun, and sexy. Since my profession required me to be physically enticing to my clients, I thought it could be both a luxury and an investment. Most of all, I really had a deep desire to please both Andris and my client.

The boutique was beautiful with a plethora of designs and styles to choose from in a vast range of colors. My eyes zeroed in on a gorgeous teal blue silk and lace piece.

"Beautiful, isn't it?"

I turned around and smiled at the saleswoman who had approached me from behind.

"It is."

"It's from our Cassia collection. This color would look great with your skin tone and blonde hair," she said, fingering the material before picking it up from the table and holding it up to my chest.

"Would you like to try it on?"

"That would be great, thank you."

I followed the lady to the back of the boutique where she offered me a luxurious fitting room to change in. After closing the door, I removed my clothes and stood staring at the lingerie that the sales lady had hung up on the back of the dressing room door. I let my hands run over the material, relishing in the soft feel of the silk and lace. I removed the bra from the hanger and placed my hands through the straps, before snapping the ends together at my back. It was a quarter cup bra that swept up to fan across my collarbones, creating a delicate opening that accentuated my full breasts. A tiny black bow completed the bra as it rested in the middle of the cups between my breasts.

I reached for the thong, pulling it on over my legs to allow the stretchy silk sides to rest gently on my hipbones. Lace graced the front of the fabric and also in the rear. The same contrasting black bow that was on the bra, sat in the front, just at the top of my mound. I reached for the suspender, pulling it on to where the lace top part swept romantically over my hips. Lastly, I put on the pair of matching thigh-high teal silk stockings and secured the black clasp at the end of the suspender to them. I turned around to look in the mirror, amazed at how the delicate fabric felt. I ran my hands down the front of my body, imagining what my mystery client's hands would feel like as he touched both my skin and my fabric. My face flushed with heat, as blood ran to my face at all the possibilities of pleasure I would get to experience with him.

"Everything okay, Sweetie?" The sales lady asked as she knocked gently on the door. I undid the lock and opened the dressing room door a fraction of an inch so that I could see her.

"Can I get your opinion on this?"

"Sure," she said, smiling. I opened the door wider so that she had the opportunity to look at the entire ensemble. I slipped back into my black heels and stood before her to be assessed.

"I think the color looks gorgeous on you. Your décolletage looks phenomenal in the Cassia bra. What sort of look or idea did you have in mind for the piece?"

"Well, I have a *special* date and want to look feminine, sexy...*wanted*."

"Well, Honey, I think you have all of those nailed down. Your date will be thoroughly pleased, I'm sure." Her smile was warm, and I appreciated her kindness.

"I'll take them, then."

"Great, when you are finished, I will wrap them up for you. Will it be cash or charge?"

"Cash, please. Thank you."

SEVERAL HOURS AND a couple hundred dollars later, I arrived back at my condo with all my new purchases. I splurged on a few more lingerie pieces for work, as well as a few cocktail dresses and a new pair of shoes. The cocktail dresses could be worn for work or play, seeing as how I did have a few clients that only used my services as a companion date, for a social functions or business dinners where they wanted or needed a companion.

I dug in my purse for the keys as I balanced all of my packages on one arm before opening the door. A crunch was heard under my foot as I stepped into the condo and I looked over my shoulder to find a white envelope laying on the floor addressed with my name. Someone must have slipped it under the door while I was gone this morning. I walked over to my couch and sat all of my packages and bags down before going to retrieve the envelope. Lifting the flap, I pulled out an intricately designed invitation to the retirement party of my former therapist, Robert Gunn. Who was also Andris's uncle. That meant that he would be there as well. Did I want to subject myself to seeing Andris again so soon? I read through the invitation and noticed that it was for tonight at eight pm. I looked at the clock and noticed it was three in the afternoon. It gave me just enough time for a small nap and then plenty of time to get ready.

My rest was fitful, when I finally fell asleep, images of the night before would begin playing on repeat. It seemed that every time I reached for my blindfold so that I could pull it off in hopes of getting just a glimpse at my mystery man, I would jolt awake before my eyes were ever uncovered from the darkness.

By the time I was finally able to shut my brain off long enough to get rest, the alarm on my phone had gone off telling me it was time to get up and get ready. I stumbled through my dark condo, moonlight savings time having the pleasure of it being dark at five pm.

The shower was soothing as I washed and buffed my body, amazed at how aware I was of the excitement I felt about getting to see Andris tonight at the party. I couldn't help but think about all the faces I would see there and wondered if I would be searching the crowd all night wondering if *he* was there.

After my shower, I towel dried my hair and rolled it in my foam rollers before venturing to my room. The Agent Provocateur bag rested on the foot of my bed and I wondered if I wanted to wear the contents that were inside. Shrugging, I decided to go for it. Maybe if my mystery client was there, he would see me and decide that he wanted to have another session sooner rather than later.

I enjoyed putting on the teal piece again, enjoying how sexy it made me feel and to have the ability to smile knowing what was underneath my clothing. I don't care what anyone says, a good pair of lingerie always makes a woman feel sexy, no matter what.

I walked over to the closet and sifted through the numerous dresses I had that accompanied some of the other lingerie pieces I had in there. The event was formal, so I needed something that would fit the events of the evening, while giving me the sexy edge that I wanted to create. I found a silk dress in nearly the exact same color as the lingerie I was wearing and decided that it would be perfect. Pulling it off the hanger, I held it up in front of me. Fate must have been on my side because I didn't realize that the top of the dress matched the top of my new bra perfectly. I looked at the tag.

Agent Provocateur.

It was a slip dress that Lexie had gotten me for my birthday this past year. I laughed at the irony and proceeded to slip into the gown. It featured two thigh-high slits up both sides of my legs that rested just to the edge of my stockings. In the back, the lace tapered from the nape of my neck down all the way to the top of my ass, exposing most of my backside. It was sexy and elegant at the same time. I needed to remind myself to thank Lexie later.

I returned to the bathroom, zapping my rolled hair with the dryer and then let the rollers sit to cool while I applied my make-up. I wanted something very sexy and simple to go with my dress, so I chose to do a simple cat-eye lined lid with a few swipes of mascara and a dab of pink lip gloss. The deep black line of my eyes made me look like a nineteen forties pin-up girl, so to complete the look, I removed the rollers and sectioned off my bangs. Parting them over to the side, I created a small pinwheel look to them before pinning them in place and then swept my long and now wavy hair over to the side to rest on my shoulder so that my back would be exposed. A few spritzes of my favorite honeysuckle perfume and I was ready to go.

After returning to my room to slip on my grey sequined strappy sandals, I grabbed a matching clutch from the top of my closet and ventured into the living room to transfer all of the items I would need tonight into it from my purse, even throwing in a few extra condoms.

You know. Just in case.

I called ahead of time for a cab, because I didn't want to stand out in the freezing cold to wait for one knowing that the wind would cut right through the delicate silk dress I was wearing, even with my trench coat on. The ride over to the hotel where the party was taking place was spent thinking about Andris and my mystery client. Since it was a business type setting, I assumed that Andris would have me address him as such as opposed to Sinclaire. The more I thought about it, the Sinclaire name didn't really fit the rugged sexiness that was Andris Gunn.

I arrived at the hotel just a little past eight pm, and as the cab pulled up, a gentleman in a well-tailored suit and white gloves opened the door for me and I felt the cold breeze hit my legs as I stepped from the cab. I thanked him, pulling my jacket tighter around me to combat the cold and proceeded up the stairs to the hotel entrance.

The New York Palace was a beautiful hotel set in Midtown that blended modern with classic New York elegance. The party was being held in a bar beneath the hotel's large grand staircase in the lobby. Trouble's Trust was modernly designed with deep red liqueur walls and embossed leather panels. It featured an intricately designed liquid metal bar, but the most impressive thing about the room was the floor to ceiling wine display.

There were probably already close to seventy people in the bar when I arrived, making it difficult to spot Andris.

Not that I was looking for him.

A gentleman at the entrance accepted my coat and I held onto my clutch just in case I needed anything inside. I made my way over to the bar, standing behind two older women who were engrossed in conversation. Their hair was immaculately styled, and their makeup done to perfection. I could tell that the women were older than what their appearance showed, thanks to the wonders of Botox.

"Madam, what may I get for you?" The bartender asked when he noticed I had picked up one of the specialty drink menus from the bar.

"I think I would like to try the 'Queen of Mean' please," I said as my eyes scanned over the rest of the menu. Breuckelen Wheat Whiskey, Ginger Beer, Red Jacket NY Apple Juice,

Averell "Damson Gin", elderflower syrup, fresh lemon, and a baked apple chip garnish seemed enticing enough to me. The bartender went to work mixing my drink just as the two older ladies turned around to look at me.

"Your dress is beyond gorgeous, my dear. If I were younger, I would have to show it off myself. How do you know my husband?"

At first I was a little shocked by her question. Given my profession, I met a lot of women's "husbands". Was she asking me if I slept with her husband? Did I sleep with her husband?

She must have noticed the furrow of my brows as I tried to search my mind for who she could be, so she reached out and put a gentle hand on my forearm.

"Doctor Robert Gunn."

"Ah, yes," I said giggling. "He was my therapist for many years, until recently." I explained to her, feeling relived that I had *never* slept with Dr. Gunn.

"What is your name, dear?"

I extended my hand to hers while her older friend looked on.

"Nicola Forbes. Pleasure to meet you, Mrs. Gunn."

She took my hand delicately in hers, rubbing her thumb on the back of my hand.

"Please, call me Dottie. That Mrs. Gunn shit makes me feel old. Nicola Forbes. You must be the beautiful daughter of former Senator Forbes."

I tensed a little. I hated it when people brought up my parents. Not that it bothered me to speak about them, but years of "I'm sorry for your loss," or hearing about how "wonderful" my father was when I knew different got rather old.

"Yes, ma'am."

"Well, how that old fart made such a beautiful woman like you is beyond me. Oh, no offense, dear."

I liked her instantly.

"None taken, trust me."

"Forgive me, this is my friend Shelby Patterson. She flew into town yesterday to surprise her husband. We go back many years. Her husband often comes to New York on business, but it is rare she gets to attend."

I really tensed then. It had to be a coincidence. *Had to.*

"Nice to meet you as well," I said as sweetly as I could to the woman. She smiled up at me and repeated the same kindness.

"Yes, my husband is floating around here somewhere. Probably bugging Robert about being too old to handle working anymore."

I laughed, though it was fake. Shit. There was no telling how many of these high class assholes that were at the party were, or still are, clients of mine. I just hoped that none of them noticed, put two and two together, or said anything that would compromise my identity.

"My nephew should meet you, my dear. He is single, you know. Are you seeing anybody?" Dottie asked with a certain gleam in her eye. Great. She was trying to play matchmaker. The last thing I wanted to be subjected to was some weasel who would spend all night trying to take me home to get in my pants. If he wanted it, he would have to pay just like everyone else, and my shit was high dollar.

"No, I'm single."

Shit. Why did I say that?

Dottie got up from her seat after tossing back the rest of her Cosmopolitan.

"Stay here, my dear. I'll go find him."

The bartender handed me my cocktail and I took a deep drink from the glass.

"Dottie means well, but she has been trying to get that nephew of hers to settle down for years. Her and Doctor Gunn never had children, so I think she has a deep want for babies running around the house," Shelby said to me and my eyes grew wide. Children were definitely off my radar. Why would I want to subject a child to my fucked up life? Why would I want to bring another human being into this world when its own mother would be incapable of loving it like a normal person would?

Shelby excused herself to run to the restroom, which left me at the bar alone. I quickly finished my drink and took a seat in Dottie's vacant bar chair, ordering another cocktail. As the bartender was serving me my second drink, a man approached me and sat in the chair that Shelby had vacated. He was an older man, dark skinned with matching dark hair. His suit was obviously custom tailored to fit his large frame. He was attractive, not overly like Andris, but for an older man he looked pretty good.

"Mind if I sit here?" He asked in a strong Italian mixed with a Jersey accent. The strong smell of his expensive cologne nearly overpowered me as he took a seat in the chair next to me.

"Whiskey, neat," he said to the bartender when he walked over.

"So, what is a beautiful lady like you doing sitting at a bar all by herself?" I raised my eyebrows at him. Surely this wasn't Dottie's nephew. Sleaziness radiated from him from the too strong cologne, to the greasy slick of his dark hair.

"I was just enjoying my drink," I said, tipping my glass up and taking a drink. I had no patience to deal with this man hitting on me all night. The only thing I wanted hitting on me tonight was the smack of mystery man's balls as he drove into me while Andris watched. The thought of him joining in, sent a glorious shiver rolling down my spine.

"Let me get you another," he said waving his hand at the bartender.

"Um, thanks."

I sat staring at the condensation on my glass, letting my fingers catch the droplets of water before they fell onto the bar. I could feel the man's eyes boring into me, trying to undress me with his eyes. It shouldn't have bothered me because I was used to it, but something about this man yelled creep.

"What is your name, lovely girl?"

"Jericho Lane," I offered, not wanting to reveal my real name to this man.

His eyes widened. No. Fuck, fuck no.

"Well, Miss Lane, if I said that I hadn't heard about you I would be lying. In fact, old man Patterson was just speaking about what you did for him just yesterday. Now that I can see you in the flesh, I think I may have to make an investment in your services."

He leaned in closer, lifting a hand to finger one of my loose curls and he traced the strand down to where it ended just at the nape of my neck and where the top of my dress began. His long, chunky fingers traced over the teal lace at my back before his fingers came into contact with my bare skin. This time the shiver I felt was not a welcome one.

"I'm sorry, but I am all booked at the moment. I am sure

there are a number of girls at the agency that would be willing to oblige."

"Surely, you would reconsider if the price is right, no?" He asked as he began to draw circles on the small of my back.

"I'm sorry, but who are you exactly? All sessions are set up through my agent, not me."

"My apologies, Miss Lane," he said, removing his hand from my back and extending it out to me. Reluctantly, I grabbed it and he pulled it toward him, allowing his wet lips to press a kiss to the back of my hand.

"Antonio Cardinelli," he said as he still held onto my hand. I pulled it away from him as if to reach for my drink on the bar, when I felt someone else approach from behind. The familiar electric shock saturated my body and I knew who it was without having to turn around and look at him.

"Nicola, there you are."

Antonio looked at me, knowing very well now that I had lied to him about my name.

"Good evening, Andris," he said before tossing back the rest of his whiskey and standing from his chair.

"Antonio."

One would have to be dumb not to feel the tension between the two men. I turned in my chair, Andris's fingers stroked across my back as I did and it sent a million tingles into my system.

"Good evening, Andris," I said, smiling up at him as our eyes met. He was devastatingly handsome. Even more so than the night he showed up at my condo in the black suit and chauffeur hat. The thought had my mind thinking. Why would a well off, sexy, powerful man like Andris, who was in one of the most prestigious families in New York, be acting like a chauffeur to my mystery client? I knew he had told me he was helping a man who had *problems*, but to act as a servant to him, and even watch and direct the whores in which his friend found companionship in, was rather strange.

"*Nicola*, here, was just telling me about her line of work, Andris. Her services sound rather interesting and I may be in touch soon for a sale."

"Well as her doctor, I am recommending that Miss Forbes takes off several weeks from her job. I don't need the stress of her *sales* getting in the way of her treatment. I am sure there are other items that would better serve your interests, Antonio."

"Perhaps."

I sat and watched the two men discuss me as if I wasn't even there. One man wanted my services and the other man was trying to prevent him from obtaining them? Why?

"Nicola, would you like to dance?" Andris asked as he tilted his head over to where a group of people were in a corner of the bar dancing. I lifted my glass, downing the remainder of my drink and eyeballing the full one in front of me that Antonio had purchased.

"That would be nice, thank you," I said extending my hand to him. Before we could walk away, I turned back around to Antonio and gestured to the still full drink sitting on the bar.

"Thank you Mr. Cardinelli, for the drink..."

And then I winked at him and walked towards the dance floor with Andris.

CHAPTER SEVEN

Andris

FIRE. HEAT. SEARING ANGER surged through me when I saw Antonio Cardinelli sitting at the bar with Nicola. The disgustingly sleazy way he fingered the strand of her hair before touching the delicate skin on her back made me want to punch him. I vaguely heard the words my beloved aunt was speaking to me as she gestured to where Nicola sat. Something about being beautiful, and single and that I should go introduce myself.

I knew she would be at the retirement party tonight. My uncle had told me that he was going to send several invitations to some of our patients that didn't require a strait jacket in order to be seen in public. The fact that my uncle could so easily mingle with the family that was responsible for using my clinic to obtain drugs legally, yet sell them illegally, pissed me off so badly I couldn't see straight. Combine that with the fact that Cardinelli had his greasy, corrupt hands on Nicola and my blood pressure was now through the roof. I had never even addressed my aunt who was going on and on about how beautiful Nicola was. No. The only thing I cared about was getting to her, and getting Antonio's hands off of her.

I led Nicola over to the dance floor, proud that the drink Cardinelli had bought for her sat untouched on the bar while she left his company to join mine. I placed my hand at the small of her back as she brought her arms up to wrap around my neck as our hips began to sway to the music.

The curvatures of her delectable body molded perfectly into mine and I could feel the warmth radiating from her skin. The beautiful teal dress she wore was thin, and as my hands caressed the fabric, I imagined ripping it from her body.

I had always been a very career driven individual. Thanks to my father, succeeding in life and becoming someone of importance was always one of my top priorities; but not only that, I wanted to make a difference in someone's life. I wanted to give them a sense of power over their disabilities and diagnoses, so that they could live as normal of lives as possible. I hated living everyday desiring success, but I was more focused on not failing.

It was also a way for me to mask my own insecurities.

Sex was something I used to break away from all the horrible things I had to see every day. It was also my escape from my own, undiagnosed condition. Something I hid from everyone, and was the biggest reason I had the arrangement that I did.

The soft scent of honeysuckle filled my senses as if dragging my brain into a lust-filled fog. Reaching up, I grabbed one of her delicate hands and held it to my chest in-between our bodies to keep me from reaching for places on her body that would be wildly inappropriate in public.

"I take it you don't like that guy," she spoke, her breath blowing across my neck and ear. Suppressing a shiver and the need to pull her closer to me, I replied.

"Like would be a tame word. That man is dangerous, and I would suggest you stay away from him."

My words sounded more like a command than a request and it had her pulling back from me slightly, cold replacing the warmth that her body had created in me.

"I deal with men like him every day. I'm used to the cheesy come-ons and sexual innuendos, Dr. Gunn. I can handle myself."

I blew out a breath of frustration.

"I wasn't implying that you couldn't. I was just stating a fact about Antonio Cardinelli."

"I know who he is."

This time it was my turn to pull back. I shouldn't have been surprised. Half of New York City knew who Antonio Cardinelli was, especially those in the wrong crowds. I watched over Nicola's shoulder as Mrs. Cardinelli joined her husband at the bar, picking up the drink that Nicola had left and downing it without a single thought. She then glanced in our direction and when she saw me with Nicola, her eyes held hardness. The cold, icy stare told me that she didn't like the fact I was dancing with her.

"So, Monday you become owner of the clinic?"

Her voice broke through as I turned my eyes away from Mrs. Cardinelli.

"Yes."

I felt her fingers begin to play with the hair at my nape. I closed my eyes, amazed at how much I could enjoy her touch without my anxiety kicking in. I enjoyed the soothing feel of her fingers as they gently brushed against the flesh of my neck. I had to fight everything inside of me to keep my dick at bay. What was it about this woman that had all my normal insecurities, all my anxiety, completely disheveled and allowed me to feel *normal* for once?

It made me want her even more. It made the desire within me to claim her body so intense, I nearly felt like I could combust. Thankfully, there was the contract.

Which she signed.

Alexandra had scanned and emailed the signed document over to me shortly after Nicola had left my office. Even though I would not get to be the one buried deep within her, *he* would be able to. I would get to be the one in control. I would get to be the one who instructed her with what to do with her body and how to do it, allowing my need for *perfect* control to be sated. As if reading my thoughts, she spoke, leaning in to whisper in my ear.

"Did your client tell you I signed the contract? That I now belong to him for the next twelve weeks?"

I nodded, trying to control how her whispering in my ear did things to my body. I was good at control. *Perfect* at it, actually, and I knew that I would be able to hold back, even though my body desperately protested.

"Is he here?"

I shook my head, and her body seemed to deflate. The fact that she seemed excited by the possibility of him being at the party made me feel jealous.

"I need a name, Andris. Any name. I—I think about the other night constantly. I feel him when I'm sleeping, and I daydream about him when I am awake. I feel things when I do. Not just pleasure, but—,"

"You feel the emotions that you have been void to," I interrupted.

"Yes."

She looked up at me, the doe shape of her eyes framed by

thick lines that accentuated the pristine blue. Not the same dark as mine, but crystal clear, like the blue of the Caribbean. I saw desire in her features, and the need for information. Taking her bottom lip between her teeth, she nibbled on the same spot that she bled from in my office earlier today.

"Don't do that, you'll start bleeding again," I said, reaching up to pull her lip from her teeth. She momentarily looked down, at where my fingers still rested on her pout long after she had released her lip. Something shifted between us and when she looked back into my eyes, I could see the want in her features, but this time instead of being for *him*, it was for me. She pressed into me more, her hips making contact with where it would soon be difficult to hide my erection.

"I like that you watched."

Fuck.

Not the words I was expecting to hear, but goddamn, it hit something inside of me. I felt my eyes glaze over like they did when I became aroused, and the familiar fog began to set into my brain. I realized that I hadn't answered her. How could I give her a name to her mystery client when I didn't even truly know it myself?

"Link. You can call him Link," I lied, trying to think of something on the spot. She pulled back, looking up at me with her blue eyes and a smile spread across her face, highlighting her cheekbones and making her eyes squint ever so slightly. I felt her breasts brush up against me as she leaned in.

"Did you enjoy watching me and Link?"

Did I? Fuck yeah I did, and it was hard to keep the jealousy at bay knowing and watching them interact, the entire time wishing it was me she was fucking. My arousal grew the harder she pressed her body into mine. Over her shoulder, I could still see Mrs. Cardinelli boring holes into Nicola and me as we swayed together with the other people dancing.

I looked at the ridged bitch, giving her a sly smile before I leaned into Nicola, making our actions seem familiarly intimate.

"You have no fucking idea. Link will be here later. He was hoping that you two could seal the ink on the contract tonight. You know, make it official," I let my lips gently touch her ear as I spoke and I felt the involuntary shiver that ran down her body. God, I wanted her so badly. I wanted to fix her—to help her feel things that only I could make her feel. I was lost in the feel of her body, the way her soft curves molded to my hardness. I was just about to tell her that we needed to get the fuck out of there when a hand clamped on my shoulder.

"Andris, can we have a chat? Excuse me, Nicola. I need to speak to my nephew," my uncle chimed in, breaking my moment with Nicola.

"No problem, Dr. Gunn. I need another drink anyway. Thank you for the dance, Andris," she said, pinching my side before she walked off towards the bar.

"What is it, Bobbie?" I asked in irritation as I ran my hand through my hair. This party wasn't anything to be desired and the only thing that made it worthwhile was Nicola.

"It seems that you have pissed off one of our guests, dear *nephew*. Let's go outside and get away from wondering ears," he said sternly as he glanced around the room. Spinning on his heel, he turned towards the exit of the bar, and without saying a word, he expected me to follow him.

Like a fucking puppy.

The same way my father used to treat me.

When we got outside, the frigid air hit me and the wind

was cold enough to bite through the fabric of my jacket. Pulling out a cigar, my uncle extended one to me, knowing damn well I wouldn't take it before shoving it back into his pocket and lighting the one he put in his mouth.

"It seems you've pissed off one of our clients tonight, Andris. I thought we were perfectly clear what was to happen when you took over the clinic. Nothing will change once you take ownership. The *arrangement* will go on as planned."

I clenched my fists, partially because it was freezing, but mainly because I felt myself wanting to give in to the anger—wanting to give into the sensations that always invaded me whenever I was disappointed. My drive to succeed sometimes fell second for my drive to not fail. But this situation was different. I was trying to do the right thing. Trying to do what I knew was going to be right for the clinic.

It ate at me.

Everyday.

"Did you hear a word I said, boy?" My uncle asked, getting up in my face, the pungent smell of cigar invading my nostrils from his breath.

"I heard you."

"Antonia Cardinelli has taken a liking to Nicola. You practically slapped him in the face when you removed her from their conversation and had your hands all over her out on the dance floor," he seethed.

"Antonio Cardinelli is married. He needs to go and have a conversation with his wife."

My shirt was pulled and my uncle was so close to me that I could feel the spit come from his mouth as he degraded me.

"I'm only going to say this one more time, Andris. You do what the fuck Cardinelli wants. When he wants, how he wants, do you understand? I still have the choice not to turn the clinic over to you. How would you like that, huh? I'll give it to someone else. I won't have you fucking shit up for us."

He pushed me away hard enough that I stumbled backwards before he turned around to head back inside the bar. I stood there, watching his retreating form, not even feeling the sting of the cold wind anymore. The wind was sharp enough to slice through my body like a knife, but I was numb.

I needed a fix.

I needed to get the fuck out of there.

Nicola/Jericho

I WAITED BY THE BAR, throwing back another cocktail as I waited for Andris to return. My head was feeling fuzzy from the alcohol. Between stares from Cardinelli, as he raked his sleazy eyes all over my body, I was ready to retreat. At the same time, I didn't want to leave in case Link really did show up.

I felt the pangs of want. The need for my fix filtered through my veins, turning my blood warm and heating my body from the inside out. I needed the needle. The penetration that invaded me and let me surrender to the sensations and feelings that I got to experience when I was with *him*.

I felt my phone buzz in my clutch and fished it out of my purse.

Unknown: He wants you outside in 5 minutes. A car will be waiting.

I couldn't help the smile that spread across my face. Like the crack addict who just got the promise of relief after a three day withdraw. I slipped my phone back in my purse and started to head towards the bathroom to freshen up when a large hand on my upper arm stopped me.

"Where are you off to in such a hurry?"

I recognized the voice of my client, Mr. Patterson, so I spun around and plastered the practiced smile that I had down to a T. Years of faking had really made me into a beautiful actress.

"Hello, Mr. Patterson. I'm just off to the ladies room before I leave for the night."

His beady eyes landed on my chest, zeroing in on the skin of my breasts framed by my dress.

Hello, asshole. My eyes are up here.

"You can't leave just yet, Jericho. Mrs. Patterson has already retired for the evening and I have another room booked in the other tower of the hotel. Cardinelli wants a session. He said he is willing to pay twice our normal fee."

I looked over Mr. Patterson's shoulder to see Antonio staring at me as he tipped up his glass before draining the liquid from his glass.

"I'm very sorry, Mr. Patterson, but I am booked for the evening. In fact, I am booked in advance for the next twelve weeks. I'm sure if you call the agency, Alexandra will find you a suitable girl."

"We don't want another girl. My good friend here has raved about you, and after seeing you for myself, I must have a taste," Cardinelli said after he had approached where Mr. Patterson and I were standing. He lifted a hand to trace his fingers down my arm, leaving a trail of goose bumps in their wake.

And not the welcome kind.

Something about this man screamed trouble. There was a

gleam of dominance in his eye and I watched his pupils dilate as he scanned my body.

"I'm sorry, I really am booked. I must be leaving. I have a client that has paid in advance and has requested my services," I said as I looked around the room, whispering so that no one could hear me. Cardinelli's eyes changed, where there was once fire, now there was ice. The fingers that were skimming my arm, encompassed my wrist, squeezing so hard I could feel my heart beat through my pulse point.

"I'll double what he is paying."

Woah.

Double the pay? Twelve weeks at twelve and a half grand a session and this man in front of me was offering twice that amount? Momentarily my mind wanted to say yes. That amount of money would put me ahead for a really long time. I wouldn't have to fuck so many sleezeballs in order to survive and I could pull back on my client list. I could even afford a vacation, new wardrobe, and anything else that I wanted.

But my body was denying me. It wanted to feel the strength of Link's hands on my body, the shudders that I felt as his cock massaged me from the inside out. It wanted the heat, the fire, and the desire, that I felt the night I was with him. I wanted to see where it would go. I was curious to see if the same feeling of desire was there when I was with him once again.

Maybe he was exactly what I needed to fill my empty soul. To bring myself out of the darkness and push myself forward to not being this vacant shell of a bottomless pit that filled me.

"Thank you for the offer, Mr. Cardinelli, but I must regretfully decline. We can reconvene once my twelve week contract is up."

His glare never relented, only continued to burn a hole

through my body. Any other person would have probably felt uncomfortable, but I just stood there, glaring back at him as my body buzzed with excitement. I needed to hurry and get outside, or I'd miss my chance with Link. I pulled my wrist away from Cardinelli, who reluctantly let go, and I turned to make my way toward the bathroom before offering my apologies to Mr. Patterson. I felt his eyes on me the entire time I was walking to the bathroom. Heat flanked my backside and I risked one more glance over my shoulder as I pushed open the door to the restroom.

He still stood there, the same spot I had left him as he rubbed his thumb and forefinger across his overly tanned jaw. A shiver ran through me as I looked away and walked into the restroom. A weird feeling ran through me as I looked into the mirror, attempting to fix my already perfect hair. It was something I hadn't really felt that much before, but I recognized the emotion as I gazed at my own reflection and saw the dullness in my eyes.

I was uncomfortable, and not in the I-fell-on-my-ass-in-front-off-a-thousand-people uncomfortable.

No, this new feeling had a hint of fear.

CHAPTER EIGHT

JERICHO/NICOLA

I DIDN'T SEE CARDINELLI, nor Patterson as I left the restroom to make my way outside, but I did have the pleasure of running into Mrs. Cardinelli on my way out of the restroom. Everything was fake about her, right down to the over large, rather expensive sacks of water filled plastic she had on her chest. Her perfume was too strong, and her make-up immaculate, to the point of being excessive. She teetered on her feet, signaling her sign of inebriation as she fought to steady herself against the doorframe.

"You think he wants someone like you?" She asked as I walked past her to head outside. Stopping in my tracks, I turned around to answer her. It was *her* husband who propositioned me, not the other way around, but her next few words stopped me by stunning me.

"Dr. Gunn. He is, what do the kiddies call it now? One fine assed piece of a man." She said as she sloshed her drink all over the floor.

She wasn't talking about her husband, but about Andris. I

was instantly brought back to earlier when she wouldn't stop looking at Andris and I while we were dancing.

"I agree," I admitted, "But the question isn't what *does he want* with someone like me, it's what *will I do to him* that will make him come back begging for more. See, the difference between your overly stretched pussy and the fine quality of mine is that it keeps men coming back for more. It even had your husband begging to be inside of me just minutes ago, so when you start using your tiny IQ of a brain to think, think about *that*."

And I walked away.

ANDRIS WAS WAITING for me when I exited the bar. Propped against the sleek black car with his palms pressed against it and strumming his fingers upon the fender, I took him in. Pulling my trench coat tighter around me, I took tentative steps toward him, drinking in the beauty of the man, who at the moment, looked like he harbored a large amount of pain or sadness. The wind whipped the bottom of my skirt around my legs and I watched as the same breeze feathered through the dark curls that rested on his forehead and the warm vapors of his breath in the air as he exhaled.

"Andris?"

He looked up, his eyes, that usually held warmth, were colder than the air that surrounded us. He pushed off the car and bounded for me, taking my hand and escorting me to the car. He was silent, brooding, as he opened the back door for me to slide into the car. My ass connected with the warm, heated leather seats, and I was thankful for the heat on my backside, but there wasn't coldness only coming from the air. Andris began to shut the door, but I extended my arm to stop him, looking up as I did so.

"You going to tell me what is wrong, Andris?"

He looked at me quizzically for a few brief moments, and I swear I saw a flash of warmth in his eyes making the gold flecks more prominent, before they darkened again.

"It's Sinclaire, *Jericho*."

And he shut the door.

Wow. Okay. So obviously he was in "character" as he referred to both of us by our other names, but it didn't explain the coldness he was portraying. He seemed to be in a great mood when we were dancing before his uncle pulled him away. Or maybe Link said something to him?

Link.

Even just thinking about his name sent warmth through my chilled body, spreading my need and desire like wildfire rampant through a dry forest. Andris rounded the car and slammed the door before putting it into drive and easing into traffic. The partition that separated the front cab of the car from the back was up, leaving me to sit with my own thoughts. This was a far different cry from the first night we were together, or even no less than a half hour ago when I was wrapped in his arms on the dance floor at the club.

"Put the blindfold on," he instructed through the speakers of the car, and I reached over to pick up the black silk on the seat next to me and placed it over my eyes. I sat in darkness and silence, the only sounds to be heard were those of cars passing by.

After blackness and silence for what felt like half an hour, the car came to a stop. Andris didn't get out of the car immediately, but after a few moments I heard the front door open and close and then my own open and the cold air rushed in relentlessly, breaking out a chill on my skin. He grabbed my hand, and I was thankful for the warmth from him, even if it was only from his touch.

I thought about this situation as we rode the elevator up to wherever it was he was taking me. I didn't think that the circumstances were about money anymore. Yes, in the beginning, I did it for the money, putting a big dent in my debt and allowing me to have stability. Since becoming an escort, I lived comfortably, very different than when I first started out. I still hoarded money, fearful of going back to the place I was in when my parents died and I was left with nothing.

The elevator doors pinged open and Andris led me into the room. The familiar smell of leather hit my nostrils and I inhaled deeply, relishing in the scent as memories flooded my mind. Hands found my shoulders and removed my jacket.

"Is Link here?" I asked into the room, not knowing if Andris was still there.

"Yes."

"Will you still be here?"

"Yes."

My ears were covered with the noise canceling headphones and a crackle filled my ears before the sound of Andris's voice came through the speakers.

"Can you hear me, Miss Lane?"

I nodded as I bit down on my lip.

"Link is here. He loves the dress. The way it forms to each curve of your body. The way your nipples pucker beneath the fabric of your bra."

A warm hand ran down the window of the dress that exposed my breasts. My breathing began to become deeper, and I closed my eyes against the darkness of the blindfold.

"Link requests that you remove the dress."

I lifted my hands immediately, wanting to please the man who consumed my body with fire. The man, the only other one besides Andris who invaded my thoughts when I had an idle moment.

"Slowly."

I slowed my pace, smiling on the inside because I knew what was *under* the dress. Unbuttoning the lace at my neck, I slowly let the dress fall from my shoulders and over my breasts before it came to pool at my waist. Pressing the fabric over my hips, I shimmied it down my thighs before letting the silk rest upon the floor. I faintly thought I heard a small intake of breath and felt pleasure on the inside knowing that Andris could also see what was under my dress. I felt a breeze cross my skin as I felt Link circle me, not being able to see him, but knowing that he was admiring my beautifully expensive lingerie.

My hair was brushed aside and I felt his lips on my shoulder before his teeth took a slight bite from my skin. Electricity and desire pooled in my belly, my clit already becoming painfully aware of his presence. Each brush of his fingers, each passing touch of his hands made my mind and my body painfully aware. I felt it. The sensation of desire, the enormity of pleasure, and the only feelings that I didn't have to face.

I sighed as he pressed his body against my back, reaching around to cup my breasts in his firm hands. His squeeze was not gentle, but just poised on that border between pleasure and pain. I felt the warmth of his skin as it connected with the skin of my back, his hard chest heaving as his desire grew. His warm breath flowed against my neck, causing my already heated body to rise several more degrees. I lifted my hands, desperate to feel him as I covered his hands with my own, assisting him with the assault of my tits.

"No touching," I heard Andris tell me through the crackle in my headphones, his voice stern, but laced with desire. Quickly, I removed my hands, something about the sound of his voice captivating me.

I have always been a pretty strong willed woman. The benefit about not giving a shit about things gave me the power to not take any shit from anyone. I was never ordered around, never told what to do. I was the one who usually gave the orders. Most of my clients, being of the more submissive type, liked it when I took charge—liked it when I old them how to do things, or how to fuck me so that I could at least walk away with an orgasm. But something in the tone, the sternness, the harsh bite of Andris's words, sent a deeper escalation of want overwhelming me. I couldn't help the hitch in my breath, nor the slight jerk of my body as Link's hands continued to trace the contours of my skin. My bra was shredded, the sound of lace ripping from behind me only moments before the bra cascaded to the floor had me gasping.

It wasn't the fact that he had just ripped a four-hundred dollar piece of fabric, but the instantaneous surge of pleasure that flowed through me. I loved that my body surrendered to the sensations I was experiencing,

God I fucking loved it.

I didn't have to live these moments pretending, faking my way through time, but instead I got to embrace and involve myself in the moment. A sharp smack of my ass sent fire burning into my flesh. I bit my lip, relishing in how wonderful it felt. How the sting could heighten my desire that much more, and how, with each moment I was in the presence of Link and Andris, my body melted even more.

His hands encompassed my waist, sliding them lower...and lower...until his fingers brushed the top of my mound.

Smack.

Heat pooled, my body responded, and I cried out into the room from the surprise of being struck in such an intimate place, my pussy convulsing, practically begging to suck his dick deep within.

"Do you like it when he does that? Link wants to know."

I nodded, unable to form a coherent sentence as not one, but two fingers were inserted into my cunt, massaging the sensitive nerve endings inside. Andris's words were a little softer now, less demanding and a husky tone was in its place. I wondered if I was turning him on. Was he looking at me with the same desire that Link was, yet felt deprived that he couldn't touch me? Was he jealous as he watched another man manipulate my body, knowing very well that I didn't feel many emotions, but to witness this side of me in person?

"Do you only ever watch, Andris?"

A thumb joined Link's two fingers and the desire to hear his answer was long gone when my pussy began to tighten, and my lower abdomen squeezed in delight as Link assaulted my pussy, quick rapid strokes coupled with the rapid circling of my clit. I could feel my legs start to shake, my knees trembling, threatening to give out beneath me as my body climbed higher and higher. Soon my body began to flood with uncontrollable sensations. I could see the end of the hill as my body began to crest over the top...

And then he was gone.

Pushing away from me abruptly, my body protested at the disappearance of Link.

"No!" I cried as my knees buckled and I fell to the floor.

"Link doesn't like it when you ask questions, Miss Lane. Especially questions about other men."

The crackle of Andris's voice through the headphones didn't hide the forcefulness that had returned to his tone. A hand cupped my chin, pulling my body up from the floor and I scrambled to work my way to my feet. Link's hand clasped mine, the feel of the calluses on his fingers touching the backside of my hand. I was led, no practically dragged to another part of the room, where the smell of leather was stronger. Link stopped walking and in return I stopped. His hand left mine and I hated the coldness that I was left with.

"There is a table in front of you, Miss Lane. Bend over, and place your hands there, spread your legs, and don't move." My hands connected with soft padded leather, the action thrusting my naked ass into the air. I heard the sound of buckles clanking together only moments before my hands were bound to the table. I felt Link caress my back with something, being blindfolded and not knowing what it was, I couldn't say. It felt like leather as it trailed down the nape of my neck and along my spine. My breathing was short and sharp. I could feel my own desire running down the creamy skin of my inner thigh as my pussy begged to be filled.

I tried to get my mind in the game, picturing what I thought Link looked like. He had to be large, bigger than me. I could feel the hard muscles of his body when he pressed into me and I could tell that his physique was either that of an athlete, or someone who worked out regularly. Since I wasn't allowed to touch him, I didn't know whether his hair was short or long, or whether he had a beard, or a smooth jaw. Not being able to see him, I didn't know if his eyes were green, brown, or the beautiful dark navy color that Andris's were.

Instantly, my thoughts were on him and the image that I saw when I walked out of the club earlier and found him leaning against the car. He was beautiful, rugged, but in a refined way. His jaw always held the perfect amount of stubble and his hair always seemed slightly too long in the front, but just enough to be incredibly sexy. Was it wrong of me to enjoy knowing that Andris was watching? Was it seriously fucked up of me to be turned on by the stare of one man while being physically turned on at the hands of another?

"Andris?" I asked when I hadn't heard anything from him in several minutes. The item that was traced down my spine collided with my ass, sending a bite of pain across both cheeks.

"You are not permitted to speak, Miss Lane, unless it is to cry out in pleasure. Link isn't pleased when you do, much less speak another man's name only moments before he fills you with his cock."

And then it happened. My hips were grabbed and Link's cock was shoved into me, burying himself to the hilt as his balls slapped against my sensitive clit. He stilled, but only momentarily, as he let my pussy adjust to his cock for a few brief seconds before he started a relentless rhythm of pounding into me. Heat spread even deeper as all the blood flow rushed to that part of my body and my pussy eagerly welcomed each thrust. There it was again. The sating of the craving, the rush of drugs to my system. My fix, flooding through my veins.

My breasts bounced against my chest as his grip tightened on my hips. My nails dug into the leather of the table in front of me as I tried to ground myself even more in this spot. The spot where everything flooded me at once, where my very few emotions came to the surface and I smiled, actually fucking smiled from the pleasure and happiness radiating through my body.

Link's hand caressed my back as the other held onto my hips before he reached up and fisted my hair in his hands, tugging my hair and making my head tilt back in the process. My mouth was open as I worked to suck in vital air at the same time I was chasing my release. It was there, teetering on the edge of bliss and total annihilation. Suddenly, my feet left the floor as Link let go of my hair and picked me up by my hips and began thrusting even harder if possible.

He drove into me like a man possessed. Like a man who was staking claim on my body, and I was loving every second of it. Hitting somewhere deep inside of me, I exploded, coming all over his cock as my body finally found the relief it was looking for—surrendering to the pleasure and flooding me with a surge of normalcy. It was wonderful getting to experience this, and even more heightened by the situation.

It was in that moment that I knew that I wouldn't be able to get enough. The sinful desires, the overwhelming pleasure I felt from being with Link as Andris watched on, would never leave my system. No one would ever be able to replace the feelings that both of these men had given me. They were a godsend, something that was quickly becoming vital to my existence and I began to feel fear as Link climaxed into me and only seconds later pulled out.

There it was. Fear again. An emotion that I didn't experience often, yet one that I recognized most in others. As my backside felt cold from the distance Link but between us, warmth filled me once again as Andris spoke into the headphones and explained that he was removing my restraints.

"Leave the blindfold on, but Link insists you stay here this evening. You can remove it once you have been taken to your sleeping quarters."

A warm robe type fabric was placed around me as Andris tied something at my waist. The headphones were removed and all I could hear was the breaths of Andris and my own.

"Is he gone?" I asked, curious about Link's quick retreat every time he came inside of me.

"Yes."

"Why does he leave like that?"

"He doesn't like his escorts to know who he is. He is a user, Nicola. He enjoys your body, but doesn't want anything else other than that."

"So, I'm Nicola now?"

I heard him sigh long and hard, as if he were fighting against something that was greater than him.

"My mistake."

I reached out to touch him, but was only met with air.

"How do you feel about my body?"

I heard him swallow audibly before he spoke, his next words cutting through me like a knife.

"Your body is beautiful, but I will not ever touch you. You belong to Link. I watch how you submit to him. I watch how you let him manipulate your body, and while it is fucking gorgeous, it is my job to provide a service, just as it is yours. Nothing else, Miss Lane."

"It's weird. How he makes me *feel*. I can't explain it. Why is it that I have such a response to him? To you as well, for watching."

"That is a question that you need to save for Dr. Gunn."

"But you are Dr. Gunn," I shot back.

"Here, I am not."

Andris led me to a room in silence, guiding me by the hand. Not another word was spoken the entire way until we reached wherever it was I was going to be spending the night. I was confused. At his office, Andris was warmer, sweeter even. Here, when I was in session with Link, he seemed colder, more distant. I didn't know whether it was because he wanted to keep his business and side job separate, or if it was because he was trying to hide behind two different personalities.

It was a challenge to me. Something that drove me to wanting to see how long Andris would hold out until he couldn't hold back anymore. I wanted him to want my body the same way that Link did, and I was going to make it my mission to see that it happened.

ANDRIS

I HAVE ALWAYS PRIDED myself on my self-control. Knowing that I had the ability to maintain authority over my actions, my choices, and sometimes even my thoughts.

But not always.

There have been very few times in my life where my constraint was tested, my self-restraint sitting on the border of complete power and complete meltdown. I was poised, educated, well-spoken and looked up to by all of my peers, many of whom were several years older than myself. It was my drive for excellence, my passion to be perfect that provided and pushed my dominance to the forefront.

Then there were things that pulled me back as well.

Like my asshole of a father, my asshole of an uncle, and now...*Nicola*.

I've been angry. I've been driven to the point of complete loss of my control, but I have managed to pull myself back from the brink, to step back from the proverbial ledge, I guess you could say.

But watching her? Hearing her? Having to endure the torture of another being pounding into her and driving her body toward a mountain of pleasure was damn near maddening to the point of insanity. My jaw ached, my palms laced with the imprint of my fingernails from clenching my fists so tight. I didn't have to see her eyes to read the desire on her face, the want, the need, the inability to maintain her own control, as she climaxed and allowed her body to surrender to Link's relentless rhythm. It was written in the curvature of her mouth, the hiss in her breath, and the throaty cry of her voice as she summersaulted into rapture.

The jealousy damn near consumed me, only moments away from pushing Link aside and taking over. To allow me to be the forethought and him the afterthought. I wanted to replace myself in her imagination as her cunt was seduced by him. I wanted the desire running down her legs to belong to me, be for me, because of me.

But, I couldn't.

Not only would it break *Link's* contract, but it would break everything that he and I had accomplished together. It was through him, because of him, that I was allowed to chase away the demons that filled me. He helped to give me the escape I needed, to not have to feel the all-consuming need to be perfect, to strive for excellence.

So instead, I let him finish while I closed my eyes, trying to drown out the visual before me, trying to lose myself into other thoughts and struggling as sweat dripped from my brow. The smell of sex infiltrated the room, the musk of her pheromones working to slowly destroy me.

The energy never shifted when they both finished, it only worked to keep the sparks alive. My breathing had quickened, my chest heaved with heavy burden as I removed my headset and threw it across the room. Link had left and all that remained was me, the man left to clean up after him. There was no telling what kind of opinion Nicola had of me, knowing what I did. She couldn't possibly respect me for the things I did. Hell, I didn't respect myself. But dammit, it was the only way for me to get through all the shit swirling around in my head on a daily basis. So when she asked me why she had the response she did to Link and the same feelings about me watching, I couldn't answer her. I couldn't speak for Link, but only for myself, and it wasn't something I could discuss with her.

I led her to a second story room in the apartment, a place where none of the other girls have ever stayed. It was a rule. Fuck them and then they leave. Neither Link, nor I had the time to deal with clinginess or idle chit chat. He got what he wanted, the girls got their money, and everyone was satisfied. But for some ungodly fucking reason, I wasn't ready to let Nicola go. I wanted to keep her close. I wanted to be able to know that she was sleeping in the room next to where I would be staying and fantasize that it was me driving into the depths of her delicious cunt instead of Link.

Fucking Link.

I had a love/hate relationship with him. I loved getting to observe his conquests. I loved getting my own satisfaction from watching him fuck girls until they had trouble walking out of the door. But I also had a hatred for him because of the jealousy I felt with Nicola. Never once had I been envious of his position—to want what he had, but somehow it's different now. My mind and eyes knew her curves. They knew the sounds she makes when she's turned on, and the soft rush of breath that always flowed from her lips right before she climaxed. I knew the throaty pitch in her voice as her desire increased, and I also knew the glow of her body after orgasm.

All without being the one to give that to her.

I was fucked up. A real sick son-of-a-bitch for what I did on a regular basis. Watching another man get his rocks off fucking a woman while I got mine off watching—sitting in the shadows and guiding their movements.

As I closed the door and walked out of the room I had placed Nicola in, I thought about it. Each step I took, hitting the nail on my coffin that stood between me and sanity.

I needed help.

I needed therapy.

Fucking ironic, huh?

CHAPTER NINE

JERICHO/NICOLA

I SLEPT LIKE I HAD never slept before, both mentally and physically exhausted from all the new shit that was overwhelming me. I stretched into the darkness, noticing the silkiness of the satin sheets I laid upon. I felt all the muscles in my body protest from the movement, the deep ache feeling more prominent as I moved. My thighs still trembled and it didn't help that the memories of last night flashed through my mind. Being bent over a table and fucked until I was nearly un-capable of forming a coherent sentence was fucking wonderful.

I smiled into the darkness, something that I didn't do a lot of. Not that I didn't know how to smile, or that I didn't want to, it was just that nothing really ever gave me reason enough to feel this happy. I was stupid happy. Like the giggling school girls I had seen on TV yet never understood, and I was smiling so much my jaw hurt.

I sat up in bed, doing my best to work my long, blonde, mussed up hair into some sort of organization. Andris had left me a t-shirt to sleep in and I lifted the material to my nose and took a deep inhale.

It smelled like *him*. It smelled like Andris. A combination of the two things had my previously darkened and nearly non-existent emotions bubbling to the surface in full force. It was almost too much, as things that I had never felt before began to flood me chin deep into the empty swimming pool I felt placed in.

I yawned, stretching once more for good measure. Opening my eyes didn't cure the darkness of the room, because when I did, I was still met with inky blackness. I felt around on the surface of the massive bed I was in (I knew it was massive because I had rolled around in it before I fell asleep) to see if I could find the ledge. I felt a chill filter through the air and suddenly I felt like I wasn't alone.

"Who's there?" I asked into the dark emptiness.

I was met with silence as I scooted toward the edge of the bed, allowing my feet to come into contact with the cold hardwood floor beneath me. I had no clue where the door was, or even if I was allowed to exit through it.

"There is a robe lying on the bed to your right. You can put it on if you are cold."

I jump, startled by the voice in the room. It sounded familiar, yet different at the same time. I had trained my ears to recognize sounds to help me associate them with certain emotions. The voice I heard was deep, dark, with just the smallest hint of what sounded like a New Jersey accent.

"Holy fucking hell!" I yelped, my voice echoing off the walls in the room and giving me an idea of just how large it was.

"You scared the shit out of me."

I heard shuffling and then the sound of shoes as they walked across the floor, sounding more distant from me.

"My apologies."

What the hell was he doing in here? Who the hell was he?

"Where is Sinclaire?" I asked him, reaching for the robe and finding it right where he had described, next to me on the bed.

"Sinclaire will be around shortly. He is busy making arrangements for your return home."

My heart rate sped up, the points in my wrist matching the heavy beating that began to form in my chest. Suddenly, something in the air shifted. It filled with electricity and I had to squeeze my thighs together to try and quell the ache that was forming.

"Link?" I asked, standing from the bed and securing the robe around my waist. The chill that I only moments before felt, was now gone and heat and warmth had settled in its place.

He didn't respond.

"I know it's you. So don't try to pretend that it isn't."

"Very well."

He spoke with an air of elegance. Someone who had grown up sophisticated, clearly very charming. The richness of it made my belly flutter, like when you go down a steep hill on a rollercoaster. I never got that feeling with men. Sure, I got a little excited at the prospect of an orgasm when I was with a client, but most of the time I was disappointed and left wanting after our sessions were over. Each time, it seemed it took me longer and longer to climax and more often than not I finished the job myself when I got home.

So why was it that just being in the presence of this man, who I couldn't even see, made me feel like I could cum just from listening to him talk? Why did my body and dormant emotions come to life whenever I was with him or thought about him?

"Why did you want a twelve week contract with me? You

could have had any number of girls from the agency, why me?"

I asked the question that had been nagging me. Of all the girls, why the fuck did he want me?

His silence nearly had me crawling out of my skin. Like there was an itch in my bones that I couldn't scratch. I was nearly ready to speak again when he finally answered.

"It was a chance encounter with you. I was expecting Kiki, but when Alexandra told me she wasn't available, I told her to send me someone else. It happened to be you. She explained to me that you were one of the most demanded girls, so I trusted her. I'm glad I did."

I shivered. His voice alone did things to my body that no man could do with his cock. It was a strange thing, feeling shit you never had before. But the feelings coming from Link were ones that were welcome. I submitted to men because I had to. It was my job to give them what they wanted because they paid me to do so. But this man made me *want* to do whatever the fuck he asked me to. Hell, I'd walk around the damn room with my thumb stuck up my ass if I knew it turned him on. My desire to have him was almost as potent as my desire to please him.

The sound of him walking toward me made me stand up a little straighter, even though my legs felt like they could give out.

"Wh—why did you make me wear the headphones and then now speak to me? I can't see you. I have no idea what you look like."

My voice faltered as I felt him at my side. Chill bumps ran up my swiftly overheating body, creating a tingling sensation to run up my arm and straight to my fucking clit. I closed my eyes and I absorbed the enormity of what I was feeling. This—this was a whole new level of pleasure that I had never experienced before. It was sexy, erotic, and damn near fucking spiritual. A connection of cosmic proportions. That would be the only way I could explain it.

Dr, Gunn had always told me that all we needed to do was find my trigger. Something that would spur and entice my sleeping emotions. I was quickly wondering if Link was that trigger.

"I like to be nondescript and faceless, Miss Lane. It keeps things impersonal. No expectations. No presumptions. No complications. It allows you to use your imagination. To conjure up your own idea of what the person looks like as he fucks you hard. Admit it. It turns you on to not know. It makes that pussy of yours quiver with excitement."

He leaned in, close enough that I could feel the warmth of his breath, the heat from his body, and hear the desire dripping from his voice.

"I bet if I slid my fingers between your thighs, I'd find your cunt ready and eager for me to take you, wouldn't I?"

I let out a staggered breath, shaking from the inside because everything he said was true. I could feel it, I didn't have to reach my own hands down to know that my pussy was saturated with want, soaked with desire, and filled with an ache that only he could offer relief to.

"Yes."

It was a one word answer, but mainly because that was all I was capable of saying. My brain seized when he was this close to me. My body responded instead, allowing my mind the freedom to allow myself to experience the sensations. I didn't have to think about them. I didn't have to search through every corner of my mind to wonder what it was that I was *supposed* to feel, but instead got to endure the physicality and awareness of what I *was* feeling.

He lifted a hand and stroked it down the back of my long hair. Through each strand, I could feel him. Each follicle giving way to tiny pin pricks of pleasure coursing through me.

"One time was all it took for me to get lost in you. I *don't* do that. I don't lose myself in anyone or anything especially a fucking hooker. What the fuck is it about you that is different? What makes your pussy golden, and everyone else's like garbage?" He asked as his fingers enclosed around the nape of my neck, using them to tilt my head to the side and he pressed a hot, open mouthed kiss on my neck and lightly grazed his teeth against my flesh. My body responded instantly, I knew he felt me jerk because he smiled against my skin.

"I like that I own you for the next twelve weeks. I get off on the fact that your sweet little cunt will be mine whenever I want it, however I want it. It thrills you too. I don't have to see you right now to know the flush of your skin. I don't have to use my sight to know how turned on you are at this very moment. I hear it in the hitch of your breath and the way you keep shifting from one foot to the other."

I think I whimpered. Like some little fucking pussy cat who was begging to be pet by her owner. I wanted him. I wanted to feel that delicious feeling of him driving into me as I climaxed around him. I felt suffocated by him, the toxicity of his presence doing funny things to my mind and body.

Suddenly, he moved away from me and I heard footsteps walking away. A bright light filtered into the room from the door, silhouetting him in the doorway. I turned my head to the side, trying to shield my eyes from the intrusion of the light, squinting and unable to see due to being in the dark so long. When my eyes finally adjusted all that I saw was the silhouette of Link as he walked out the door, closing it behind him and leaving me in the darkness, alone once again.

ANDRIS

"WHAT THE FUCK did you just do? How could you lose your shit like that? Your actions don't only affect you, you know. Think with your fucking head and not your goddamned cock all the time." I scorned Link. Exposing himself to Nicola was a bad fucking move. If she found out who he was, the shit could possibly hit the fan and it would drag me down with him too. I knew what we were doing was wrong, but dammit, it was the only way I found to be able to deal with the shit storm that was my life. The pressure that I was getting from my uncle as well as the added pressure of Cardinelli and his Barbie doll wife had my mind going in a million fucking directions. Now, add to that the fact that Link actually fucking spoke to Nicola, and my blood was boiling.

"She is different from the others."

"That's not a fucking excuse. She's my patient. I could lose her as a client. Hell, I could lose the fucking clinic if she decided to sue the shit out of us."

It was just after ten in the morning, yet Link walked over to the decanter on a table in the room where he fucked Nicola not once, but twice now, and poured two fingers worth of amber liquid and tossed it back like it was medication to his system. Then he looked me in the eyes through the mirror on the wall in front of him and laughed.

"If you think losing her as a client is the *only* reason you could lose your clinic and go to jail for life, then you have bigger issues than I thought."

He didn't have to say what he was talking about. I already knew. Writing fucking prescriptions to a fucking mob boss so he could obtain a controlled substance, then turn around and sell them illegally would end my fucking career and my life.

"You know I'm trying to stop that shit," I growled, feeling my nails dig into the palms of my hands with my anger building. Link knew how to get to me. He knew just how to push my buttons. He also knew it was the way to keep me coming back to help him get what he wanted.

"Well. You take care of *that*, and I'll take care of *her*."

"Fuck you," I sneered, my upper lip damn near pulling back to expose my teeth like a fucking caged dog.

I needed to get Nicola out of there before he or I did something that I would regret. I grabbed my keys off the wall and headed back down the hallway to the room where Nicola was, stopping to grab a pair of sweatpants and a clean t-shirt from the room that I stayed in sometimes when it was too late to go home.

I loved this apartment. It screamed luxury with red velour wallpaper framed with gold trim, decorating the walls. Plush red carpet was spread throughout all of the floors, except in the three bedrooms and kitchen. Decorated with clean lines and simplicity wrapped in luxury, it was comfortable.

I paused outside of Nicola's room, taking a few moments to get my bearings. Everything that Link had said was true. She *was* different than the others. There was something mysterious, intriguing, and fucking sexy as hell about her. Her beauty went beyond her physical appearance. It was the more damaged parts of her that got to me. She made me hungry, and was the only one who could feed me. She was the same dream I had had over and over for the last few days that kept waking me up in the middle of the night. She was a kink in my armor of control, and I needed to get my shit together. Taking one more deep breath, I pushed the door open.

I turned on the dimmer light gently so that I didn't harm her eyes with sharp light. I found her sitting on the bed, wrapped in a robe with her arms wrapped around her knees as she rested her head upon them. Her golden blonde hair draped over her legs like a curtain of sunshine. She looked up at me with a solemn look on her face before she saw it was me and smiled.

"Are you Andris or Sinclaire right now?" She asked as her blue eyes bore through me like she could see through to my soul. There was no way she could know what was going on, but still, I had that nagging feeling in the back of my mind she had an inkling."

"I should probably still be Sinclaire, but for now I can be Andris."

"Okay. Are you the Andris I danced with earlier, or are you Dr. Gunn?" I chuckled slightly as I approached her. She extended her long legs in front of her and brushed her hair off of her shoulders, a movement that exposed her tanned, smooth neck. I willed my dick to stay soft. To not give in to the physical beauty before me, but when she bit her lip and arched her brow at me, he betrayed me.

"I'm only Dr. Gunn at the clinic. Right now, I'm just Andris. Here. I brought you some clothes to change into so I can drive you home."

She took the linens from me and our fingers brushed during the exchange. She pulled back sharply, a hitch in her breath slightly noticeable like I had shocked her.

She felt it too. The spark and tension that was between us. Just like the spark she felt with Link. I needed to leave the room so she could change. There wouldn't be any way I could witness her stripping down without wanting to grab her and throw her down on the bed and fuck her for the rest of the damn morning.

"I'll be waiting outside the door when you finish. Just knock and I'll come in to help you with the blindfold."

"Link was in here. Earlier."

"Yes, I'm aware."

"You sound angry about that."

"You are recognizing anger. That is a good sign."

"Don't analyze me, *Doctor*. Not here."

I nodded.

"Why does it upset you that Link revealed himself to me? Are you afraid he won't want you with us during the sessions anymore?"

"No, I'm not worried."

She exhaled a long and slow breath. I watched her throat bob and she swallowed before she spoke.

"Good. Because I feel safer knowing you are there."

My brows furrowed after her statement.

"Nicola, Link would never hurt you. He isn't like that. I wouldn't let him near you if that were the case."

"It's not that I am fearful of my safety. He unsteadies me. Makes me feel unbalanced. It isn't something I'm used to. It feels weird. If feels strange and new, but having you there is kind of soothing. I think—I think Link is my trigger. He is the only person in my entire existence who has allowed me to feel the things I've only seen or read about. Knowing you are there to catch me if I were to break, brings me a bit of comfort."

A tiny bit of pride filled my chest. I had watched her interactions with Link, seeing how much she needed and was going to need in order to get past her void emotions. I was jealous to know that he could be the one to do that to her and not me, but to hear that she did in fact need me too, just in a different way was fucking amazing.

"We can discuss that at your next appointment, if you wish. Right now, if you'll get dressed, I'll take you out for breakfast before I take you home."

"That sounds amazing," she said, her stomach growling right on cue. We both chuckled and she stood up, letting the robe fall off her shoulders, leaving her exposed in only the shirt that hit her just above mid-thigh. My eyes zeroed in on her toned thighs and I had to force myself to turn around and walk away.

CHAPTER TEN

Jericho/Nicola

ANDRIS TOOK ME to a hole-in-the-wall, mom and pop streetcar diner somewhere on the outskirts of Manhattan. I was only allowed to remove my blindfold when we were a safe distance from where we were and closer to where I lived. We were seated in a corner booth, him cleanly shaven and dressed in a suit and me still in the baggy t-shirt and sweats that he had given me to wear home. People in the restaurant were looking at us strangely, probably thinking we were an enigma. Him with his sophisticated class and me with my black smeared mascara eyes and comfortable clothes like some random person he may have picked up off the street.

Good thing I didn't give a fuck. When people would stare, I waved at them and smiled. Andris would laugh and it went on like that throughout most of the meal. I was getting to see a different side of Andris as we ate and engaged in idle chit chat. He told me about how he was in prep schools when he was younger and I told him about my wonderful adventures in boarding school. I noticed that he didn't talk much about his father, and didn't ask me questions about my own family. I was glad. I had nothing graceful to say about the two people who brought me into this world. I was nothing on the inside to them, so they thought it fit to leave me with nothing when they died. Even in death they were assholes.

"What made you want to become a psychiatrist?" I asked him as I took another bite of my scrambled eggs, savoring the creamy cheddar that was incorporated into them. I noticed that Andris started to shift the food around on his plate after my question and wondered if maybe the subject was a sore spot with him. He was interesting and had me intrigued. I found myself wanting to get to know him better, learning about all the little things that made him who he was today. The good and the bad. It was almost as if we were two kindred souls, both burned by people who were supposed to mean something to us.

"It was expected of me. As you know, my grandfather started the clinic and my father joined him after he completed school. My uncle joined a few years later, so it was just kind of instilled upon me at birth." I watched as he took a long draw from his coffee cup before setting it back down. His eyes, ones that had seemed more alive only moments earlier, were now back to a deep, brooding blue.

I changed the subject, but no matter how hard I tried, I couldn't get Andris back to the place we were when we first attended the restaurant. When we finished eating, Andris paid for the food and escorted me back out to his car. We drove in an uncomfortable silence back to my apartment where he escorted me to the door, and placed a kiss on my cheek before turning around and walking away. I was confused by his sudden mercurial shift in mood and shook it off as I entered the apartment and headed straight to my bathroom. Turning on the taps, I made sure the water was a comfortable temperature before I removed the clothes Andris had given me and sat them on my sink counter. I looked at them briefly, wondering if they were Link's or Andris's.

The warm water of the bath was soothing to my skin as I lay down and emerged myself all the way up to my neck. My muscles were still tender from Link's thorough fucking the night before, but they also held a lot of tension from the confusion I felt with Andris.

It would have to happen. For the first time in my life, I was feeling *feelings*. I was experiencing normal emotions that I had never felt before until this point, and it was all due to two different men. One, my doctor and person who was paid to help me try to get past all the vacant shit inside of me, and the other one who paid me to get past the bad shit that seemed to be inside him.

When I finished my long, luxurious soak in the tub, I threw on some more comfortable clothes and climbed back into bed. Most of my clients were night time customers, so I wasn't used to being up during the day, but seeing as how contractually I am not allowed to see any other clients, I might as well enjoy the benefits of leisure time. I grabbed the remote from my nightstand and turned on the TV, mindlessly flipping through the channels. I don't remember when I fell asleep, but I did know that when I did, all of my thoughts and dreams were filled with two men. Two men, who both did things to me I couldn't explain. One of the men fucked the hell out of me, while the other one gave me a climax of a very different kind.

FOUR DAYS.

I haven't heard from Andris nor Link in four fucking days. The last images I had of either of the men were of them walking away from me, and I didn't like it. Had Link decided he no longer wanted to fulfil the terms of the contract? Surley he would have called Alexandra and let her know, wouldn't he?

I got dressed methodically this morning, working in robot mode like I normally did, trying to go about my days like I would under normal circumstances, but it was damn near impossible. Every time my mind had an idle moment, which was a lot lately, my thoughts strayed to my two men.

Ha.

Two men.

Well, if I weren't already a fucking escort, people would think I was a whore. The thought made me laugh.

I ventured downtown to the flower shop to meet with Lexie. We had a weekly meeting where all of the girls came together to discuss clients, tips, tricks, and etcetera. Ten women in one room resulted in a lot of hen talk and too much clucking for my taste, so I usually sat back and just let it all go by. If I spoke up, that meant that we would be there longer, and then we would be there until nightfall.

I had my bi-weekly appointment today with Andris. If I said that I wasn't nervous or excited to see him that would be a fucking lie. That was the thing. Most of the time, my appointments were just another robotic thing I did during the week, now, they gave me something to look forward to.

"Jericho," Kiki said coldly as she hobbled in on crutches and took a seat next to me.

We all sat around an oblong table, something that Lexie found necessary, saying that it helped us all to "connect." Well, more often than not, I wanted to "connect" my foot with each of their asses. The meetings were basically a bitchfest, with each girl having to complain about their clients. If you didn't like the business, get the fuck out.

"Kiki."

Kiki was shorter than me, by several inches. Where I had long, blonde hair, she had shorter dark hair. Whether Kiki was her real name or not, I didn't know. Hell, I didn't even use my own name to my clients. They all knew me as Jericho Lane. Only Andris, and probably Link, knew that I was Nicola Forbes. Kiki's last name was chosen, because only a girl who had tits that looked like they would consume her face would call herself "CHESTfield." The dumb bitch probably fell forward from the weight of her medically enhanced frontal balloons and that is why she was on crutches.

"I hope you are taking care of my client. I will be back to normal soon and he will want me back. I appreciate you filling in for me, even if it isn't what he is used to."

She tried to make her comment sound pleasant, but I heard the disdain dripping from her voice. She was always one to try and get a rise out of me, but once again that was a benefit of not giving a fuck.

"I'd take all the time you can to recover. He's covered for the next twelve weeks."

"What the hell are you talking about?"

"I'm under contract with him for twelve weeks."

She huffed out a disbelieving breath as she let her crutches slide down to the floor, lading in a metal thump.

"That's absurd. He only pays a session at a time. I should know. He's been my client for the better part of two years."

"Maybe you don't know him as well as you think you do."

"Whatever."

Lexie started talking to the group as we all sat and listened. I was restless, eager to get out of there so that I could make it to Andris's office on time. I still had plenty of time to get there, but the thought of being close to where I knew he was made me feel better. The closer I was to Andris, the closer I felt to Link.

After our meeting, Lexie retreated to her office and I watched Kiki follow her. I made small talk with some of the other girls who I didn't really mind being around while I gathered my things. As I ventured down the hall to prepare to head to Andris's office, I heard Kiki's voice coming from Lexie's office.

"But he's my client. Lexie! She was supposed to only fill in for me until I recovered. The doctor said I would be fine in another week, and you are telling me he has her for another eleven?"

"It's out of my hands, Kiki. That is what he wanted. I can't go against the client's wishes. He wants Jericho, so she signed a contract with him for the next eleven remaining weeks. We can renegotiate after that, but until then, what's done is done."

"This isn't fair. Why the fuck does she get all the good clients?" Lexie's door burst open and Kiki came stumbling out on her crutches, giving me an evil glare before she retreated down the hall. I tried to walk past Lexie's door unnoticed, but I didn't have that much luck.

"Jericho."

I turned around and smiled brightly at her, sarcastically of course.

"Cut the shit, Jer. Antagonizing Kiki is uncalled for. That contract was supposed to remain quiet and you told Kiki about it."

"Well, she was the one who started in on me. I was just

putting her in her place."

"Well, stop. Now she knows and if she goes running back to your client, he may nullify the contract. Do you want that? Do you want to lose out on all that money?"

"No."

"Good. Now go to your appointment. Maybe your therapist can talk some fucking sense into that head of yours."

I left, wishing that were true. The last thing on my mind was *talking* to Andris, and more among the lines of fucking the hell out of him.

Andris

I GROANED.

My fucking ten o'clock appointment would be here in a few minutes and the last thing I wanted to deal with was Barbie Cardinelli.

The clinic was now mine. I owned it. Signed the papers and sent my dickhead uncle on his way to happy retirement. Now, I needed to get things together. I had to pull this clinic out from under the Cardinelli family if I wanted it to be a respectful, moral environment for my employees as well as my clients.

I walked out into the waiting room to retrieve my client. She sat, like she did the week before, in the same chair but with a different fashion magazine in her lap. Her grey eyes turned to me and smiled with a silky seductiveness as she placed the magazine down and retrieved her purse before rising and walking in my direction.

"Good morning, Dr. Gunn."

"Mrs. Cardinelli. Right this way."

She walked into the hallway ahead of me and proceeded

into the direction of my office. I shut the door behind us and walked around my desk to sit facing her, trying to exude a sense of authority. I was sick of feeling pushed around by her and her husband.

"How are you doing today, Mrs. Cardinelli?" I asked in fake sincerity.

"We can skip all the pleasantries, don't you think, Andris?"

"Then what do you want?"

"The usual. With extra this time."

"I can't do that and you know it. It will flag the pharmacists if I write over the amount normally subscribed. Do you want to tick them off as well as the authorities? I don't think so."

She tapped her overly long, manicured nails against the soft cushion of the chair in which she sat. Even though it was padded, the sound was still like nails on a chalkboard to me. Everything from her posture to the tone of her voice was irritating, like an annoying little tick that wouldn't go away.

"I'll just have to make sure that Antonio's boys make an appointment then. The demand is up, and the normal supply we are getting from you isn't cutting it anymore."

"I can only write prescriptions for thirty days at a time, Barbie. You know that. I won't give you anymore."

She rose from her chair, rounding my desk, walking perfectly in her sky-high stilettoes and sat down on the edge of my desk facing me. She crossed her legs and leaned in to grab the silk of my tie and threaded it to through her fingers.

"Maybe we can work out an arrangement then. Maybe you could prescribe me a different *medication* that will help me get through my days."

"You don't have any medical issues and you know it, Barbie. It's all in your fucking head. The only reason you are here is because your husband sends you to do his fucking dirty work for him."

"Maybe so, but he is just trying to protect the family name by sending me instead. We all know women are better at negotiating anyways."

"I'm not negotiating anything with you."

"Oh, I think you will," she said as she leaned in closer. "See, I'd hate for people to discover *your* little *side business* you have going one. One that involves a pretty little blonde and her *services*."

My head snapped to meet her eyes with such force, I could have given myself whiplash. I saw determination and also victory in her eyes. There was no use in denying her accusations. Her husband had the means to find out anything on anyone. It would ruin me, and Nicola both if anyone were to find out about my side ventures.

"So, this is what is going to happen. You are going to make both me and my husband happy. We'll send in a few extra 'clients' a week to you to get the extra we need, and in the meantime, you will give me what I need."

She stood up, slowly unbuttoning her blouse and letting it fall from her shoulders before unbuttoning her skirt from the side and allowing it to fall to the floor at her feet. She stood before me in nothing but her stilettoes, bra, and panties. Her bones nearly visible beneath her overly tanned and malnourished flesh. She had nowhere near the amount of sinful curves that Nicola possessed. She didn't have the same sexual radiance as the woman who invaded my dreams. But I had no choice right now. I was being blackmailed and at risk of losing both my clinic and Nicola.

I stood. Grabbing the skeletal form of Barbie Cardinelli, I

dropped my pants, rolled a condom on, and proceeded to fuck the hell out of her there on my desk, the entire time trying to imagine Nicola long enough to keep a hard-on.

BARBIE LEFT AFTER I gave her not one, but two orgasms, sealing the deal in the fucked up hand of cards I was dealt. This game was a gamble, and the odds were against me. It wouldn't matter so much if I were the only one effected, but the livelihoods of all my employees as well as Nicola were at stake and it wasn't a chance I was willing to take. I had to comply with the Cardinelli plans until I found a way to get the fuck out from under them.

I sat at my desk after Barbie left, trying to calm my racing mind and my body. I was painfully hard, not able to climax into the plastic form of Mrs. Cardinelli even with thoughts of Nicola. The room still reeked of her overly floral perfume and I could still smell the sweat of her body coming from my skin. I tried to put some order back into my desk as the intercom on my phone buzzed.

"Andris, Nicola Forbes is here for her appointment." Laura Lee stated.

Fuck.

My dick was still swollen with no relief in sight. There wasn't any way I would be able to walk out into reception to greet Nicola, so I buzzed Laura Lee back.

"Could you send her to my office, please? I am just finishing up a few things."

"Yes, doctor."

I scrambled, trying to get everything back into place before she arrived. How the hell I was going to sit through a session with her with my cock as hard as granite, I didn't know. How was I going to face her after four days of silence between us? I hadn't called her, nor had I made any other forms of contact with her via Lexie like Link would do. I would probably have to speak to him soon. Regardless of whether he needed her tonight, I knew I was going to.

CHAPTER ELEVEN

JERICHO/NICOLA

I COULDN'T GET TO Andris's office fast enough. I practically raced into his building and waiting room with an eagerness too strong to describe. I checked in with his receptionist when I arrived, fully expecting Andris to meet me at the door like he had prior, to escort me back to his office. Instead, his receptionist instructed me to head back by myself.

I began walking down the hallway as a woman approached from the other direction. I recognized her immediately from Dr. Gunn's retirement party.

Antonio Cardinelli's wife.

I walked a little taller and pulled my shoulders back as I continued down the hall. Our last interaction wasn't too pleasant and I didn't feel up to dealing with her shit today. She had a smugness about her, a sly smile out of the corner of her mouth. She looked slightly disheveled, different from the perfectly put together appearance that she portrayed at the retirement party.

When we were close enough to see eye to eye, she lifted her hand to swipe at the bright pink lipstick I had noticed was smeared across her mouth.

Then the bitch winked at me.

Fucking winked.

If I weren't on a mission to get to Andris, I would have followed her out of the building and did some facial augmentation on her myself with my fist, but instead I chose to keep walking. What the fuck was that all about anyway? Why the hell did she see it fit to fucking taunt me when she didn't even know me?

I knocked on Andris's door just before I pushed it open to find him arranging papers on his desk. He wore a dark, steel colored suit that showcased the broadness of his shoulders and a blue silk tie that matched the darkness in his eyes. His hair was slightly disheveled, like he had been running his hands through it repeatedly. He didn't look at me right away, which was strange considering he heard me knock and enter the room, so I closed the door and took a moment to take him in, sighing silently as I did so.

"Come in, Miss Forbes, and have a seat," he directed as he shoved some papers back into a file and placed them into a file holder on his desk. I rounded one of the chairs, having a seat in front of him and placed my bag on the ground, while he silently went on about his task. When he finally finished, he sat down in his chair and folded his hands together in front of him before he looked at me for the first time. I noticed the strong floral scent that lingered in the air of his office and knew that Mrs. Lipo-Fanatic had to have been in here. It made me sick to know that he was behind closed doors with that heap of wanna-be plastic and my lip snarled up in distaste.

"How have you been?"

"Why haven't you called?"

He let out an exasperated breath, something he looked like

he had been struggling to catch since the moment I walked in. His restless posture and fighting hands made me wonder what was going through his mind. His body language hinted at unease, or anxiety, and he kept staring at his desk in distaste as if recalling an unwanted memory.

"I figured you might ask that when you got here today. Things have been busy for me here at the clinic since I took over. I'm sure you can understand that."

"Okay, then why hasn't Link called? I was under the assumption that with the contract I would more than likely be engaging in more than one session a week."

"Link has been very busy as well."

"Let's talk about you, Nicola. Obviously the sessions you have had with Link thus far have flipped a switch within you somehow. How are you doing with this new onset of feelings?"

I licked my lips as I recalled those two sessions. The first time was amazing, but the second one was overwhelming in the best possible way. In a weird and twisted way I always felt blessed for not experiencing some of the shit other people had to deal with on a daily basis. But if I had known I was missing out on the intense feelings that I had with both Andris and Link, I would have done everything I could to seek out the cure or whatever the fuck it was I needed, to get past the giant wall inside of me.

"I feel full. Like he climbs inside of me to help me *feel*. When I am with him, with you, I feel like you both are a glitch in the process that stops me from expressing or being involved in feelings I had never been able to understand before. I've always felt pleasure. I've always been more in tune with the physical side of things. But with you and Link, it isn't just physical arousal. It is emotional arousal as well."

His eyes darkened if that were even possible. I noticed the slight tick of his jaw and watched as he adjusted his position in his seat. He was aroused by the idea of me telling him that he aroused me.

"Why do you think that is?"

"I don't know. What I do know is that the connection between us could not only be felt, but grasped. I can put my feelings into words. I understand them, even if I don't understand what is happening at the moment."

He nodded and cleared his throat before leaning back in his chair as if to put distance between us. I've always been an honest person. Saying what comes to my mind first had always been easy for me, but somehow my next words were a little harder to pass through my lips.

"I'm afraid of what I will lose once the twelve weeks are over."

He stilled and I looked up into eyes that were just as eager as mine. Heat pooled in his orbs as his gaze made my body feel like it was on flames. It felt almost like a betrayal to Link for me to feel that way about Andris when he wasn't with us, but the thing about that was I have had Link. Link had been inside me. Andris has touched me only once physically and that was when we danced. It wasn't even a touch of seduction or one of pleasure, but only the pleasure of being in his company while we moved on the dance floor. Yet, I clearly felt the same things with Andris that I did with link without as much as one orgasm.

"It doesn't have to end, Nicola. You know now what triggers these emotions you are feeling. Use that information to carry on."

Even as he said the words I could tell he didn't mean them. I smiled inwardly because he knew that carrying on meant me fucking other men for money. My occupation would see to that. I stood up out of the seat and walked around to his side of the desk. He sat completely still, nothing moving but his head and eyes that were glued to me. My tight, black pencil skirt showcased my curves and the cream form-fitting sweater I wore accentuated my breasts. The thigh high boots that adorned my feet made me taller, giving me a confidence boost. I wasn't naive. I knew I was pretty. I had been told my entire life how beautiful I was, by both men and women alike.

I could feel his stare as he swiveled in his chair when I walked past him to the framed documents on the wall, scanning all of his achievements hanging and on display for all too see.

"Have you ever wanted something so bad that you felt almost desperate to have it?" I asked as I ran my fingertips across the glass of his PhD certificate. "Imagine one of those things you want was your own feelings. Your own emotions, but no matter how hard you try, you can't turn them on. You can't cause a stir within yourself to flip the switch that turns everything on. You get to watch others around you feel love, passion, excitement, and even pain, yet all you feel is nothing. I'm a blank canvas, doctor. Untouched and impassive. Bare of any color or vivid hue that could turn it into something truly beautiful."

"Nicola, you are beautiful."

"Cut the shit, Andris," I said, turning around to look at him. He sat with one leg across his knee as his other bounced unceremoniously on the floor, his fingers clasped in his lap.

"That's not what I'm talking about and you know it. I can go all day feeling deadpan and expressionless, but the second I am with you and Link, it's like someone has taken a huge amount of beautiful colors and splattered them all over my blank canvas. Instantly it comes to life—I come to life. I feel human, normal for once in my life."

He only nodded slightly as I slowly approached him and sank down onto my knees in front of him. Placing my hands on his thighs, I absorbed the feel of his tight muscles beneath the palms of my hands as I slowly ascended them up towards his torso. I was affecting him just as much as he was affecting me, as he worried his jaw and his clasped fingers became fists in his lap.

"Nicola," he said in warning, his voice just loud enough to sound stern, but still soft enough to be classified as a whisper. "You have no idea what you are getting yourself into."

"Oh, but I do, *doctor*. I also know that this can't stop. I need it to continue."

My hands met the hardness of his abs and I could feel the ridged lines of his muscles through the fabric of his shirt. I had never seen him naked, but I didn't need to see him to know that he was cut beneath his clothes. I spread my fingers along his chest and he removed his foot from his knee, allowing me to nestle between his legs. I witnessed my effect on him as his cock grew with arousal and he swallowed audibly. My heart was beating frantically in my chest and I could feel it in my fingers as they splayed on his pecs. I fingered one of the buttons on his shirt before I smoothed my hands along his jaw. I leaned in closer, desperate to get a taste of his mouth. Our lips were only a breath away when I noticed something on his collar.

It was pink.

The same pink that fucking Barbie Cardinelli had on.

I moved his collar to the side and noticed the same hue across his neck.

That was why he was so nervous when I came in.

I pushed back from him so abruptly that I landed flat on my ass. He must have registered the heat in my eyes and could tell it was no longer heat of arousal. He lifted a hand up to his neck and wiped gently before pulling it away and looking at it.

"Shit."

I scrambled to my feet and rounded the desk before he had a chance to even get up from the chair. This was certainly a new feeling I was experiencing. Jealousy was an ugly son-of-a-bitch and I didn't like it.

Not at all.

If I thought the *good* feelings I had with him were overwhelming, then this one was a fucking powerhouse.

"Nicola, wait," he stated sternly as I made my way to fetch my purse on the floor. He reached me before I had the time to grab it and haul ass out of there.

"Will you just wait one goddamn second?" He growled as he grabbed ahold of both of my arms and spun me around to face him. "It's not what you think."

"Oh really? So it's completely normal for you to be wearing that horrid shade of lipstick on your neck then? Honestly, I didn't take you for a cross dresser, Andris."

"You don't understand."

"I understand *completely*. The contract stated that I couldn't fuck anyone else, but clearly it wasn't the other way around. Why am I even upset by this? I'm not even in a contract with you! It's with Link."

"The contract is with me too."

"But Lexie said…"

"Lexie must not have read the fine print. I have a copy if you need to see it."

I tried to shove away from him, but his grip was too strong. The smell of his cologne was doing things to me and I needed to get away from him before I either beat the shit out of him, or fucked the hell out of him.

"Let go of me."

"Not until you calm the fuck down."

"Did you fuck her?"

"What?"

"Did. You. Fuck. Her."

His silence was all the answer I needed. I attempted to pull away from him once more without success. That is when his lips crashed to mine, creating a tingling sensation in my body. It wasn't a gentle kiss. It was rough, bruising, punishing. For a brief moment, I savored the taste of him. I melted into the curvature of his mouth, and relished in how we fit together perfectly. My head was spinning and my knees felt week. I opened my eyes when he tried to slip his tongue inside, and that was when I saw the lipstick again. I pulled back, angry that I had let myself surrender to him when I was pissed off at him. Angry that he had his lips on me only minutes after he had them all over another woman.

I reared back and slapped him across the face. I'd never been so upset that I had hit a man, or anyone for that matter, before and it had my hands coming up to cover my mouth in shock.

I needed to get out of there.

Without a backwards glance, I raced out of his office and out of the building. I don't remember hailing a cab and riding all the way to my apartment. My head was in a jealous and confused fog. I do remember however bursting into my apartment, slamming the door and marching down the hall toward my room where I did something I had done only once or twice in my life.

I cried.

ANDRIS

I WANTED TO CHASE after Nicola. I wanted to tell her that every time I drove into the fucking bag of bones that was Barbie Cardinelli, it was her that I was thinking of. It was her that I imagined beneath me. But I couldn't because my next patient was due in fifteen minutes.

I knew I shouldn't have kissed her. Especially not in my office, but I couldn't control myself. I couldn't control the need that rose in me to show her how much I wanted her. I didn't think I would be able to hold back anymore and watch as Link fucked her. I knew that my jealousy was becoming an issue, just as hers had reared its ugly head when she found out about Barbie. In a sick, sardonic way, it was a comfort to me because it showed that she did care. I made a woman, who had previously been void of emotions, feel something for me. It was a reward and a burden at the same time because I knew inevitably, that either Link or I would destroy her. Possibly both of us.

I made it through my next four appointments in record time. Offering solutions to the patient or just listening to their concerns. Trying to keep a clear mind and not focusing on Nicola was proving to be a difficult task. I had been so career-driven in my early life that I had no desire to settle down and have a relationship. They were just a distraction from the perfection that my father, and soon myself, came to expect from me. I had dated, but nothing serious. Now that Nicola had come barreling into my life, suddenly the thought wasn't so atrocious.

The fucked up thing about it? She was my patient. The other fucked up thing? I was just as fucked up in the head as she was. I was a conundrum, a fucking hypocrite to my own profession.

But all I knew was that I needed her. I needed to be the one to divulge in her body, to lose myself inside of her so that I could release my demons and help her release hers. I just had to get Link on board.

NICOLA/JERICHO

Andris: *The car will be there at 8pm. Be ready.*

I stared at that damn text message for what seemed like an hour. I never used to have to deal with this shit. I never used to get nervous, or even excited about having to see a client. But ever since the day I took over for Kiki, my head has been all sorts of fucked up.

I now wonder when he will call. I wonder what Andris and I will talk about in my sessions. I wonder how it would feel to touch Link, or what it would feel like to have Andris inside of me while Link watched.

I threw the phone onto my bed, frustration getting the better of me, and rose to go and comb through my closet to find something to wear. I was still angry, jealous, and disgusted by the fact that Andris fucked Barbie Cardinelli. If he had her on the side, then what the hell did he need me for? Technically, Link was the one who fucked and paid me for my services, even though all I did was pretty much bend over and take whatever Link gave to me.

I wanted Andris to feel some of the hurt I was feeling.

Yes. I was *feeling* hurt, and it fucking sucked.

It was this experience that made me want to go back into that dark place I had been in most my life. I had never imagined what this would actually feel like to experience, and I wasn't liking it one bit. The thing is, Andris and I weren't in a relationship. He was my damn doctor for Christ's sake! Not once had he ever given me any reason to think that things between us would be anything but professional, even with the contract.

But I saw it in his eyes. I felt it in the heat of his body whenever we were close to each other. There was no way that I could imagine that. I never felt that with any one of my clients before. Over the years, I had fucked politicians, high profiled people, even celebrities. None of them had ever had the impact of the two men who now consumed nearly all of my thoughts.

I sorted through my collection of lingerie with new determination. Was I a bitch for wanting Andris to feel even a small amount of jealousy I was feeling? Yes, maybe, but it wasn't going to stop me. I couldn't go back on the terms of the contract or risk losing the money, so I was going to have to get to him the only way that I could.

Through Link.

CHAPTER TWELVE

Andris

NICOLA CAME WALKING out of her building at precisely eight o'clock. Her normally long, flowing hair was pulled up with just a few ringlets that cascaded down to frame her gorgeous face. Her makeup was minimal, more natural than I had seen before and it only aided in capturing the vastness of her beauty. My eyes raked her trench coat clad body, trying my best to use my head and imagine what it was she could be wearing underneath. My cock was instantly hard, begging to be eased of the pressure she created just from being in the same place she was. My heart beat triple time in my chest, and even though it was damn near below freezing outside, I felt sweat bead and roll down my spine.

She didn't look in my direction, nor meet my eyes as I held the door to the town car open for her. She brushed past me, the smell of honeysuckle filtering through the air in her wake had me closing my eyes and inhaling the addicting floral scent. It took all the strength I could conjure to shut that door behind her and not follow her into the back of the car and pound the fuck out of her with my cock right there on the busy New York street.

I put the partition up between us after making sure she secured the blindfold over her eyes before I pulled out into traffic. I knew she was still angry with me. She was giving me the silent treatment and I was okay with that, because I knew that by the end of the night she would be very *vocal*.

Fucking butterflies danced in my belly and I gripped the steering wheel tighter as I drove through town to the apartment. Whether Link was fully on board with what I had planned for tonight, I wasn't sure. He damned well better be because tonight, I was making Nicola mine. I would have her. I wanted it to be me who drove her to the edge. I wanted it to be me who filled her thoughts, her actions and her little pussy until she had nothing else to do but take all of me.

The drive to the apartment seemed to take forever. Traffic was stop and go and it only made my anxiety grow as we finally reached our destination.

You're not good enough for her, Andris. You will be a failure at fucking her and giving her pleasure, just like you fuck up everything else in your life. You are a sad excuse for a fucking human being. You will never be good enough.

My father's ghost filled my thoughts, creating the fears inside of me as he always did only this time, he was making me doubt my ability to be with Nicola. He did that whenever I got enough nerve to go after what I wanted. It was the same way his father was with him and my uncle. No one was good enough. They always saw me as this royal fuck up. Someone who didn't have the balls to go after what he wanted in life.

Well, I was going to prove them wrong. I wanted to show them that I could have anything I wanted. I would prove to my father that I could be everything Nicola needed and more.

All I needed to do was convince myself first. Especially living in the shadows of the man who *could* give her what she wanted.

Pulling up to the apartment, I turned and looked up at the immaculate building. There were six apartments inside, the top two having been renovated into one large one. It was an investment I had made not long after I joined the clinic after college. It wasn't my home, but instead my escape. It was a place of refuge whenever I was stressed or needed to vanish from life if only for a few hours. It is where I left my father's nagging, insulting voice at the door and could be Sinclaire, the man who controlled everything and who aided Link in his own perusal of demon banishing.

I stepped from the car, my legs a little shaky due to my sudden onset of nerves. This would be the first time that I would be the one fucking the woman, not Link. I was such a fucking hypocrite. I always prided myself on doing the right thing, yet, here I was going to do something I knew was wrong. And the even sicker thing was, I didn't give a fuck. My need to be inside her overpowered my need to strive for perfection. It was honestly the first time in my life I had ever felt that way.

Back in the office, Nicola had told me that Link and I helped her. That we managed to bring forth her vacant feelings. Well, I had to say that it went both ways. When I was around her, I didn't feel like I had to be perfect. I didn't have to be flawless or spotless, but instead I could be myself. I could feel natural without thinking I had to try so hard. She calmed me, soothed me in ways I could never describe. She subdued and tranquilized my demons as well as the haunting inner dialogue, my long dead father, insisted on having in my thoughts.

I stepped out of the car and into the cold. Snowflakes melted against my skin the instant they came into contact with my face. My body was hot with desire, warm with the knowledge of what was going to occur upstairs and even the freezing temperature of the New York winter weather wasn't enough to cool me down. I opened the door, reaching down to grab Nicola's hand to help her from the car. The blindfold was securely in place and she had a firm expression of her mouth. It was tight as if she were trying to hold back from saying something to me by clenching her jaw. Since her hair was up, I watched as the snowflakes danced across her neck, chilling her and creating a pattern of goose bumps on her skin.

We walked up the stairs and into the warmth of the building. She walked with grace. Even though she had never been in the building without the blindfold, she knew exactly how many steps there were to the elevator. She knew how many taps of her heels it was to the door of the apartment, and she knew how many strides it took her to get to the bed in the center of the room.

"Would you like a drink?" I asked as I poured myself a large tumbler of dark whiskey, taking a large draw from the glass and appreciating the burn in my throat and my belly. I walked over to where she sat on the bed, her back ramrod straight and her lengthy, smooth legs crossed over one another. I held the glass to her lips, and watched as she inhaled the liquor before opening her mouth for me to allow some to pass her lips. There was something devastatingly erotic about watching her lips on the same glass that mine were on only moments ago. Even though we were both afraid to let go of our insecurities, and yes, she had them, I felt like sharing the glass with her was allowing two pieces of ourselves to unconsciously blend together.

"Where's Link?" She asked after she swallowed, the dark amber bringing out a huskiness to her voice.

"He'll be along shortly," I lied. I had to keep up the façade, because her anger with me would probably turn to outrage if she knew that I was going to be the one who would be fucking her tonight.

She pulled off her jacket and laid it on the bed next to her, smoothing out imaginary wrinkles as she did. There she sat in a garnet red, silk mini-dress that exposed the garters holding up her stockings due to how short it was. The top was nearly sheer, exposing the darkened areolas of her breasts, and the pertness in her nipples through the thin fabric. I swallowed the rest of the whiskey down before setting the glass back on the table next to the decanter. Making my way over to the stereo, I picked up the headphones and turned on the system and retrieved my own headset so that I could still speak to her if I needed to, yet allow my hands to be free to roam her body.

"I'm going to place the headphones on you now."

She only nodded, clearly still not speaking to me. Good. She could use that anger, that aggression she was harboring and channel it into how I was going to fuck her. Only I had plans for how I was going to carry it out. Placing the headset onto my own head, I spoke to her.

"Can you hear me?"

She nodded again.

"You have to speak to me sometime, Nicola. Although, your silence won't last very long," I said, sexual innuendo prevalent.

"I have nothing to say to you, Doctor. Where is Link? Can we just get this over with?"

I reached for her chin, tilting her head to where she would be staring into my eyes if it weren't for the blindfold.

"I told you, when you are in this place, I am Sinclaire. Do you understand?" I asked as I brushed my thumb across her bottom lip.

The tiniest hitch of her breath didn't go unnoticed before she nodded.

"Good. Now, scoot back onto the bed and extend your arms and legs out."

She did as I instructed, laying back and extending all of her limbs toward the four corners of the bed. Her breasts heaved as she did, clearly being affected by the situation. My control was slipping and I needed to get inside of her before I lost it. I attached both her legs and her arms to the soft leather cuffs on the bed, making it clear she wouldn't be able to move. This is what I needed to ensure that my demons wouldn't come to the surface while I was with her. If she were to try and get up and leave, it would wreck me. I couldn't take that kind of rejection.

Not from her.

I undressed, making sure to take my time and breathe through the flood of desire filling my chest. My cock, standing rigidly at attention was objecting to the aching slowness of my removal of clothing. I had to be sure that I was in control before I took the chance with her.

I climbed onto the bed, feeling the mattress dip as I did. Slowly, I placed my lips against her navel, dipping my tongue in and causing a slight jerking reaction in her body.

"Link?" She breathed, something funny in the sound of her voice. "I've missed you," she whispered.

What?

"Quiet," I demanded through the headphones. She stilled along with the silence in her voice. I began to trail kisses up her body.

"Are you ready?" I asked.

I KNEW WHAT I was about to do was wrong. I knew that in the long run it could damage the trust between Andris and me, but I didn't care. I had never felt hurt before, but the first time I had, it was like a devastating blow to my chest. The thoughts of him fucking Barbie Cardinelli wouldn't leave my mind and I wanted him to feel the same jealousy that I was consumed with.

My years of being a female escort, hooker, prostitute, whatever you wanted to call it, gave me good practice at being an actress. I could make any man feel like he was God of all things sex when he was with me. I knew how to make them cum longer, faster and better than they ever had in their lives with just the sounds of my voice. I was a highly trained professional with years of field practice.

"Link? I've missed you," I stated in a breathy whisper.

"Quiet," I heard Andris bark into the headphones. I smiled inwardly, knowing that it would work just from the one phrase alone.

He trailed kisses up my torso, causing my breath to quicken. A sharp pain radiated in my right breast as his teeth clamped down on my nipple and converted to pleasure when he licked it soothingly through the fabric. My body instantly heated, my blood beginning to pump faster in my veins.

Truth be told, I really did miss him. Link had the powerful ability to make me feel, yet also had the ability to mask those feelings in a way that only had me feeling pleasure. He was a calming fortress to my newly racing thoughts and emotions. The harder he pounded into me, the less I had to actually think about the emotions and instead could immerse myself in them.

My dress was pushed up past my hips and the top was pulled down, exposing my breasts. Two warm palms came to rest on my breasts and he squeezed my nipples, sending an electric current running strait to my clit. My back arched off the bed, pressing my breasts harder into his hands.

Soothingly, one hand caressed the side of my face. It was new. It was almost…intimate. Something Link had never expressed before. It scared me slightly because my thoughts were now running wild in my head, making it difficult for me to keep my mind on my task.

I moaned softly as he nudged my thighs apart and settled his body between my legs.

"Link, please," I begged in a desperate voice that I clearly didn't have to fake. I did want him, but I also wanted to get to Andris.

"I love how you feel when you are inside me. I love it how your cock fills me so completely. I love how hot you make me feel."

His hands squeezed my thighs and I yelped out in surprise.

"That is enough, Jericho," Andris said sternly, his breathing coming faster.

It was working.

"Link. Fuck me."

"I said quiet!"

I didn't have time to respond because Link climbed up my body and straddled me. I felt the tip of his cock as he rubbed it across my lips and I opened, allowing him to gain access to my mouth. I couldn't hear him, but I felt the rumble of his body as I worked my tongue around the tip of his dick. He hardened in my mouth, the velvety smoothness of his skin stretching even further. This was the first time in the few sessions we have had together that I had gotten to taste him. I enjoyed the salty presence of his precum. I relished in the feel of his hands as he placed them behind my head and guided my movements.

I put everything into sucking him off, something that was hard to do with my arms being restrained. My neck protested, the muscles there burning with each bob of my head as I worked to pull him deeper into my mouth. His grip tightened on my head as he pulled on my hair. Prickles raced down my spine. I was enjoying this. I felt empowered as his thighs tightened at my sides, signaling his approaching orgasm.

Suddenly he was off of me, leaving me wanting the explosion in my mouth. I wanted to taste him as he lost himself over to me, knowing it was me who gave him that insurmountable pleasure.

My panties were pushed aside as he settled between my legs again and I felt the hot tip of his tongue take a long, slow swipe against my clit. My hips bucked in pleasure, my mouth opening to allow the sudden rush of breath to escape from my body.

"Link, oh my God," I said as I tried to squeeze my thighs together, clearly not able to complete the task with them restrained. I heard Andris growl into my ear at the same time that Link groaned against my pussy and it sent waves of pleasure circulating through my body. My legs began to tremble and I gripped the sheets beneath me and squeezed them in my fists as my body began its slow trek towards crescendo. I felt my clit stiffen as Links relentless tongue lashed against it. My body was desperate to get away from the torture of his tongue, yet ached for him to continue at the same time.

It hit me suddenly, no warning. Just pure bliss and elation as my body exploded from his tongue, stiffening as I felt the rush of fluids between my legs. My mind momentarily traveled into a state of trance, going absolutely blank as if I were in a state of meditation. As I came down from my high, I felt my body weaken and I opened my mouth because the need to breathe deeper was desperate. I let go of my grip on the sheets and allowed my body to relax into the bed.

Link climbed over the top of me, settling his hard chest against mine and pressed a single chaste kiss to my lips, allowing me to taste my own desire on his. I felt the tip of his dick press at my entrance and even though I felt weak, I opened for him, my body still not through with the pleasure he could give me.

My clit was still sensitive as he started pushing inside of me in one long, slow thrust. He stilled at the hilt, allowing my body to adjust to his size. This is where things took a turn. In all of the sessions I have had with this man, he had fucked the hell out of me so hard that I felt the remnants of him on my body for days after. He made me sore, giving me that constant reminder that he was there each time I took a step. But this time, he went slow, pulling out and pushing in at a slow, leisurely pace. I noticed that Andris was unusually quiet and it made me wonder if the desperate sound in my voice as I begged for Link to fill me, really got to him. Suddenly I didn't feel so great about wanting to torment him the way I had been, after I found out about him and Barbie.

"Andris?" I breathed into the air as Link continued to slide in and out of me. The action made every single nerve ending come to life. My mind couldn't adjust to just one sensation as it tried to filter through all the tiny ones that riddled my body and my mind. I felt Link's hands caress my arms that were held by the cuffs and soon his fingers were linked into mine. I stiffened momentarily at the intimacy of the gesture.

What the hell was he doing? This wasn't fucking. This was slow, sensual and almost like what a man would do if he was making love to a woman, wanting the feeling to last because it was greater than any other that they had ever experienced.

Panic began to rise in my throat, but the pleasure Link was creating in my body took precedence over the panic.

In.

Out.

In.

Out.

It was like he had a perfect rhythm set. Each inward thrust matched the length of him pulling out of me causing me to feel each ridge, each hard line of his cock as it entered and exited my pussy.

My mind began to be overwhelmed by a foggy haze as my body began to climb once again. My eyes stung, the pleasure too much. His actions too much. I wanted Link, but at that moment, I had a desperate *need* to hear Andris's voice. I needed him to tell me that the sensations I was feeling at that exact moment were normal, and that I wasn't losing my mind.

"Andris, please. I...I..." I couldn't say what my heart wanted me to say. To admit to needing someone felt almost too vulnerable and I didn't want to upset Link at the same time. There was a difference in the two men that I couldn't describe. Link was the man I wanted. The man who made my body come to life. But Andris was the man I needed. The one who gave me reassurance when I started traveling down this dark road of awakening feelings. He was my light at the end of a long traveled, dark tunnel. He was also blinding though. Something that I felt that if I got too close to, I would get burned.

My second orgasm hit me just a fiercely as the first, but the waves took longer to subside. My body continued up a ridged mountain until it reached a cliff and took a nosedive off the edge. For a moment, I couldn't breathe as I fell rapidly towards the ground below, and just before I hit, Link kissed me. There was something familiar in the way he explored my mouth, soothing me and the after effects of what he just did to my body.

Pulling back from our kiss he gently undid the cuffs at my wrists, taking the time to massage my flesh there before moving to my feet and completing the same task. Then he was gone. I felt his presence leave the room. I was desperate to take off the blindfold, not wanting to see where I was but, desperate to seek the navy eyes of Andris. I needed him to tell me that I was okay. I needed the reassurance from him that whatever the hell it was I just experienced with Link was real.

I needed him to tell me I wasn't crazy because I was clearly falling for two different men.

CHAPTER THIRTEEN

ANDRIS

MY SESSIONS WITH NICOLA continued both in the clinic and at the apartment almost in a comfortable schedule over the next three weeks. On Mondays and Wednesdays, we had sessions where we discussed her newfound abilities to experience emotions she had never had before. We discussed strategies on how to deal with them when they became overwhelming or too much for her to be able to handle. Our interactions away from the apartment were professional, but her eyes told me otherwise. She never brought up the subject of Barbie again, and I never did either, instead hoping it would pass. Barbie had come to me twice more since the day I fucked her on my desk, and each time, I sent her packing and out the door with her required prescriptions.

I had combed my mind over and over trying to find a solution to get away from the Cardinelli family. Each week, there were more and more "patients" coming in, and my associates and I were writing more and more prescriptions. We were probably weeks away from having the Feds come down on us. I had no doubt in my mind that the pharmacists were keeping track of the amount of medication that was coming out of my clinic and I had hit my limit. What was the worst thing that the Cardinelli family could do to me? They could threaten me all they wanted, but if I continued complying with their demands, then the clinic would be shut down anyway and I would be hauled off to jail.

The contract was my excuse to have Nicola. My clinic was my excuse to keep seeing her even after the terms of the contract ended.

I didn't want it to end.

I felt dread and sick to my stomach at the thought of not having her. Each passing day, the strength of my feelings grew for her to the point that I was daydreaming about her while with other patients. I thought about her when I was at the store, or especially when I sat alone in my apartment at night wondering what she was doing.

I knew eventually the truth would come out. I knew eventually that the comfort of my relationship with her would come to an end, but something told me that I needed to keep a hold of her. I wasn't ready to let her go, and even though we still had several weeks remaining in our contract, I needed to start doing something to solidify things so that she continued to come back.

First, I needed to get rid of Cardinelli.

I made an appointment for him to come see me, choosing my office as a safe place for him to come. If I needed to call security, I could, and a police station was right down the road. I gathered evidence. Copies of all the prescriptions I had written to him as well as family members and a majority of his staff members. I needed to be able to present the evidence to the authorities if need be, and also prove that the people who weren't family were employed by him.

Cardinelli came into my office, basking in an air of authority. Scrunching his nose, he made his way over towards my desk, two of his goons flanking at his side.

"You certainly have filled your Uncle's office well, Gunn."

"Don't come in here trying to exchange pleasantries, Antonio. Sit down," I gestured toward the chairs in front of me. The smell of strong cologne and cigars filled the room to the point I wanted to gag. I hated the look of his face, the over-tanned leather of his skin made him look far older than he really was. I had done a lot of research up to this point about the Cardinelli family. They were rumored to be involved in drug rings, money laundering, and a vast number of other law breaking activities. There had been arrests made on some of the crimes, but the case was usually thrown out in court on some technicality.

I knew the move I was about to make could potentially be a fatal move on my part, however, I couldn't continue to run this clinic under his thumb. Regardless of the shit that went on in my personal life, I *would* run this clinic with integrity.

"You called me here, Doctor. What can I do for you?" Cardinelli asked as he placed his elbow on the chair arm and held his chin in his hand. His Italian accent more prominent as agitation was clearly evident.

"I'm done, Antonio."

"I'm afraid I don't follow, Doctor."

"I mean I'm done with you using *my* clinic to run your business. I'm finished with you trying to drag the reputation and integrity of my business into the ground. I don't give a shit what the contract or negotiations you had with my uncle were, this is *my* clinic now."

The two men standing next to Cardinelli stepped forward,

pushing back the sides of their jackets to reveal the handguns nestled at their sides. With just the wave of his hand, the two men stepped back as Cardinelli silently signaled for them to do so.

"You have balls of brass, young man. I'll give you that. There aren't many people that will stand up to me or tell me no."

"I'm serious, Antonio. You will not get another prescription from me unless it is medically necessary to do so."

He nodded his head, sitting up straighter in the chair and raking his two index fingers over his lips, all the while never taking his eyes off of me."

"Carl, Pedro. Leave us." He demanded to his side hands.

"Are you sure about that, boss? What if we need to stand in?"

Cardinelli didn't say anything in return, only turned and looked at the men. It was all it took for both of the sidekicks to tuck their tails between their legs and leave my office. When the door shut behind them, he turned back around to face me with a small smile on his face.

"I'm glad you find the situation amusing. I do not."

"I'm sure you don't, Andris. I'm a man of business, plain and simple. You should understand that being one yourself. Here you are telling me that I can no longer run my business and that presents a small problem to me."

"That isn't my problem."

"No, it's not. But like I said, I'm a business man, and I'm willing to cut a deal with you."

"I'm not cutting any deals. I'm just cutting you off."

The sardonic chuckle that came from his lips was bone chilling. If I said that I wasn't a little scared by standing up to a man like Antonio Cardinelli, I would be lying. My legs trembled slightly under the armor of my desk in front of me. In the blink of an eye, Cardinelli was standing and had a fistful of my shirt and tie as he pulled me closer to him from across the desk. The stealth move was shocking, especially coming from a man who was clearly pushing seventy years old.

"Listen you little dick head, if you think that I need you, you are mistaken. I have plenty of resources, so your involvement in my dealings isn't even a blip on the radar. My wife has taken a liking to you and it keeps her out of my fucking hair. You fuck her and I don't have to. Fucking bag of bones. But if you think for one minute I am going to let you think you have power over me, you are in for a world of hurt."

He pushed me away, causing me to stumble as I held my hand out to grab my chair to keep from planting on my ass. He sat back down in the chair in front of me, smoothing out the imaginary wrinkles in his suit. I stood there staring at him, thinking that standing while he sat gave me back a little bit of my dignity and power.

"Sit down, *Andris*"

Slowly, I retreated into my chair and I kept my trembling hands underneath the desk. Yes he scared me, but I didn't want to give him the satisfaction of knowing that. After taking a deep breath, he continued.

"As I was saying, I am a businessman. I'm willing to work something out with you. There has been something that has caught my fancy and I haven't gotten it out of my thoughts since. You have connections and I want to put them to use."

"I don't have anything that you want, Cardinelli."

He pulled back the lapel of his jacket and retrieved an envelope from inside and threw it down on the desk in front of me. It was thick, the contents clearly enough to fill up the envelope.

"What is that?"

"Why don't you look for yourself?"

I picked up the envelope, not knowing what to expect on the inside. Pulling back the flap I retrieved a stack of pictures from inside.

I froze.

Heat and fire spun through my body as my breathing increased.

Picture after picture of Nicola and me. Some were on the streets. Some were in my very office. But the ones that were most disturbing were the ones of Nicola blindfolded as I drove my body into hers. Her eyes not able to see me but the camera was clearly capturing the erotic contortions of her face as her climax hit her. Her body, clearly on display for the camera. Pictures of me handing her the brown envelope that contained her fee.

All there in evidence before me.

Incriminating me.

"As you can tell, doctor. Not only could your involvement with me shut you down and have you put away, but it looks like your own extracurricular activities could have the same effect on you."

I continued to flip through the pictures in my hand, each time begging that the contents would change, that I wouldn't see Nicola's face and mine staring back at me.

"I'm sure you are well aware of the consequences that the American Medical Association would have on you if they were to find out..."

"I'm well aware of what the AMA would do," I interrupted, as I felt my eyes darkened with anger. I was seething. Not because of the fact that I had been caught. It was one of the many things that I wasn't shameful for. I used sex as medication to get over my own psychological problems just like people depended on oral medication to get over theirs. No, my anger was because it was Nicola. If my name was dragged through the mud because of my own fucked up tendencies, that was fine, but if it were to bring her down with me, it would devastate me. She didn't deserve that shit.

I was her fucking doctor for Christ's sake. I know it would look like I had preyed upon one of my patients, conning her into contracting into a sexual relationship with her. That would lead to medical malpractice and not only would the clinic be shut down and ruin my life, but also the lives of the other doctors in the practice. Some who had families and small children.

"So I'm damned if I do, and damned if I don't. Is that what you are telling me, Cardinelli?"

"I told you I was a businessman. I'm willing to negotiate our terms if you oblige."

"What terms?"

"Well, we have a large supplier we have been relying on for some time now, so our little operation with you is meaningless so to say. It was just convenient."

"Then why do you continue to abuse the privilege?"

"Like I said, you keep Barbie happy and it was convenient. I'm willing to let you have your 'morals' as you so call them in exchange for something."

"What?" I bit out, eager to learn what it was that would get me out of this situation.

He nodded his head toward the pictures I still held in my hands.

"Nicola? You want Nicola?"

"Spot on, ace."

"Fuck no. No way in hell am I letting you have her."

The thought of anyone touching her made me fucking sick to my stomach. Even the idea of Link getting to be with her was no longer settling well. The fucking disgusting man in front of me was no different. In fact, it was worse. No doubt Nicola had had worse than him given her profession, but I didn't want her to do that anymore. While she was in the contract with Link and me, she couldn't fuck anyone else. I didn't know what I was going to do once the contract was up, but I just knew I couldn't let her continue.

"Well then. You'll continue to provide for me then. All I want is one night, one time to show her what a real man does when he fucks a woman. No doubt after all the pencil dicks she has had throughout her years as a prostitute, she needs some good dick."

"Over my dead body."

"That can very well be arranged, Andris."

"Are you telling me that you will kill me if I don't comply?"

"I could. I have no issues whatsoever of telling Carl and Pedro to pump lead into you or your little girlfriend. I'd much rather watch the AMA do you in, though. It would be less painful, but more drawn out to watch your life unravel."

He stood, snapping his fingers loudly and instantly Carl and Pedro were walking back into my office and stood at his side.

"I'll even be the nice guy here and give you two weeks to answer."

"How very generous of you," I sneered.

"Oh, and uh, keep the pictures. I have extras," he threw over his shoulder as he walked out of my office.

Fuck.

WEDNESDAY ROLLED AROUND and Nicola was right on time for her eleven a.m. appointment. She came in, looking more beautiful than ever. Dressed in simple jeans, a sweater, boots, and a blue jacket that matched the color of her eyes. She was stunning. Probably even more so than when she was made up for our *other* sessions. Her normally loose hair was pulled back into a low ponytail, allowing her fresh looking face to be clearly seen. I took a few moments to admire her as she settled into the chair in front of my desk.

"Good morning," I said when she finally met my eyes. The clear blue of her irises reminded me of warmth and summer. Even though I had been under a shit ton of stress the last few days with the whole Cardinelli situation and my body felt cold as ice, I could always count on her to be the heat my body needed.

"Good morning," she replied as she smiled shyly at me. Although our sessions in my office have been strictly professional, the electricity between us still remained. I would catch her smiling at me or looking at me when she didn't think I was looking, and vice versa. I couldn't help but stare at her. I couldn't help but want her.

Ever since Cardinelli had come to my office, I had been trying to come up with an idea to get out from underneath his blackmail. There was no way in hell that I would let that fuckwad have Nicola, but I sure as hell didn't want to go to jail for medical malpractice. If we were going to continue our extracurricular sessions, then I was going to have to give her to one of the other doctors to provide her care. I didn't want the AMA thinking I was acting unprofessionally as well as unethically so I had to change things up a bit. That included our personal relationship.

"How are you?" I asked her, sitting back in my chair and staring at her with a cocky grin on my face. She brought out the playfulness of my personality. I loved some of the banter and innuendos that I had become accustomed to between us.

"I'm okaaaaay…" she replied, drawing out the word and arching her eyebrow at me. "What has you in such a great mood?" She laughed.

"So, you recognize that I'm in a good mood?" I asked, arching my brow right back at her.

"Andris. You know damn well I can. You know a lot of things have changed for me. Things I feel, recognize, and all because of…"

She paused as a glassed over look in her eyes made desire shine full force in her gorgeous features.

"Because of Link?"

"And you."

Just her admission alone was enough to send my cock into a raging hard on. Knowing that it was me as well as my protégé who became the triggers to a woman that was once filled with nothing, was amazing. Add to that the fact that she was sexy as fucking hell, a genuinely good person, and did I say sexy as hell?

I smiled.

"You're playful today, Doctor."

"You're beautiful today, Nicola."

She paused, looking at me quizzically. I've never commented (much) on her looks, but felt the need and also had to say something to get on her good side. Having to explain to her that I was passing her off to another doctor was probably not going to go over so well. I was interested in seeing if I could possibly take our personal relationship to the next level. Well, lack thereof.

"What do you want?" She asked, smiling back at me.

"I have no idea what you are talking about."

"Cut the shit, Andris," she said, giggling. "You want something."

"You're right. I do *want* something."

Her eyes grew wide as I rose from my chair and rounded my desk to where she sat. The slight squeeze of her thighs against one another didn't go unnoticed. I knew what she was thinking, and for a few moments, I allowed her to think it. Did I *want* her want her? Fuck yeah. It was taking all the control I could find in my body not to lift her from her seat, throw her on my desk and bury myself inside of her for the rest of the day.

Over the last few weeks, I had come to wonder if my feelings for Nicola went beyond sexual. We seemed to get along really well as well as connected more on an intellectual level. Many of our session in my office had been spent basically getting to know each other. She would tell me how shitty her childhood was and how she was basically ignored by her parents, friends, and classmates for being the "weird" girl. I told her about my strange relationship with my father, leaving out the details about how he made me feel like a piece of shit on a daily basis. I didn't tell her that a ton of the emotional shit I went through in my adult life was because of him. She didn't need to know that her doctor was probably more fucked up than she was.

"Andris...we can't...we can't do *that* here," she said, swallowing. I watched the smooth skin of her neck bob as she struggled to keep reins on the desire I could clearly see in her eyes. The sexual tension between us had been so strong you could cut it with a knife. I could still see her want for Link, though, as well. It pained me to know that another man filled her thoughts. Thoughts that I wanted to belong to only me. I wanted her to think about me when we weren't together. I wanted her to want to see me when we weren't. I wanted her to beg me to fill her over, and over, until she was so sore she couldn't take anymore. I wanted to consume her, make her invisible to others so that I was the only one she saw.

"Get your mind out of the gutter,'" I teased. "I was just thinking that maybe we could go out for lunch."

"Lunch? Are you serious? What about our session?" She asked as she looked around my office, her pony tail brushing across her back as her head whipped from side to side. I perched my ass on my desk, crossing my feet at the ankles then crossed my arms over my chest, allowing the desk to support my weight.

"Do you really want to sit here and talk about the same crap over and over, or would you like to get the hell out of here and have a nice lunch with a very sweet, charming, sexy doctor that I know?"

"Sweet? Maybe. Charming? Possibly. Sexy? Well, that is still up for debate."

I extended my hand out to her and she reached for it, allowing my larger one to fold her smaller one inside. She stood quickly, and suddenly, we were toe to toe, breath to breath. She breathed life into me. Made me feel more alive than anyone or anything in my life. She was a rare gem in a field full of diamonds. The funny thing about diamonds was that there were never two that were exactly the same, but yet, it was still a diamond. A clear stone that everyone had and everyone wanted. A girl's best friend.

Nicola wasn't a diamond. She was more like tanzanite. She brought out spiritual awareness and psychic insight. She was just as strong as the blue-violet stone, and it even had to match the gorgeous hue of her eyes.

I could smell the soft cinnamon scent of her breath and could taste her on the tip of my tongue. Honeysuckle surrounded me, clouding me in her familiar scent, and it had all of my senses working in rapid time to try and absorb as much of her as I could.

"You're staring."

"You're staring," I retorted, my lips tipping up on the ends.

"Well, Doctor. You planted the idea of food in my head. I suggest you take me somewhere so I can fill the insatiable appetite you have created," she teased and both of her hands pressed into my chest softly as she pushed me away. I watched the curve of her ass as she turned around to grab her purse. My hand itched to smack her right across the ass. Then I wanted to sooth it, pinch it, and cling to it as I drove into her.

Fuck. I needed to get a grip. I adjusted myself in my pants before she turned around to look at me.

"Ready, doc?"

WE CHOSE A SMALL deli a few blocks away from the clinic. It wasn't a large place by any means, but it was packed. Most of the tables were full when we arrived, but a few had opened by the time we got halfway to the counter to order.

"Why don't you tell me what you want, and then go claim one of those tables while I get our food?" She nodded, giving me her order and then going to have a seat at a booth towards the back of the deli that faced the busy New York street. Another fifteen minutes later and I was joining her at the table with food in hand.

"Wow, I didn't realize how hungry I was. Thank you."

"My pleasure." *And your pleasure…later.*

We both dove into our sandwiches while making idle talk. I was stalling. Putting off the inevitable. I had chosen for us to go out to lunch on purpose because I wanted to, I guess you could say, be on neutral ground when I broke the news to her that I wouldn't be her doctor anymore. As much as my fucking chest hurt with the idea of seeing her less than what I already did, I knew it was what I had to do to try and beat Cardinelli and his fucking blackmail.

"So I have some news for you."

"Really, what kind?" She asked as she wiped at the corners of her mouth with a napkin. She dabbed at her lips like a true debutant would, clearly having been taught to do so from an early age.

"Kind you probably won't like very much."

She stopped chewing and her eyes met mine, fixing me in her gaze as if I were trapped in a glass house looking into something I could see, but couldn't touch.

"As of next week, you will be seeing one of the other doctors in the clinic."

There, I said it. She resumed chewing, then swallowed before lifting her glass of water to her lips and taking a long, slow draw from the liquid. Her silence was deafening to my ears. I was used to not getting a reaction out of her in some situations, but not when it came to us and our strange…*relationship*.

"How do you feel about that?" I asked as I rubbed at the condensation on my water glass, watching the water bead and trickle down to the napkin on which it rested. Out of the corner of my eye I could see her set her glass back down on the table. I don't know why I was so nervous about breaking this news to her, but I was even more nervous about the fact that she wasn't showing any kind of reaction to it.

"Is this why we came to lunch? You wanted to break the news to me...gently?"

I looked up and saw it. I heard it in the tone of her voice when she spoke. She was angry, yet trying to hold it together as if to prove what I had told her wasn't getting to her.

"Partly. But I also really wanted to have lunch with you."

"Why?"

The hurt in her tone was evident. I reached over and grabbed her hands and held them in my own. I felt the strength of her grip on my own hands.

Fear.

"Why am I giving your care over to another doctor?"

She nodded.

"Well, I have a few reasons for that. But my biggest reason is because I'm not allowed to date my own patient," I replied, adding a smile to my face and hoping that she caught on to what I'd said.

"I'm confused," she said, knitting her brows together as she nibbled on her bottom lip. I reached up, releasing her lip from her teeth and allowed my thumb to brush against the bottom of her full pout. Her lips were soft, begging me to kiss them. If we weren't still in a public place, I would have. I would have ravished her if there weren't nearly sixty other patrons in the deli with us. Besides, who knew if Cardinelli was watching us right then as well?

"I want to date you, Nicola. I want to go to dinner. I want to spend time getting to know you on a more *personal* level."

Her eyes widened, revealing even more of the beautiful hue that I had come to love. I could get lost in those eyes. Even though at times she doesn't show a large amount of physical signs to her emotions, I could read her most days and judge how she was feeling just by looking into them.

"I don't know what to say, Andris. I...what about Link?"

"Let me handle him. There are only a few weeks left in the contract. We'll work it all out. So? How about it?"

She looked around the deli. All the tables were full, many with couples who looked lovingly towards each other. I knew she had to be struggling with the decision. I knew she had feelings for Link, but I also knew she had feelings for me. If I could get her turned on to the idea of *us*, then maybe I wouldn't have to fight Link for her thoughts or her heart. I wanted her for myself, no longer wanting to share her with him, with anyone, and this would be the first step in rectifying all of that.

"Okay."

"Okay?"

"Okay." She smiled.

Fuck yes.

I threw my napkin down on the table and rose, reaching for her hand, pulling her close to me. Patrons and Cardinelli be damned. I couldn't resist the opportunity to be able to capture her lips with my own. The next few weeks were going to be difficult, fending off Cardinelli and trying to transition her connection with Link and the escort business all at the same time, but if the end result was that she was mine, I would fight till the death.

I pulled her closer, feeling the warmth of her body absorb into mine and lightly pressed my lips to hers. I didn't take it any further, instead feeling like this small, innocent looking kiss was much more than it perceived to be. It was a promise, not only to her, but to myself. I would go to any lengths to protect her, especially from Cardinelli.

"So I take that as you are okay with it?" I asked her as I stroked the smooth skin of her cheek as my fingers threaded into the hair at her nape.

"I don't like it, but—," she said leaning in to whisper in my ear. "If it means that I get to finally see you naked? Then I'm all for it."

Damn. My dick hardened in my pants. I couldn't wait to have her, no blindfolds, and no darkness between us. The thought made me both pleased and anxious at the same time. My arrangements with Link had always seen me through my sexual desires. Sometimes he would have the girls, and other times I would have them. Never once had either one of us fallen for one of the women until now. Link seemed to be different with her just as I was, and it made me wonder if I was up for a big fight.

Link wasn't the only thing that gave me anxiety. I've never really been with a woman on a normal level. Sure, I'd fucked girls in high school and college, but this was different. This was a woman that I could imagine spending most of my time with. When she wasn't consuming all of my thoughts, she was at least in a vast majority of them.

We walked from the deli hand in hand and snuggled up close to each other to combat against the wind that threatened to carry us away. It felt nice to live normally for once. I allowed all the bad shit to slip away and just enjoyed the moment with her. I was fucking giddy like a schoolgirl as we walked down the busy sidewalk back towards the clinic. The entire way men stared at her, women turned their heads and wished they could be her.

That's right. She's mine.

And I wasn't going to let anyone, or anything get in the way of that.

CHAPTER
FOURTEEN
JERICHO/NICOLA

I COULDN'T WIPE the smile off my face as I left the clinic after lunch with Andris. We went back into his office after we made it back to the clinic and he barely had enough time to shut the door before he spun me around and pinned me against it. When his mouth seared over mine, it was intense. I could feel the need for him to have me and it matched my own. I kissed him back with equal fervor until we were both left breathless, yet panting for more. We probably would have fucked right there on his desk if it weren't for his secretary buzzing the intercom and announcing that his next patient was waiting in reception.

As happy as I was about the idea of developing a relationship with Andris, because seriously, who wouldn't want a relationship with a fucking sexy as hell doctor who knew how to guide a woman to ecstasy without even touching her? I was also apprehensive because of Link. It wasn't just that I had feelings for Andris, feelings I have *never* had for anyone until now, but I also had feelings for Link. Even though I had only spoken to him once in the darkness of the room I had spent one night in, I felt this overwhelming connection to him. He knew how to mold and manipulate my body to feel things and experience them like never before. In my heart, I felt that it was he who ignited the fuse of my vacant emotions so that I was able to open up to the idea of maybe falling in love with someone. No matter how scary it was to do so.

I left the clinic building and relished in the cool air as it hit my overheated face. Andris had warmed my body to all new heights and I was more than giddy for our first actual date tonight. He told me to dress nicely and be ready for a good time.

The only good time I wanted was to feel him inside of me all night.

I walked towards the end of the sidewalk to hail a cab, to go to Fifth Avenue. I wanted to invest in something to wear tonight and maybe also pick up something that I could guarantee Andris would enjoy taking off later.

I had nearly made it to the end of the sidewalk when I crashed into a very large body. I made my apologies without looking up, but decided to go ahead and offer my eyes to the stranger in which I had offended, when I froze in place.

Antonio Cardinelli.

"Hello, Nicola," he drawled in his thick accent. His voice was dripping with something. Disdain? Desire? I didn't know what it was, but it made me shiver, losing any of the remaining warmth that had been left there by Andris.

"Um, hello, Antonio," I stammered, trying to walk away from him. I was in a good mood and I didn't want to talk to the creepy man who always gave me an unsettling feeling.

"Just finished seeing the good doctor, eh?" He asked as I raised my hand in the air to signal a cab. The quicker I could get away from him, the better.

"Yes, if it's any of your concern. Excuse me, but I really must be going."

"Why such a rush, my dear? You know, I've been meaning to get in touch with you. I am still very much interested in your services."

I turned to face him, standing up to my full height that didn't even manage to bring the top of my head to the level of his chin. Two large, younger men stood off behind him, ogling me and him as we stared at each other. My eyes flicked back toward the two men, and then I lifted my head to look at Antonio.

"I told you *Mr.Cardinelli*, that I am under a contract. I cannot provide any services for at least another four weeks. Like I said before, if you would give the agency a call, I'm sure Lexie can put you in touch with someone who can accommodate you."

I started to walk away in the other direction, ignoring the cabs and choosing to walk instead. I had a bad feeling of dread in my stomach and I tried to quicken my pace, weaving in and out of the people who were also walking on the sidewalk. I was stopped in my tracks when a hand clamped over my arm and pulled me backward. If we were in any other city other than New York, people maybe would have noticed, but not in this city. I could be lying on the ground bleeding to death and people would just step over me and be on their way. So when a big crime boss grabs you by the arm and pulls you backward, no one gives a fuck about that either.

"I think that the terms of your contract will be negotiated," he spoke in my ear and the smoky smell of his cigar breath made me nauseous. I tried to pull away from him, but didn't have any strength and my attempt at escape was unfruitful. A black car pulled up to the curb and the two men standing behind him rushed over to it as one of them opened the passenger side back door.

"Get in the car, Nicola. We have business to discuss."

"I'm not discussing anything with you. Let. Me. Go."

I was ignored as I was pulled and then practically shoved into the back seat of the car. Although the warmth of the heated leather seats was welcome to my body, the uneasy and fearful feeling that threatened to overwhelm me was not. Antonio climbed into the back seat next to me and sat uncomfortably close. The unpleasant smell of tobacco mixed with his cologne filled the back cab of the car, nearly choking the breath from me. The two men that had been with him climbed into the front seat and we soon pulled out into traffic, heading towards God knew where.

"What do you want?" I asked as I shoved my purse next to me, trying to create some sort of barrier between Antonio and me.

"You know what I want, Nicola, don't try to act coy. You just come off being bitchy." I turned around in my seat so that I could look him in the eyes, showing him that I was not about to back down.

"You will *never* have me. You're pompous and arrogant if you even think that is a possibility."

"Trust me, my dear, you'll change your mind."

He ran the tip of his pinky across my jeans, and even though he didn't touch my actual skin, it was like his touch scorched me. I didn't want this man's hands on me. In fact, I've never turned down someone who was willing to pay me, yet something about Cardinelli sent warning signals flashing through my mind. I jerked my leg away from him and he smiled with a cocky and sardonic attitude.

"You and the good doctor have gotten close."

My head snapped in his direction. No one knew about my arrangements with Andris other than Lexie. She was the only person other than Link, Andris, and myself who knew the terms of that contract, and suddenly my warning signals started flashing stronger and brighter.

"He is my doctor. He treats me and I pay him for his services."

"And he in turn pays you for *yours*."

I froze. It scared me that this man, this mob man, knew about my arrangement with Andris and Link. Andris had a reputation to protect. His clinic, his employees, all of them could be devastated by the aftermath of the public finding out about our strange relationship. Although Andris was working to separate our relationship from his business, we did still have the contract, and Antonio knew that.

"You know nothing about me, or my relationship with Andris," I spat out. "Besides, you are married. What would your wife say about you propositioning me?"

"My wife is occupied by your good doctor. It doesn't bother you that Andris not only fucks you, but her as well?"

I sat still in the seat for a moment. I knew of one time that Andris had fucked her, but he had never given any indication that he continued to do so. Am I blinded by these strong developing feelings for him? Is he still fucking Barbie?"

"I can tell by the look on that gorgeous face of yours that you didn't know."

"You're lying."

"My wife sees him twice a week. She comes home happy every time and doesn't bug me for sex. You do the math."

My heart sunk at the possibility that Andris was still fucking

Barbie. If he was in fact doing so, then that means that he broke the contract. As much as it hurt me to think that he did, did I also really think I could trust Antonio Cardinelli's word?

"I don't believe you."

"Believe what you will, doll. I still want my night, and I will have it. That is if you want to make sure that you and your boyfriend stay out of jail. I'd hate for you two to be separated by cell bars."

"Andris has nothing to do with any of this. Leave him out of it."

Antonio's chuckle sent a shrill, bone-chilling shiver through my body. I had no doubt in my mind that this man had connections. I had no doubt that he knew people and could get anything he wanted.

And what he wanted was me.

"Dr. Gunn has everything to do with this," he said, gesturing between him and me with a wave of his hands.

"Oh, my dear, if only you knew how deep your good doctor was. How he could go to jail for things far worse than contracting a hooker to fulfill his fantasies."

What in the hell was he talking about? Since I had known Andris, he had never wanted to do anything but good. The only time I had seen him sort of let go was at the place he takes me to be with Link. He even sacrificed himself for another man. He watches while I have sex with him, all the while it probably kills him to see me do so.

At least I hope it did.

"Secrets are a funny thing, Nicola. But somehow, they always seek their way out. They never stay hidden for long. The truth will always prevail."

"I don't have to fucking listen to this."

"No, you don't, but I think you will want to."

He reached for a compartment just to the side of the door, and opened it, revealing a decanter of liquid. He pulled two small tumblers out of the same compartment and extended one to me and I tightly shook my head, refusing. I waited damn near impatiently as I watched him pour the liquid with a steady hand into his glass before placing the decanter back into the compartment along with the empty glass I had refused. With a painstaking slowness, I watched as he brought the glass to his overly tanned and dry lips and took a long draw from the liquid and then swallowed leisurely as he swirled the amber ale around and sniffed the aromas of it by bringing it to his nose.

His dark eyes sparkled with mischief, but also held a coldness about them that left me wanting to crawl out of my skin if only to escape it. The dark brown hue of his eyes bore into mine, never breaking contact as if trying to assert his dominance over me. I never felt intimidated by anyone or anything before in my life, but Antonio Cardinelli was a mythical dragon. Something you only ever envisioned seeing, but also hoping at the same time you would never have to come face to face with. I'd never really known fear, but if this was it, I never wanted to feel it again. Putting a hand to my chest, I tried to calm my racing heart and even out my breaths that had become more rapid. I couldn't show this man that he was getting to me. I had to keep strong not only for me, but also for Andris. Cardinelli knew far more than he was telling me. He could ruin not only my life, but Andris, and even Link's if word got out about our contract. Andris's reputation would be tarnished and he would never be able to practice as a doctor again.

Antonio finished his drink and then rested the glass on the edge of his knee as he massaged the smoothness of it with his fingers. A small squeak filled the cab of the car as his thumb slid back and forth upon the glass. It was worse than having to hear nails on a chalkboard, or an annoying high pitched car alarm.

"Will you just get to the point, Antonio?" I snapped as my patience began to wear thin.

"Andris and I have… I guess you can say…an *arrangement*. One that he inherited so to speak. It is his intentions to break that arrangement and even though I told him it wouldn't hurt me if he did, it in fact would be rather detrimental to my business."

"I don't understand," I said, shaking my head, my ponytail sliding along the back side of my jacket.

"Andris works for me, Nicola. He writes prescriptions for me to gain access to the drugs that I need that I cannot get from my other suppliers. Ever since you became his patient, he keeps trying to cut ties with me. I do not like that."

"You're lying. Andris is too good of a person to be involved with a fucking sleaze ball like you," I hissed through clenched teeth. My jaw began to ache from the pressure I was putting on it and I could feel an angry flush fill my face as it heated while my temper grew. Antonio reached into his pocket and produced his cell phone, sliding his finger across the screen to awaken it and gesturing it towards me before speaking again.

"If you don't believe me, give the good doctor a call."

I stared at the phone like it would burn me if I touched it. Part of me told me to ignore the accusations that Antonio was saying about Andris, but a large part of me knew that they were true. A man like Antonio Cardinelli wouldn't be trying to attack Andris through me if it weren't true.

"Ah. I see it in your eyes, Nicola. Deceit is a nasty thing. The fear hits you right in the chest and you become angry and frustrated." His hand came up and a finger traced along my jaw. I didn't move. I didn't flinch. Partially paralyzed by the fact that Andris could keep something as vital as his involvement with Antonio Cardinelli away from me, and partially because I didn't want to let Antonio see how much it was affecting me.

"Your beauty astounds me. I could give you anything you want. You wouldn't have to sell your body and your soul to the highest bidder in order to survive."

I held my head high, even though his words sliced through me. I hated this. I hated myself. I was scared, frustrated, and pissed off all at the same time. For someone who until recently didn't experience any of these emotions, I quickly found myself wanting to go back to that place. Back to the old me who didn't have to feel anything—didn't have to care.

But I did. I did care. I cared about Andris. I cared about Link. I wanted to protect both of them. I have had to do some vile things in my life to survive. This would be no different. I could handle Antonio Cardinelli just like any other shit storm of an event or sick bastard that had crossed my path.

"What do I need to do?"

CHAPTER FIFTEEN

ANDRIS

THE LIGHTS WERE LOW and candles bounced, illuminated flickers of light off the walls. The aroma of chicken masala filled the air as I stood looking around my penthouse apartment. I have never had a woman over to my real place before. I have never wanted to. The direction in which I was venturing to take my relationship with Nicola was teetering dangerously along a fine line. I wanted her. Needed her in fact. She was my glimpse of sanity in the world of messed up shit I dealt with every day. I faced demons and pasts of others on a daily basis, but never took the time to manage my own or to come to grips with the reality of my own mental struggles.

I paced up and down the hall, hands clasped firmly behind my back as I wore out the carpet between my room and the space between the living area and the dining room. I was the one who was always asked for help, but tonight, I called upon my friend for help. I knew it could possibly be a mistake to involve him, or to let him know of my newly developed relationship with the woman in which he was fucking, but I couldn't let another day go by without making her mine.

I approached the mirror in the hall, pausing to adjust the line of buttons on my shirt until they were perfectly in place above my belt buckle. My hair was tamed with styling gel and my tie matched the color of my eyes. Tilting my head side to side, I tried to relieve the tension in my neck and shoulders. When I next opened my eyes, I was staring straight at him.

"Are you sure you are ready to take this step, Andris? Are you sure that you can handle the pressure? I won't be here to help you should she change her mind. I won't be here to guide or protect you if her rejection hits you full force."

I stared at my friend. My confidant. The one person who I could count on to help me get through the shit that swirled in my head on a daily basis. He had always been there for me. Someone who I could trust with my words, thoughts, or my own life if necessary.

"I can't keep living my life in fear of him, Link. I can't keep letting the insecurities my father instilled upon me keep me from living my life. I have never had a desire to want to get past all of the crap I have been through, but she makes me want to. She makes me want to try and defeat him. To finally, once and for all, prove that he was wrong."

"Your father has been dead for years, my friend. He is not here any longer to put those lies in your head or to make you doubt your abilities. Yet, you still let him in like he were standing here before you today."

"That is what happens when you are told practically from birth that you are a 'nobody'. That you are a fuck up. A metaphorical hole-in-the-condom accident that only existed because my mother was too moral of a person to abort me."

I felt a warm hand on my shoulder. I tensed even though I

knew it wasn't my father's hand. Although it was meant to be a comfort, it still made me jump every time someone made the gesture. You see, it wasn't always just words from my father that cut deep, but also the searing pain from the back of his hand, or his fist when it collided with my ribcage. My mother, too afraid to stand up to him because she would also be on the receiving end of his wrath, was only able to stand by and watch as he took out his anger on me.

"Your father was an imbecile who had to compensate for his on insecurities by taking it out on you, Andris. Since I have come into your life, I have watched you grow. I have watched you fight him and the lingering effects he has left on you as a person. And since Nicola has entered it, I have watched you become so much more. That is why I don't want you to let the fear in. I don't want you to allow your father's memory, or thoughts, seep in and taint this evening for you. I want you to be with her. Be normal. Make love to her without the blindfolds, without the restraints. This is what I have primed you for. This is what our arrangement has been working towards since the very beginning. You can do this, Andris."

He walked away, as I stood there staring in the mirror. I felt a little lighter from the conversation with him. I allowed Link's words to flow through me like an antibiotic attacking the venomous virus left behind by my father. When I looked in the mirror, I saw his eyes staring back at me through my own. I looked so much like him, yet never wanted to have anything to do with being like him.

Straightening my shoulders, I took one last look at myself before I turned to walk down the hall and out of the apartment before I even allowed him the opportunity to invade my psyche. I had a woman to pick up for our date. A beautiful, sexy, intriguing woman, who after tonight, would belong to me.

NICOLA/JERICHO

Dear Journal,

Andris suggested that I write down anything that I feel so that I can start recognizing those feelings and then maybe be able to better understand them. It is strange that in just a few short weeks, I went from being this vacant hole, to someone who experiences a thousand new and different emotions all at once. Not only is it thrilling, exhilarating, and exciting, it also makes me feel apprehensive, scared shitless, and overwhelmed.

I admit it seemed rather stupid at that moment when he gave me this to write in, but the more I thought about it, and even more now that I've put pen to paper, I have to admit that it was a good idea.

There are so many things I want to say to Andris that I am unable to. He told me I didn't have to let him read what I have written in here, but that he would discuss them with me if I wanted him to.

I am more than excited for tonight. To have a chance at a real relationship, with real feelings is the part that excites me the most. Each new moment I spend with Andris awakens more and more emotions within me that I never imagined would ever be possible.

It isn't that I never wanted to have emotions. I tried. Desperately. I begged my mind to let go of whatever shield it was holding up that prevented me from being normal. I watch my friends in school experience things and feel different feelings that felt unreachable to me. I always wondered why I was born with the inability to feel. I knew my mother didn't have a drug problem, so I couldn't blame it on her. I always thought it was due to the lack of emotions they seemed to show to me. I blamed it on my lackluster childhood, the sense of abandonment that I had only read about in my psychology textbooks. I took classes in high school, trying to better understand the things that were happening, or rather weren't, happening to me. I got to live life everyday bare and expressionless, completely empty. I was seen as weird, or unsociable. A real sociopath. People thought I was crazy or that something was wrong with me. Not only was I looked down upon by my peers, but by my own parents, even the doctors who tried to "fix" me.

Andris is the only person who has looked at me like a real person. He doesn't make me feel stupid, or suggest that I am holding back. It is almost as if he can see through me—to the real me. The little girl who has been screaming on the inside to break through the shell that I've lived in. To the woman inside of me who wanted a normal life, a normal way of feeling.

He is the only person who has ever ignited a spark within my soul, the only person to ever make me feel the flames of desire. I get warm from one look, I grow like a fiery inferno from his touch. My body and mind buzz to the point that I succumb to sensations. My mind gets to wonder and think for itself instead of having to try and analyze every detail that unfolds before me.

He has become a craving, a need so powerful that I no

longer have control when he is near me. I welcome it. I want to submit to the feelings over and over as they overwhelm me. They drive me to the point that I could spontaneously combust, and fail to exist in my past anymore and only be enclosed in the present and the future. My body and mind feel as if they have awoken from a long eternal slumber. I feel resurrected from death and brought into a new light.

Andris is my light. Link is the flame behind the light.

Link.

How can my feelings for someone I have never truly seen be so powerful? I've never had the pleasure of looking into his eyes, but I've had the pleasure of the glorious feel of his hands on my body. I've felt the enormity of his presence and how he has the power to obliterate any rational thought to the point I am left with nothing but ecstasy.

But with the pleasure also comes something that I've rarely gotten to feel, but now experience it tenfold.

Pain.

Several different types. Not only do I feel torn between two men who make me come to life in many different ways, I am now also in the predicament that I have to protect both of them. If I were to lose either of them, I don't know what I would do. How is it that I have come to the point in my life where two people are completely detrimental to my survival?

My thoughts wanted to continue to flow on the pages of the leather bound journal, only a knock at my door broke me from my written confessions. With a trembling hand I placed the pen down on my desk and closed the journal and slid the strap into place to lock it. I felt the need to perform the ritual as if it would seal my thoughts inside the bindings. I could never share with neither Andris nor Link the information I had written on the pages. If they knew what I had agreed to do in order to protect both of them, they would never want anything to do with me again.

Being a whore had never bothered me before. Being a slut used only to pleasure men and for my own monetary gain never crossed my mind as being wrong or dirty. Now that I had two wonderful men in my life that I felt extreme feelings for, it did bother me. It made me feel disgusting for all the times I nonchalantly let a man inside of me. It made me feel weak for letting a man, who could have been married and even had a family waiting for him at home, penetrate my own body. For years they invaded my body unharmed, but now that I had Andris and Link, all of those men in the past began to penetrate more than my body. They are now ghosts of my past actions and mistakes that threatened to invade my thoughts. I'd never let them in before. Never allowed anyone in, but now that the shield was down, the army of my sins began to triumphantly march inward to where I was sickened with agony over my actions.

Another knock sounded at the door and I opened the drawer to place the journal inside and stood up, smoothing the imaginary wrinkles on the front of my red Valentino cocktail dress. My body trembled with excitement, but it also shook with anxiety. I had never been nervous for a session before, but this was no ordinary session. This was a date. My first real one in my life. I chuckled slightly, thinking about the fact that I was in my mid-twenties and just now experiencing the things that most normal girls did in their teens.

I looked in the mirror, adjusting the spirals of curls that cascaded over my shoulders and checked my makeup in my reflection to ensure that it was perfect. Taking a deep breath, I let it out before I left the comfort of my room and made my way down the hall to my condo's front door. With a trembling hand, I reached for the knob and opened it completely unprepared for what was waiting for me on the other side.

I felt sucker punched in the gut at the sight of him as if all the air had left my body. My eyes roamed over him clad in a light grey suit that accentuated the muscular build of his body. His tie matched the same blue of his eyes, making them stand out even more. His normally messy, yet sophisticated hair was now controlled and styled so that it left more of his gorgeous face open for my viewing pleasure. His smile was devastating, to the point that if I didn't breathe soon, I would very possibly pass out before him from lack of oxygen.

"Hi," I forced out when I was finally able to find my breath once again.

"Hi," he replied with confidence as he too used his eyes to make love to my body without so much as a single touch. We stood there, assessing each other's appearance as if looking at the beauty of one another for the first time. I guess you could say that we were looking at one another in a new light. We were taking our relationship beyond the contract, beyond the professionalism of him being my doctor and pushing it into a one way freight train heading for something unknown.

He took a step towards me, but I didn't move as I felt the warmth from him even from several inches away. His scent invaded my nose, threatening to turn my brain into mush to the point I couldn't form a coherent thought. In the next instant, my back was against my door, his hot lips on mine and my leg hiked up to encircle his waist. His hands sought past the fabric of my dress as he pushed higher and higher up my thigh, nearly leaving my ass exposed to the occupants of my condo's building.

I didn't care. All I could concentrate on was the expert way he explored my mouth. The way he kissed me as our tongues danced together, and the way I felt like he was absorbing into me. I felt my nipples pucker beneath the fabric of my dress and my toes curl as he squeezed the flesh of my ass. I felt weightless, as if floating from the earth, as his other hand came up to cup the back of my head as he tried to deepen the kiss. When he finally released my lips from his, I felt the painful absence.

"I'm sorry. I've been thinking about doing that the second you walked from my office earlier today."

I smiled from his confession, having had the same thoughts throughout the afternoon.

"Well, who am I to stop you, Doctor?" I smiled, meeting his equally sparkling eyes that matched the same desire of my own.

"If I don't stop, then we will never leave your condo. Besides, I think your neighbor behind us was enjoying the show."

I looked over his shoulder to find old man Winters staring at us with wide eyes. I leaned in and placed my forehead on Andris's shoulder, unable to control the giggles I was trying so hard to suppress. The old man stared at us only seconds longer, before I heard the sound of his condo door shutting and Andris and I both laughed. His warm hand cupped my chin and lifted my face to where our eyes met. Even through our fit of laughter at being caught making out like a couple of hormonal teenagers, I could still see the fiery desire in his eyes. They danced with luminosity as he stared directly into mine, silently letting me know what was to come later in the evening without a single word passing his lips.

"Are you ready to go?" He asked, leaning in and brushing

his lips across the shell of my ear. The act made my body shiver with a glorious delight. Even if I didn't feel the wetness already pooling between my thighs, other parts of my body would have been a dead giveaway about the readiness that I possessed.

"Sure. Let me lock up and grab my purse."

I turned off all the lights and grabbed my coat and purse before locking the door to my condo. I turned back around and found the heat of Andris's stare upon me, lighting me up from the inside out. I felt addicted to the force of his gaze, like it was the greatest high I had ever been on. His beauty hit me like a freight train every time I had the pleasure to just look at him.

He crooked his arm and I slipped mine into his as we set off down the hallway towards the elevator. I was instantly brought back to the first night that he led me to the place where I fulfilled the duties of my contract with him and Link, only this time it was different. Whereas before I wore a blindfold, I could now clearly see where we were going. Yet, I still didn't know where we were going, just like before, both physically speaking and relationship wise.

We were assaulted by the cold air as we stepped outside my condo's building. Waiting at the curb was a very masculine looking supped up pick-up that had wheels that looked like they were my height. It was sleek, yet sexy. Mysterious, yet powerful looking. I arched my eyebrows in Andris's direction as I looked from him then back to the monstrosity of metal in front of us.

"It's a four wheel drive. The forecast has called for heavy snow tonight so I wanted to be sure I could get you home safely."

"Oh," was all I could reply. I couldn't help the small sense of defeat I felt at the prospect of him wanting to bring me back home. The silly, inner-girl within me had hoped that he would invite me to stay over. Isn't that what people in a relationship did? Maybe I was thinking too far ahead, not knowing yet where the diameters of our arrangement stood.

"Although, if I have anything to do with it, you won't be leaving for quite a while."

My heart seriously skipped a fucking beat. My body flushed with excitement.

"What if we get snowed in and I have to stay a while? You may grow tired of me."

"Oh, I'll be *tired* all right, but it won't be *of* you, it will be *because* of you."

He winked at me as he opened the passenger side door of the truck and offered his hand to me to help me climb into the cab. Warm, heated leather molded to my backside, adding to the warmth of my body that Andris had created with his words. He shut the door and walked around the other side to climb in. I had a small sudden flash of fear as Link came to mind. How would he feel about my new relationship with Andris? Would he be angry? Would he even care? Did I want him to?

Thoughts and questions swirled in my head until Andris finally climbed into the cab of the truck and broke me from my thoughts.

"Wow. That was an intense look."

"Hmm?" I asked, looking over to him.

"You looked very serious when I climbed in just now. Are you sure you are okay with this, Nicola?"

"Already trying to analyze me, Doctor?" I said with amusement in my voice and a smile upon my lips. When he didn't return my amusement, I placed my hand on his thigh, momentarily lost in the feel of him beneath my hand before I found my voice.

"Of course I'm okay with this. More than okay. I was just thinking—how—how does Link feel about this?"

Andris started the truck and the rumble of the motor could be felt through the leather seats beneath my body, enhancing with synchronization the already intense buzz of my body with the closeness of Andris. I moved across the bench seat of the truck until I was shoulder to shoulder and thigh to thigh with him. The familiar electric spark of heat hit me the instant we touched and for a brief moment I allowed my eyes to close and relished in the feeling. It felt amazing to finally feel that sort of feeling with another person, especially with a man who, with every second that passed, became that more etched into my soul.

"I saw Link just before I came over. He is okay with our arrangement. However, you are still under the terms of the contract for three more weeks."

"Are you okay with that? I mean, are you going to be able to allow me to be with another man outside of our—"

"Relationship. You can say it, Nicola. In fact. I want you too. I want to move forward with the idea of you and me. That is, if you want it too."

"I do. I must be honest with you, though. I—I also have feelings for him as well."

He sat back in the seat, resting his head against the seat as he closed his eyes.

"I sort of thought you might. I appreciate your honesty. I must warn you about Link, though. For him it's all about sex, Nicola. He doesn't have the same feelings that I do."

Woah.

"What feelings would that be?"

"That I can see myself falling in love with you."

How many times could a person's heart skip a beat in one night? Warmth radiated through me and I leaned into him instinctively and placed my lips on his. I probed until he opened to me and I slipped my tongue inside, devouring the taste of his mouth and completely loosing myself in the feel of his mouth on mine. I may have initiated the kiss, but he quickly took control, cupping my head and tilting it ever so slightly so that our mouths were aligned perfectly. We were both breathless when we finally detached from each other and I worked hard to try and catch the breath that was trapped in my lungs.

Wow.

Putting the truck in drive, Andris pulled out into traffic, one hand on the wheel, the other hand threaded through mine. In therapy, many doctors had given me romance novels to read to try and trigger an emotion or thought within me. There were several ones where a young girl would ride next to her crush or boyfriend in a pickup truck just like the one Andris and I were in now. Back then, I never even thought twice about what the girl was feeling riding so close to her man, but now having the experience myself? I had to say it was fucking awesome. I felt seventeen—experiencing love for the first time.

I couldn't wait for what the rest of the night held in store for us. With the looming cloud of worry that hung over my head at what I had agreed to with Cardinelli, I didn't want it to seep in and taint the evening that Andris had planned for us tonight. For a few hours I could put aside the dark and step back into the light that Andris created within me.

CHAPTER SIXTEEN

ANDRIS

IT WAS TAKING ALL the control I could find not to pull the truck over on the side of the road and peel the sinful dress from Nicola's body and ravish her on the spot. Her close proximity to me in the truck wasn't helping to diminish the rapidly growing desire for her that nearly consumed me. Her scent filled the cab and my nostrils, and on its own it was an aphrodisiac.

The ride back to my apartment felt like it took forever. I drummed my fingertips on the steering wheel to keep from groping her in the truck. The whole drive over I had to try and convince myself that I was doing the right thing. She was no longer going to be my patient, so ethically I could make her mine. Emotionally, however, I was struggling. My feelings for her grew fast and hard, repercussions be damned. I didn't have time to slow down or be able to think about how it would affect her if she found out the truth about me. I didn't want her to find out how weak and insecure I was when it came to women. Link had helped me to conjure some confidence before I went to pick up Nicola, but not enough to shake that flagging niche in the back of my mind that told me I was going to fail at this.

If I ever wanted anything to work in my life, it would be her.

I helped her from the truck, enjoying the warmth of her palm as our fingers laced together. I felt the slightest tremble in her hand and it echoed my own. She was nervous too, and in an odd way it was comforting to me to know that.

When we got to my penthouse, the scent of the chicken masala I had prepared earlier hit us as soon as I opened the door.

"Wow, something smells wonderful," she said as she shed her coat and once again revealed the red dress that was doing powerful things to my cock. Nicola was beyond beautiful. She had to do little to her appearance in order for that beauty to reflect her, yet the small touches that she did do only enhanced it. She had a model quality about her, as clichéd as it sounded. She could give any movie actress a run for their money and make even the most committed man want to have a sinful affair with her.

"I made dinner before I came to get you. I hope you have no food aversions."

"Wow. So many talents, doctor. I do believe I hit the jackpot," she said in a playful tone.

"Have a seat and I'll serve it."

She walked to where I had an elegantly decorated table in the dining room that was connected to the kitchen. I picked up a lighter from off the bar and lit the tall pillar candles on the table and then dimmed the lights to where the flames danced upon the walls. The tall vase of red roses in the center of the table filled the small space with a sweet, floral aroma that accented the wine from the chicken masala.

All throughout dinner, I could barely contain myself. Even

the way she chewed was turning me on to the point I felt like my body was going to rupture from the growing tension. It needed her. I needed her, but I also wanted to take this slow. When it came to Nicola, fucking up wasn't an option.

We retired to the living room where I pressed a button on the remote that instantly lit the fireplace. We sat closely on my oversized couch, enjoying a glass of wine and engaged in conversation.

"Dinner was wonderful, thank you."

"My pleasure. Cooking is something I have always enjoyed."

"Lucky for me then, because I suck at it," she giggled before she took another sip of her wine. I watched her throat bob as she swallowed, my lips begging to be pressed against the smooth, tanned skin of her neck.

"How could you suck at it?"

"Well, growing up I had cooks or maids who did it all for me. In school, all of our meals were either cooked for us or catered. I never got the opportunity to learn, really. When my parents died I ate whatever was available to me. Mostly that consisted of gas station junk food or takeout."

"Well, maybe a cooking lesson will be in order. Next time we can make our meal together."

"That sounds like fun."

We sat in silence for several moments. I watched the heat from the fire match the heat in her eyes. We were both holding back, afraid of what would happen if either of us made that first move. I had thoroughly enjoyed her company so far, but dammit, if I didn't have her soon I was going to go crazy.

I sat my glass on the coffee table in front of me before I reached for her, pulling her mouth to mine. The sweet taste of wine mixed with the normal taste of her mouth was incredible.

She had quickly become something that I craved constantly. She lit me up. I was a stick of dynamite and she was the fuse that ignited something inside of me that only she could. She made me burn with need, and I would gladly go up in flames just to be with her.

"Nicola."

"Hmmm?" She replied as I pressed hot kisses to her throat just like I had daydreamed about only moments before.

"I want you."

"Oh thank God," she breathed as if she had found the relief that she desperately needed. I sought her mouth once again, allowing our tongues to mingle and dance together in a perfect rhythm. Her hands came up to loosen my tie as I reached behind her and slid down the zipper of her dress. Removing her arms from the top, she allowed it to pool at her waist, exposing her sheer black lace bra to me. It was a sharp contrast to the firelit creaminess of her skin. I shed my shirt and tie leaving both of our upper torsos exposed to one another. This time when we embraced, our flesh touched and it was a glorious burning sensation that reached deep down into my chest.

You're mediocre.

No. Fuck no.

You don't deserve her, you worthless piece of shit.

I tensed as my father's words echoed in the back of my mind. I had worked so hard not to allow him to invade my thoughts. Nicola had been a wonderful distraction and helped me keep him at bay all evening, but now that we were so close to intimacy, he came barreling in full force.

Nicola looked at me for a moment, recognizing something. Did she see my fear? My anxiety?

You've never had a woman that wasn't blindfolded. You know she will run the moment you even try with her, so why even bother?

I closed my eyes tightly before opening them and finding Nicola looking right into them.

"Is everything okay?" She asked as her thumb stroked my cheekbone in a tender caress. I swallowed almost audibly, trying to rid the heavy lump that had developed in my throat. I wish Link were here. He would tell me what to do. He would tell me that my bastard father wasn't actually here to hurt me. He would tell me that I deserved someone like Nicola. He would tell me that I deserved to be loved.

As if sensing something were wrong, Nicola pushed me back and stood up. This is what I feared. My lack of confidence to be able to make love to a woman like a normal human being was quickly becoming a reality. She was going to walk out, not wanting to be with a fucked up head case like me. I was prepared for her to retreat when instead, she pushed her dress down her hips, exposing her matching lace panties and garter belt. Briefly, my father's thoughts escaped me and my mouth watered at the enormity of her beauty.

I was surprised even further when she dropped to her knees in front of me and caressed my thighs with the palms of her hands before she reached for my belt buckle and released it.

"You know, I may still be new at this whole emotions thing. I am now better able to understand and recognize things in others. I have you to thank for that, Andris. You have done something to me that has flipped a switch that was long hidden within me."

She undid the button of my pants and I lifted my hips, allowing her to remove them, and leaving me exposed in my boxer briefs.

"You saved me. You brought me out from a dormant and

vacant life, Andris. You have woken up my soul. I feel so many different things with you. Everyone always wanted to know what I was feeling or what I saw. I see a fear in you right now. I don't know what it is, and you don't have to tell me if you don't want to. Just let me help you get past it, like you helped me."

With tentative fingers she pulled down the waistband of my boxer briefs, completely exposing my ridged cock to her. Nudging my knees apart, she steeled between my legs, tracing her delicate fingers across my thighs. I shivered with delight. Nearly bounced on the spot with anticipation. Sweat formed on my brows and my balls ached to the point I could barely stand it.

Gripping me in her hand, I grew even harder, and when her head descended down and she took the tip of my cock into her mouth, I nearly died. The warm, moist confines of her mouth nearly had me coming as she swirled the tip of her tongue around the tip. My head rested back on the sofa as she took me deeper with expertly practiced movements. She went slowly, painfully so.

"Oh fuck, Nicola."

"Mmmm." She moaned against my dick and the vibrations she sent through me nearly made me come undone. She continued in an unrelenting rhythm until I was forced to stop her, or explode in her mouth.

"I wasn't finished," she protested as she wiped at the corner of her mouth. Damn, she was fucking perfect. She didn't ask any questions nor seek any answers when I began to behave differently, she just took the reins and made me forget my torment.

"Well, you have had your dessert, now I want mine."

"Well, who am I to deprive you of that?" She teased before rising from the floor. Unhooking the clasps of her garter, she seductively slid her panties down the smooth skin of her thighs, before allowing them to pool at her feet. She teased me in delightful ways. Knew exactly how to drive me to the brink of insanity, to where there was no room for my father's ghostly torment, only thoughts of burying myself inside of her remained.

Taking her hand, I gently pulled her down onto the couch and guided her to where she was lying on her back facing me. I placed my hands on her knees, guiding her legs apart before coming to settle between them. Through the flames that flickered around the room, I could see her desire. I was exposed to the glistening evidence of her desire as I traced a single finger through her wet core.

"That feels amazing," she breathed as her back gently arched off the back of the couch. Not wanting to waste any more time or allow my father's voice to gain access to my thoughts, I concentrated solely on her as I spread open her lips and traced my tongue around her sensitive clit. Her body jerked with the first touch and continued to make small acknowledgements of my presence as I began to pick up the pace until I was at a rhythm that had her writhing beneath me in only a matter of moments. I drew my power from her. The pleasure that she was experiencing from my tongue drove me further. I relished in her taste, claiming her as mine with my tongue before I would claim her as mine with my body.

The look on her face was enough to satisfy me. Her eyes were closed and her perfect mouth hung open slightly. I focused on her breath, synchronizing swipes of my tongue to match her pants, creating a pleasure within her as well as myself like neither of us has ever known. I gripped her thighs more firmly when she tried to close them, and when her hands fisted in my hair, the prickly sting at my scalp was a welcoming feeling.

"Andris..." she moaned, my name sounding erotic coming

from her lips. Knowing that her thoughts were filled with me drove me to the brink of madness. So many times I had to witness her sessions with Link. So many times I had to experience the chemistry and heat between them, and so many times it left me feeling inadequate…second hand.

But to have her before me, writhing and on the brink of climax gave me all the power and courage I needed. She made me feel like I was enough. She gave me the ability to see past my own fears and to overcome any obstacle I faced.

"Andris, please…" she begged.

I inserted a fingertip, gesturing in a "come hither" motion as I began to stroke the sweet spot inside of her that made her even wetter. I felt her thighs tremble and her breathing begin to hitch.

"That's it, Nicola. Feel it. Feel me."

"I…oh God…I'm going to cum."

And she did. Gloriously. Fully. Like her body had just been granted pure and unadulterated ecstasy. Pressure having given way to release.

When she opened her eyes, they were clouded as if she had just had an out of body experience. I could still taste her on my tongue and leaned in so that she could taste herself on me.

"You are so beautiful when you cum." I said between kisses and I lapped at her tongue and gently bit on her bottom lip. She reached to rid me of my boxers and I stopped her.

"Not here."

I picked her up bridal style, the smooth creaminess of the backs of her thighs resting on my forearms and her arms snaked around my neck, pressing her breasts towards my face. As I made my way down the hall to my bedroom, I leaned down and captured one already hardened nipple and playfully teased it to where it puckered even more.

Gently, I placed her down on the bed before joining her and laying my body on top of her to absorb the warmth. She looked around as if searching for something.

"What are you looking for?"

"There aren't any restraints in here."

"No, there isn't."

"No blindfolds?"

"Nope."

"Any kinky sex toys?" She slightly giggled.

"No," I asserted with seriousness even though she was being playful. Her amusement was cute, but right now my mission was to prove to her that there was just me and her. No toys, restraints, or barriers to come between us.

"None of that here, Nicola. Tonight it is about you and me. It is about seeing your eyes when I make you cum. To watch the glistening flecks of your irises as you fall over the edge. To see the pleasure written on your face as I bury myself deeper and deeper inside of you. I want skin on skin. Breath to breath. I want you to touch me. See me, and only me. I want your full attention, your trust. Mostly I want you to know that you belong to me. With me."

"Okay. You know, doctor, a girl could get used to this kind of flattery. I like it when you get all bossy and tell me what to do."

"Get used to it. Because I plan on making you cum so hard, you will forget who you are."

"Bring on the amnesia, doc."

I reached over to the bedside drawer and produced a foil packet. She once again reached between us and this time, I allowed her to slide my boxers down and expose myself to her.

For a brief moment I stilled, poising the condom over the head of my dick as fear once again threatened to overwhelm me. This will be the first time in my life to make love to a woman no holds barred, literally. There were no holds, no restraints. Only the woman that I was falling deeper and deeper for every day. She was my only chance to break free. I had forgotten what it was like to feel *okay* before her, but I also knew she could be my downfall.

As if sensing my hesitation, she took the condom from me and rolled it onto my cock, her fingers massaging my shaft on the way down. I shook away the darkness, no longer content with living among the grey of my shitty life and instead embraced her light instead of fighting it.

I lined myself up to her entrance and in one slow push, I was inside of her and it felt like breathing for the first time. It felt like I had been reborn from the hollow and sorry man I had become and was now birthed into someone who wants to be better than that.

"Oh God," she breathed. My arms trembled as I poised myself over her, beginning an easy rhythm and enjoying the feel of her pussy as it clamped around me, pulling me deeper inside of her, like she was greedy for our bodies to connect.

"You feel even better than I remembered," I admitted in a whisper as I pressed my lips to the spot on her neck that flirted with her jawline. She tilted her head to the side, allowing better access as her hands roamed my skin, reaching and searching for something that I'm sure she herself wasn't even aware of.

"Open your eyes," I commanded and was met with desire, want, and need all at the same time when she complied. I cupped her face with my hands, forcing her to keep her eyes on me as I continued to rock in and out of her.

It was like heaven to finally be with a woman without any restraints or barriers between us, but not just any woman. It was a privilege to be with her. She was something I never envisioned happening to me, but everything I ever wanted.

Our lips met as we made love to each other with our bodies and our mouths. It was a high like no other that I had ever experienced, and I never wanted to come back down.

When we finally both climaxed in a rush of hot breaths and sweaty skin, it was together. Both finding our release in each other. Two broken souls made complete by being with one another.

CHAPTER SEVENTEEN

Jericho/Nicola

MY NIGHT WITH ANDRIS was beyond anything that I could ever imagine. Never having felt or truly experienced love, it was something that I now craved more than my next breath. I yielded to the comfort of his arms and I counted each and every lazy breath he made while he slept beside me.

Light filtered in through the window and cast shadows on the walls. It was almost peaceful and serene if it weren't for the looming sense of dread I felt hanging on my shoulders. I felt a cataclysmic unbalance as I sat and relished about my night with Andris, mixed with sad and painful thoughts of how our relationship was going to survive what we were aiming for.

I felt Andris hold back a little last night before he finally let go of whatever demons were plaguing him when we finally made love. I've never made love with a man before. I was built to fuck, built to not care about my sinful acts, but being with Andris was earth shattering, soul embracing.

"Someone is deep in thought," he said in a sleepy, yet husky voice. His baritone radiated through me and made me tremble.

"How long have you been awake?" I asked as I stroked the skin of his forearms with the tip of my nails.

"Long enough to hear those wheels in your head turn faster than the huge ass wheels of my truck."

I chuckled.

"Just reliving last night in my head."

From the floor, a cell phone alarm sounded annoyingly loud into the silence of the room and Andris reached down to retrieve it.

"Fuck. I have three early patients this morning. But I'd much rather stay here with you all day."

My heart swelled to the point of bursting. I still couldn't believe how easily he could give me that warm and fuzzy feeling, even if it were only from his words.

"It's okay. I need to get downtown to meet up with Lexie anyways. I haven't talked to her in a few days and if I don't make an appearance, she may send Big Joe out looking for me."

He arched a questioning brow in my direction.

"Big Joe is her husband/bouncer/protector dude. He is the cavalry that is sent in when clients aren't behaving themselves."

Andris grew suddenly still next to me, very much so that I feared he had stopped breathing. I propped myself up on my arm and held my head in my hands so that I could look at him.

"You aren't going back to work are you? Technically, you are still under the contract with Link for three more weeks."

"I know, but I need to have a talk with Lexie about after the contract."

He sat up quickly, a look of disdain on his face. His hand came up to rub at the shadow of hair that had formed over his face throughout the night. I wanted to reach up and caress it with my hands, to feel the roughness beneath my palms.

"Nicola, I know this is all new to us, but I am not comfortable with..." He trailed off, looking out of the window where the snow had formed on the windowsill. The sun reflected off the white fluff, making it seem brighter than it actually was outside.

"You aren't comfortable with what?" I prodded, eager to know what he was going to say.

"I'm not comfortable with your profession, alright? I know I sound like a douche, but I don't want you to go back to work after the contract," he stated, his voice raising an octave.

"You're right, you do sound like a douche. It's my job, Andris. You can't expect me to just quit. I have to have the means to live. I have a condo to pay for, food to buy. Just because we are in a..."

"Relationship. It's okay, Nicola. You can say it."

There was almost a bitterness in his tone that I was unaccustomed to hearing. It made me coil back into myself. Why was he acting like this? Was he regretting what happened between us last night?

"I'm not afraid to say it, Andris. I'm also not afraid to tell you that you have no control over my choice of profession. It's all I know. It's all I've done. But if you would have given me the opportunity, I would have told you that I was going to Lexie to tell her I needed to cut back."

He slammed his fist down on the bed and I could hear the mattress springs scream out in protest from the force.

"Dammit. You don't get it. I don't want you to cut back. I want you to *quit*. I won't have my girlfriend—"

"Whoring around? Is that what you were going to say?" I grabbed the sheet to cover my naked flesh. I felt dirty. Cheap.

For the first time since I became a prostitute, I felt disgusting. I regretted what I had chosen to do. I've *never* felt like that before, and I wasn't liking it.

"That isn't what I was going to say."

"Yes, it was."

"Nicola, I don't want to argue with you. I was just expressing my feelings about the matter. You really think I would like the idea of you being with another man? Do you really think I could just sit back while another man puts his dick inside of you?"

"You don't seem to have a problem watching Link do it."

"That was a low blow."

"Why? Why is it any different? You sit back and watch him fuck me. Hell, you guide my damn movements!"

I clutched at the fabric of the sheets to keep from pummeling him. His hypocritical feelings were starting to make me angry. Something that was also new to me, and I did not like it either.

"Link is an *arrangement* made prior to our relationship. Besides, it is just different with him. He is my friend."

"Oh, so it is okay for me to sleep with your friends, just not any perspective clients that would provide an income for me, is that it? What, you want to be my pimp now?"

"Don't be fucking ridiculous. You used sex in the past in order to feel something. Well, now that you do, you don't need that anymore, Nicola. You don't have to look or turn to perfect strangers in order to feel pleasure. I can give that to you."

"And Link."

"Yes, and Link. But that is only temporary."

He reached over and grabbed my hands, causing me to release the sheet I was clutching to my chest. Circling his thumbs, he massaged the top side of my hands as he sighed heavily.

"Look. I'm trying to tell you that I want you to be mine. Only mine. Link included. It is just complicated where he is concerned. He is a friend. Someone who has helped me through some really bad shit in my life and I feel like he is a part of me. But I also know that I cannot let him have you forever. After the three weeks are over, that is it. No more contract. No more sharing you. Please tell me you want that, too."

I looked at him, my eyes glistening as I tried to get up the courage to tell him that I wanted only him. Truth is though, it would be a lie. I had a strong connection with Link. It may only be physical, but it was a connection and one that I wasn't yet prepared to break. I didn't know if it was due to the fact that I was terrified to fall any deeper for Andris out of fear that he could break me. Not once in my life have I ever been gentle or soft. I've always had a hard exterior that shelled an even harder interior.

"I want that too, Andris…"

"I'm sensing a 'but' at the end of that statement."

"But…I also have feelings for Link."

He didn't say anything, and even though the sun was shining in through the window, I felt the whole room cloud in darkness. It looked like a thousand different emotions crossed his face, half of them I still didn't understand, but a vast majority of them, I did.

"I'm sorry. I wanted you to know the truth."

He released my hands, reaching up to scrub his face with both palms, frustration clearly written in his features.

"You can't tell me that you didn't know."

He blew out a rush of breath, wiping his lips with the pad of his thumb.

"Of course I knew. I just thought that maybe I was…"

He stopped and turned to face away from me. I reached up and placed my hand on the smooth skin between his shoulder blades. I felt the tension in his muscles and felt the anxiety in his posture. Soothingly, I rubbed his back, trying to offer some sort of comfort in place of what was obviously affecting him deeply.

"You thought what?" I asked, leaning in and placing a kiss on his shoulder. A soft shiver raced through his body and could be felt through my lips.

"It was nothing. Forget about it."

He rose from the bed and left the bedroom before I even had the chance to protest the way he dodged my questions. He returned a few moments later with a toothbrush hanging from his mouth and made his way over to a dresser staged in the corner of the room.

"I'll take you to your agency on my way to the clinic. It snowed quite a bit last night, so I would feel more comfortable driving you instead of you taking a cab," he said, his words half mumbled due to the toothbrush in his mouth.

"So that's it, huh? You really aren't going to tell me what you were going to say?" I half pouted as I began to rise off the bed. My legs felt weak from the lovemaking we did, not only the first time, but again when he woke me in the middle of the night for round two.

"There's nothing to talk about. Get dressed. We need to leave in a few minutes."

He walked back out of the bedroom and the next thing I heard was the water running from a shower. A big part of me wanted to stay naked and go in and join him, to offer him comfort because he was obviously upset about something. But the other part of me was pissed that he was dismissing me so easily.

I marched down the hallway and found my dress, slipping it back onto my body before sinking down onto the couch. Showing up at Lexie's office in the same clothes I had on from the night before wouldn't be a shock to anyone. In fact, it was rather common among all the girls.

I sat there silently, trying to go over in my mind how the atmosphere between Andris and I went from scorching last night to frigid this morning. I felt a little guilty about confessing my feelings for Link, but I wanted to be honest with him. Several weeks ago, I wouldn't have cared whether or not my confession hurt someone. That was the benefit of my non-existent emotions, but now that Andris and Link have triggered a switch in me, it was hard to be dismissive of what Andris had to be feeling. It also made me wonder if Link would have a similar reaction. Andris had said that Link was only about the sex, but a part of me hope that wasn't true. I hated comparing my feelings for both of them, when one was physically and metaphorically invisible to me, while the other was present in true form. One was willing to give himself to me completely, while one hid behind the mask of my blindfold.

Andris emerged from the bathroom dressed in another one of his well-tailored suits. It was stupid of me to be jealous over something as frivolous as clothing, but I was. I wanted to replace each piece of fabric on his body with my hands, or my tongue, or *both*.

"Are you ready to go?" He asked as he shoved some files into his briefcase on the bar that connected to his kitchen. I nodded my head and stood, reaching down to retrieve my purse from the floor. I noticed the blinking light of my cell phone flashing angrily from inside, but ignored it. No one really called me anyway, except Lexie, and I was on my way to see her anyway, so

I could save myself time by waiting to talk to her until I got to the flower shop.

When I looked up, Andris was standing before me. I breathed in the masculine scent of his cologne, getting lost in the smell of his deep, woodsy scent. It was like an aphrodisiac that made the bones in my body feel like rubber, and I wanted to fall at his feet and beg him to take me over and over again.

I placed the strap of my bag on my shoulder and met his gaze. His eyes revealed so many things that he would or couldn't say with his words. We stood there, neither one of us flinching or moving as our eyes never left the other. Heat sizzled between us like a flame gaining vital oxygen. I could feel a buzzing in my finger tips and toes, and the sensation was nearly a direct replica of the buzzing of my clit. Not only did I want him, but my body did as well, gaining a mind all on its own.

He threw the briefcase down on the couch and took a step closer to close the space between us. My breathing increased, never tiring of the way he made me feel alive when he was near. Reaching for both of my hands, he cupped them in his own, drawing me closer to him to where my hands splayed on the chest of his dark blue sports coat. I reached for the silky silver tie that was around his neck and played with the fabric between my fingers.

"I'm sorry I got so angry earlier. It just really makes me mad to think about you continuing to be an escort. I don't like it, Nicola. Not one fucking bit. But I'm also not going to be the asshole boyfriend who starts making demands and telling you what you can and cannot do."

He looked defeated, having probably practiced the same exact speech to me while he was in the shower. I had so many questions swirling in my own mind while he was in there as well.

"I understand, Andris. I'm going to talk to Lexie. I don't know what I am going to do for an income, but if it means that much to you, I'll quit. Although, you know that I have to fulfill the terms of the contract with Link?"

"Yes, I'm aware."

He reached up, smoothing a strand of errant hair away from my face by tucking it behind my ear. His touch was gentle. It said *I want to cherish* you, but his eyes said something more along the lines of *I want to bend you over this couch and fuck you seven ways to Sunday*.

"If you don't stop looking at me like that, I'm going to be dreadfully late for work. How would it look if the boss came in late because he was too busy indulging himself with the beautiful body of his girlfriend?"

"I'd say his girlfriend was a lucky girl," I smiled. He leaned in and pressed his lips to mine as his hand came to cup my jaw. He still tasted like minty toothpaste, and I grew painfully aware of the fact that I hadn't brushed my own teeth yet. It didn't matter, though. When Andris kissed me like this, no other thoughts were in my head, other than him. My head was clear of thoughts about Link, Lexie and my job, or even of the shitstorm I was going to create when I had to fulfill my obligations to Antonio Cardinelli. Instead, I wrapped my arms around his shoulders to deepen the kiss as my heart swelled even more in my chest.

I never wanted this feeling to end. I was a woman, albeit a grown one, who felt like a giddy teenager. I've never been in love, or really felt love toward anyone in my life, but with Andris, I was on a road heading on a collision course straight for it.

I rode in the middle of the truck, just as I did the night before, only this time, I snuggled into his side. Sure, I was cold from my brief encounter outside before we climbed into the massive beast on wheels, but I wanted to be close to him to warm not only by body, but my soul. It was a heat that only he was able to provide me, and I planned on absorbing as much of it as I could on our drive to Lexie's office as I could.

He kissed me goodbye with the promise of calling me as soon as his last patient left the clinic. As I walked through the flower shop and said hi to the employees out front, my phone vibrated from inside my purse. Reaching in and pulling it out, I was only able to read the name of the person sending the text message before it died and the screen went blank.

Antonio Cardinelli.

ANDRIS

"HE TOLD ME HE WOULDN'T cheat on me. I believed him. Just like I believed all the others. Just like I believed my father wouldn't lie to me."

I tried as hard as I could to focus on my patient in front of me. She was a gorgeous young girl with golden blonde hair, that wasn't quite as blonde as Nicola's. Her eyes were almost too large, and weren't the same vibrant blue as Nicola's.

It didn't matter what the fuck I did to try and concentrate on her, the one woman who invaded nearly every vacant space of my mind wouldn't go away. I found myself smiling throughout the day when I thought about how we spent last night, although I frowned when I thought about the morning. I knew that I shouldn't have let my father's desperate attempt to affect me from the grave alter the events of my life, but he was. These last few months have found me turning to Link more than ever, and now that I had Nicola, I both wanted him here and wanted him gone.

"You have issues of trust with men, Gabrielle. That is understandable considering the circumstances you have been in. Have you thought about why it is that you keep choosing the same kind of man? Have you considered maybe attempting to look for someone that you never would have thought you would be with?" I said to my patient to fill the silence that had developed between her and me. I needed to get my shit straight because my father's inflicted insecurities were now trying to seep their way not only into my personal life, but my work as well.

I helped people. I reached into parts of their psyche to help them break through walls and to develop into an individual capable of letting go of their fears to be able to function normally in society.

Too bad I couldn't do that for myself.

"I've never thought about it like that," she stated as she contemplated what I had just said.

Reaching into my drawer, I pulled out another leather notebook and handed it to her. She accepted it, turning the leather binding over and over in her hand.

"Your homework for our next session, Gabrielle, is to write down a list of qualities you feel are important in a mate. Not what you find attractive, but what you feel would help match what you are. Then bring it back with you next week."

She shoved the journal into her bag and shook my hand before retreating from my office to probably go and find her next unsuitable male. I rested my head in my hands to take a moment to breathe. Two more patients to go and I would be done for the day, but my next patient wasn't slated until another hour and a half from now, so I had a little time to kill.

I looked up when there was a knock on the door. Bradley, one of the other doctors in the practice, stood staring at me from the doorway. His arms folded gently across his chest as he leaned against the doorjamb.

"Rough day, Andris?"

"You could say that," I said with a slight chuckle.

Bradley was older than me by several years. He wasn't as old as my uncle, but not young enough to be classified as my generation. He was also a damn good psychiatrist and the only person at the practice who knew about my issues.

"Feel like talking about it?"

I nodded and he entered the office and shut the door before coming to sit in one of the chairs in front of my desk. Throughout the years that I had worked at the clinic, Bradley always tried to reach out to me whenever he saw how hard I would strive for excellence. He saw past the hard exterior I tried to let the world see, to recognize the boy inside of me that was still affected by the wrath and hatred of the one man in my life, who was supposed to love me unconditionally.

Crossing his legs, he relaxed back in the chair. He was a tall man, towering over me by a few inches. His build was slim, which made him appear even taller. Salt and pepper speckled his hair, showing the signs of his age, but his smile was still that of a vibrant eighteen year old boy. For some strange reason, I always felt that I could confide in him, almost looking up to him the way I never did my father.

"How are you handling taking over the clinic, Andris?" Bradley asked me as he gave me his full attention.

"Well, the day to day stuff is completely manageable, it's the other stuff he left behind that is a pain in the ass."

"You mean the Cardinelli situation?"

My eyes snapped up to meet his and I saw understanding through his grey irises.

"You know about that?"

He nodded as he let out a frustrated breath.

"Yeah. I walked in on him and Cardinelli in a heated argument once. Apparently your uncle tried to pull out and Cardinelli wasn't having it."

"Really? That's news to me. I always assumed that he wanted the arrangement."

"Partially, but I think that after he saw how deep he got, he knew it was a bad decision."

"Yet he still pushed me to keep the relationship with Cardinelli."

"I think that was more pressure from Cardinelli himself than your uncle."

I contemplated what he said for a moment. It was strange to think that my uncle, who in a vast amount of ways, reminded me of my father.

"Seems to me, that isn't the only thing you are troubled about. How many times have you called on Link lately?"

It wasn't a shocker for Bradley to discuss Link with me. I had confessed my need to have Link in my life with Bradley before, and he knew Link was my way of hiding behind my so-called imperfections.

"Several. Although you will be pleased to know that I am now seeing someone without hiding behind Link and the blindfolds."

He arched his eyebrow at this, and at first I thought it was in surprise, but then he smiled and I knew he already knew. Of course he did.

"It wouldn't be that beautiful blonde whose file you sent

my way, would it?"

A vision of Nicola flashed into my mind, particularly the look on her face as she climaxed while I drove into her over and over. I could even see the trickle of sweat that developed on her brows and the way her mouth fell open in ecstasy.

Bradley snapped his fingers in front of my face, bringing me out of my sexually induced daydream.

"You got it bad, man."

I could only nod. There was no sense in denying what I already knew was happening.

I was falling in love with her.

If my jealous actions this morning over her employment were any indication, I'd say I was already there. It was both a blessing and a curse, because not only did *I* have a shitty amount of baggage, but Nicola had her own as well.

"Does she know about Link?" Bradley asked me.

"She does. She's met him. She slept with him before she ever did me."

"I see. Is this something you and she have discussed? Is she okay with it?"

"We've talked about it to an extent. She doesn't know the full truth."

He rose from his chair, and placing his hands on the desk, leaning in closer towards me.

"Nothing good has ever come from secrets, Andris. If you truly feel anything for this girl, and if your face is any indication, then I know you do, you need to be honest with her. She has her own demons that affect her. Hell, she is a patient, and one I'm glad that you handed over to me. The last thing you need is a malpractice charge or an ethics issue. You are a very talented doctor, Andris. Have faith in that, but be honest in every aspect of your life, not just your professional one."

I rose to shake his hand. I had the deepest respect for Bradley. Losing his wife to cervical cancer several years ago could have ruined him, but he still remained calm, collected and professional. Any man who could go on living after the love of their life had passed on was a hero in my book.

"Thank you for the talk, Bradley. I appreciate it. I trust you to take care of Nicola for me in the absence of my care. You are correct about my feelings for her."

I followed him across my office and just as he reached the door, he turned around and cupped my shoulder.

"I know your old man never treated you right. It simmers down to the way his old man, your grandpa, treated him. I'm not making excuses for him, Andris. Even though you might disagree, I know he is looking down on you and is proud of you. I know I am."

Then he walked out. It wasn't the first time that Bradley had said something similar to me before, but for some reason it sucker punched me in the gut a little more this time than to any other times prior.

He was proud of me.

For what? For *still* being under the thumb of the Cardinelli clan? For falling for a woman who didn't deserve to have to deal with all of my issues, and one I had to lie to on a daily basis?

My feet felt like lead as I walked back to my desk and picked up the file containing my next patient's information.

I didn't believe Cardinelli one second when he said that he didn't need me. These kinds of regulated drugs were hard to come by and were in limited supply on the black market. He needed me more than he thought he did, which made me wonder what he was really up to.

My phone vibrated on my desk and I picked it up to reveal the alarm that indicated my next appointment would be here soon. The stress of the day and the weight on my shoulders were starting to take their toll on me. As much as I wanted to lose myself in Nicola tonight to rid my mind and body of the relief, I just didn't know if it would be enough. They say old habits die hard, and they couldn't be more right. As much as it hurt my guts to think about her with anyone besides me, I knew that a session tonight is just what I needed.

Nicola wasn't the only one not ready to let Link go.

CHAPTER EIGHTEEN

JERICHO/NICOLA

HIS HANDS SKIMMED gracefully, yet possessively over my body. His mouth made my skin feel as if it were on fire. A soft sheen of sweat had developed, coating my body as he explored each of my erogenous zones. I was wound up beyond comprehension, and each second he delayed my gratification drove me further to the brink of insanity.

"Link thinks you are fucking gorgeous like this, Jericho."

Whispered words of encouragement rang through the headphones on my head. Andris guided all of my movements with his words as Link guided my body with his hands. I was strapped down, unable to move, and the only thing that supported me was the bench-like contraption that I was bent over. My ass was poised in the air, my thighs spread apart, and my hands bound at the wrists in front of me.

Once again I was left to the darkness behind the blindfold as one, two, three strikes landed on my ass. I could feel the heat begin to rise on my cheeks from the impact, the evidence of my arousal growing between my legs as a result. Andris's breath could be heard through the microphones as he watched me submit to the man behind me.

Breathing in, I sought comfort in the smell of leather and arousal. It turned me on even more to know that Andris was aroused as well. Even though he had told me he didn't like the idea of me being with Link, there was no hiding his own arousal at the sight of it.

My bi-weekly sessions with Link have almost become an addiction, just as my lovemaking with Andris has. With Andris, I loved that I got to experience something new. I got to actually feel the emotions that he had so easily stirred within me. With Link, I didn't have to think. I didn't have to analyze or make decisions. All I had to do was fall victim to the pleasure, the euphoria of the moment.

Link had yet to enter me, but I was so close to coming. All it would take would be one or two more touches and I would be cresting over the edge. With Link, it was like climbing a mountain. It was a steep grade of indulgence. My calves burned, my thighs burned, and the higher I climbed the more my legs would quiver. It wasn't a quick build-up, but more of a long and torturous crescendo that bordered on pain and pleasure. He drove me mad, more insane that I already was on a normal basis, but he had a way of making my thoughts nearly non-existent.

"Keep still, Jericho, or Link won't let you cum. Your submission turns him on. Your willingness to display your own control is fucking beautiful to him."

I tried to keep my body as still as I could, but the closer that Link's hands came toward my pussy and the clit that was now violently throbbing between the lips of my sex, the harder it was for me to control myself.

I bit down hard on the strap of leather that Link's hand

placed in my mouth, my teeth sinking into the skin of the hide. I wanted to cry out for him to touch me. I wanted to beg for him to slam his cock into my aching pussy, but I knew if I did, he would remove his hands from my body.

I wanted to ask Andris to join him. I wanted to feel the hands of both of my lovers on my body. I wanted the feelings that each one of them gave me to merge, creating a pleasure in me so cataclysmic, I could denigrate.

Fingers plunged into the wetness of my core, hitting the sensitive spot in my inner walls. My body jolted from the multitude of the sensation. I could feel Link's body as his thighs connected with mine, and his dick laid heavy and thick on the top of my ass. If I had the ability to push into him, I would have, but being bound in the position I was in, I couldn't move.

I was so close. Chasing for something that was always just outside my reach. The pressure was building and my body trembled violently from what was just below the surface. I felt like I was drowning in a sea of ecstasy, falling deeper and deeper into the dark end of a pool.

And all I wanted to do was surface.

"God, Nicola. You are so fucking sexy."

I paused in the midst of pleasure. My orgasm slipped further and further from my grasp as I realized what Andris just said. He called me *Nicola*, not *Jericho*. As long as I had been having these sessions with them, wherever the fuck it was that he always brought me, did he ever say my real name.

Without notice, Link slipped his cock inside of me, burying himself to the hilt. I was very wet, which made him glide in with ease. From this position, I felt full and all thoughts of Andris saying my name melted away. Link was unforgiving, pumping in and out of me with such fervor, that I had no doubt I would have bruises on my legs from the force. His hands gripped at my ass as he continued his assaulting rhythm. It wasn't long before my body began to soar once again and I felt myself gliding through the water of my pleasure to reach the surface. I could see the light glistening just overhead and my body swam faster. I was fearful for what would happen when I climaxed, never having felt this enormous amount of pleasure before. But I was also fearful of what would happen if I didn't. Would the pressure keep building to the point that I couldn't handle it anymore?

A sharp, yet welcome pain flashed through my clit as Link reached around and pinched it between two fingers. It was the spark that ignited the flame and I cried out in a muffled voice with the leather still in my mouth. My eyes, although still shielded from the blindfold, were wide open and for a moment I felt like the world actually stopped. My heart seized in my chest, my breathing paused, being held hostage in my lungs.

It was perfection in the highest form, the hit of heroin that relaxed me after a five-day drought. Link collapsed onto me, the slickness of our two bodies combined into one as I felt his chest rapidly rising up and down. It was almost like he was embracing me, yet hiding it in some way. Normally, whenever Link came inside of me, he withdrew himself almost as quickly, but this time he lingered. My heart swelled, thinking that maybe, just maybe, some of the feelings I had for him were being reciprocated.

And just like that it was over and I was left cold, missing the warmth of my lover's body. If Andris had witnessed the little interaction, I didn't know. All I heard was shuffling of clothing and then I was unbound from the bench before being lifted up and carried off. I left the headphones over my ears, not having had permission to remove them.

It was several minutes before I was placed on a soft bed, one that I had been placed on many times before. The sheets cooled my skin as I fumbled around in the darkness of my blindfold to position my naked body underneath the covers. I didn't realize how incredibly tired I was until my head hit the pillow. The headphones were removed from my head and the blindfold as well, yet I was still in the pitch blackness of the room, unable to see anything. A hand gently caressed my face. Calloused hands, familiar hands stroked my cheeks with tender care before I felt him rise from the bed and heard the footsteps cross the room, growing more distant with each step that he took away from me. When the door opened, a small soft light cast a shadow over my lover, silhouetting him through the darkness. I couldn't tell if it was Andris or Link.

I laid there for what seemed like hours, tossing and turning in the soft sheets. One minute I was cold, the next my body felt on fire. I was exhausted, but sleep wouldn't come for a long time, because tomorrow was a day I wanted to skip. Tomorrow was going to alter not only my own life, but the life of the man I loved. I wanted to talk to him desperately, but knew that there was no possible way that I could, not being permitted to leave the room.

THE NEXT MORNING, Andris took me to my condo on his way to work. There was something different about him on the ride downtown, but I left it to the fact that it was my first session with Link after Andris and I decided to be a couple. It did feel awkward fucking another man while I was in a relationship with someone, and suddenly I felt the enormity of how all the women at home must have felt when I was fucking their husbands. My sins never bothered me before. I never cared. Never even wanted to, but now they weighed heavily on my shoulders.

Damn emotions.

My talk with Lexie went as I thought it would yesterday when I told her that after my contract expired with Link, I wouldn't be returning to the agency. After pitching a fit, she reluctantly accepted my resignation and even offered me a job scheduling for the other girls in place of my last position. As great of an opportunity that it would have been for me to accept, I knew that I needed something legitimate if I was sincere about my relationship with Andris.

Like it would really matter, though.

There was a small café not too far from where my condo was. It had a great little deli section, an enormous menu of coffee and drink options, and a fun yet laid back atmosphere. The owner was an older Italian woman with more wrinkles on her face than cracks in a dried up riverbed. Her Her Her smile was contagious, but she was stubborn and hard headed.

I loved her immediately.

I had noticed her help wanted sign in the window and decided that it was probably something I could do. I mean, after all, I was previously employed in the *service* industry. Instead of serving my pussy on a platter, it would be a hot, steaming meatball sub and chips.

Letta had a thick accent. Her hair was always pulled back tightly into a bun at the nape of her neck, and she was never seen without an apron on that contained remnants of flour from her homemade bread. This woman could run circles around the teenage girls she had employed.

"You want work here? Why?" She asked in her heavy Italian accent as she sat a steaming cup of café latte in front of me before joining me at the table.

"Well," I began, "It's close to home, I need a job, and this place has some of the best damn bread in the city."

She tried to hide the hint of pride in her smile. I didn't lie though, she made some kick-ass bread.

"Ah, you know way to my heart," she replied as she patted her aging hand on top of mine. "You need eat more. Put meat on you bones. The men, they lika the curvy women. No skinny." She winked at me and we chatted for several more minutes before she retrieved some paperwork for me.

I got the job.

I filled out all the information, using my real name for the first time in ages. After that was all completed, she showed me around the back of the shop before grabbing me some employee shirts and told me to come back tomorrow for my first shift.

I sat in my condo for hours after meeting with Letta. Even though my body was still, my heart and mind raced at a million miles an hour. I had my appointment with the new doctor that Andris had arranged to take over in his place, and I was nervous about even going to the clinic at all. The text messages have been flooding my cell today to the point that I finally had to turn it off. Cardinelli's goons were waiting outside of the café when I had left. They didn't speak to me, didn't have to. I knew why they were there.

Intimidation.

Cardinelli wanted to make sure that I was still following through with his request and sent his little men to ensure that I wasn't trying to renege on the agreement.

My leg began to bounce unceremoniously in rapid rhythm as I gazed up at the clock. The second hand was the most torturous thing in the world as I watched it tick closer and closer towards what I was ordered to do. No matter how hard I tried, I couldn't get enough air in, suffocated by my impending iniquities.

I couldn't help but think about Link. How would all of this affect him when the shit hit the fan? If I didn't do this, Andris would suffer, but it also meant that Link would suffer when Andris finally lost his shit with me.

And then I would lose not just one of them, but both.

For the first time since Andris and Link ignited the flame that switched on my vacant emotions, I hated them. I'd give anything to be able to go back to that vacant, cold-hearted human being I used to be. I wanted my mind to feel blank, my heart to not feel every beat, and for my conscious to take a fucking hike.

Rising from the couch with dread in my stomach, I walked over to where I had my phone charging and switched it on. Within seconds, a thousand notifications flashed before my eyes. Most of them from Cardinelli, making sure I was going to go ahead with the plan today. But there was one that nearly broke me. One that nearly stole the very breath from my body.

Andris: **I can't wait to see you.**

CHAPTER NINETEEN

JERICHO/NICOLA

THE CLINIC WAS RELATIVELY quiet when I arrived. I really wished it wasn't. I wanted noise, distraction, anything that would take my fucking mind off the shit swimming around in it. The lobby smelled like him, as if his scent left a tiny breadcrumb trail to where he was. I felt how close he was as I approached Laura Lee at the reception desk. The hairs on my arms stood on their ends and the faintest of shivers ran down my spine. My body tingled as it remembered his expert hands on me. It came alive as it reminisced about how wonderful it felt, as his cock filled me so completely. My heart remembered just how much I cared for him.

All from his fucking scent.

"Hello, Miss Forbes. Dr. Chambers will be with you soon. Dr. Gunn, however, has requested that he see you prior to your appointment," she said, winking at me before placing a stack of folders into a pile. She buzzed the door that led to the offices and on unsteady legs I made my way toward Andris's office.

His door was cracked open and I saw him sitting at his desk, doing what looked like paperwork. One hand held up his head, while the other wrote furiously on a piece of paper. I took a moment to just look at him. Really look at him. I loved the way his dark hair fell over his eyes giving him a mysterious look. The strong structure of his jaw gave him a deeply masculine appearance. The broadness of his shoulders filled out his dress shirt, nearly exposing the deeply chiseled muscles he hid beneath the fabric. I smiled when I remembered how great they felt just as my hands explored his back, feeling not only his strength, but his deep need to be inside of me. Although he tried to go slow, to savor the moment between us, I felt the tension there and the lurking of his urgency beneath the surface.

As if sensing I was watching, he looked up to find me staring at him from the doorway. I did something I didn't think I had ever done before.

I blushed.

I was caught ogling my man and he smiled knowing it.

Smug bastard.

Throwing the pen on the desk, he rose from his chair and made his way towards me. My heart pounded furiously, in sync with each step he made in my direction. Not saying a word, he reached for my hand and pulled me inside his office and closed the door behind us.

Standing there in the middle of his office, he let go of my hands and placed them on my hips pulling me closer to him to where our bodies touched. Heat began to simmer just below the surface, but we didn't once take our eyes from each other.

"Hi," his voice was deep, heavy with all the pleasure I knew he could supply to me.

"Hi," I managed to reply. The heaviness of the way we left things this morning fell to the wayside as I saw the glimmer in his eyes, which no doubt matched my own.

"God, I've been wanting to do this all fucking day."

And then his mouth was on me, seeking, devouring, and quenching his own thirst for me while relieving me of my own for him. He tasted sweet, like candy mixed with hints of coffee. My skin bathed him in as he took control of the kiss, dipping his tongue deeper into my mouth. My arms uncontrollably reached up and wrapped around his neck, tugging on the hair at his nape with my fists, on instinct. There was something damn near primal about our connection, and I didn't know if it were something natural or the fact that my heart, mind, and body were all fully invested in him. When I was with him, I never wanted to close my eyes, fearful that if I did, if I blinked, he would disappear.

When he finally released my lips, I struggled to stand upright as my breathing labored to catch up in my lungs.

"I needed that," he stated, smiling at me and dropping one more kiss on my lips. He led me by the hand over to the couch in the corner of the room and gestured for me to sit down as he sat next to me. He laced our fingers together, and I absorbed the warmth of him.

"Care to tell me what happened this morning between leaving Link's place and you dropping me off at Lexie's?"

I could see the hesitation in his face. He didn't want to tell me, but it had been eating at me since then.

"I don't want to share you anymore."

I sighed. It was exactly what I had expected him to say. What do you do when your heart belongs to two people? What do you do when you are faced with the ultimatum of having your heart ripped in two? I knew Andris. I could see him, feel him, and even be with him out in the open. I existed in his world more than just a few moments of bliss in the privacy of the bedroom. But I also never felt more alive than I did when I was with Link.

"Andris…"

"Nicola, please, just…just listen for a second. I'll never be able to spit this out if you don't. What if I introduce you to him? What if you meet him and see that he is not what you need? Will you see then that you are exactly what I need?"

His hands trembled with nervousness as his brows furrowed together. This normally strong man looked pale in comparison to the one I was used to being with. There was a child-like hesitation about him, like a kid who had done something wrong, yet was trying to hide the truth.

"Just promise me something."

"I promise, Andris. You can tell me anything. It isn't going to change anything."

"Nicola, I'm falling…fuck…no, I *have* fallen in love with you. I just need you to promise that you aren't going to run in the other fucking direction once you meet him."

"Seriously? He couldn't be that horrible. Are you afraid that I'll run away from him based on his appearance? Or his attitude? I've seen and heard some pretty bad shit in my life, Andris. I don't scare easily," I chuckled, trying to lighten the mood. He looked up and his eyes were filled with torment. I wanted to grab him and pull him close to me. The vulnerability radiating off of him truly had me concerned.

"No. I'm scared you'll run away from me."

"Andris…"

I was interrupted by the sound of Andris's intercom buzzing and he excused himself to go and answer it.

Run away from him? Why would I run away from him? Wouldn't it be Link that I should be concerned with?

"Dr. Gunn, could you come out to reception? There is a concern about a patient and Dr. Lewis needs your assistance," Laura Lee's voice said, sounding a little shaken up.

"I'm on my way."

He came back over to the couch and reached for my hand, leading me towards the door with him. When we got there and before he opened it, he turned around and kissed me once again. Not long enough to satisfy me, but long enough to put his heart behind the action, telling me with his lips what his voice was hesitant to say.

"I'll be back soon. If I'm not back by the time of your appointment with Bradley, his office is the fourth one down on the left. You can wait here in case I am able to come back."

"Okay."

He left the office and I closed the door behind him, leaning my head against the heavy wood. I concentrated on my breath for a few moments, trying to get up the courage for what I was about to do.

With determination, I pushed away from the door and made my way to his desk. I didn't know exactly how much time I had left before he would return, so I needed to act quickly. I searched the top of the desk first in hopes that what I needed was in plain sight.

No such luck.

I began frantically pulling open the drawers of his desk, making sure to glance up every other second to be sure that no one was walking in. My hands trembled as a bead of sweat trickled down my spine.

Pens.
Notebooks.
Candy.

I started getting frustrated until the last drawer produced the pad of paper I was looking for. Several of them, in fact. Without any hesitation, I grabbed them and shoved them into the oversized purse I brought with me today before I had the chance to change my mind. I barely had enough time to place them there and practically sprint my way back to the couch in the corner before a knock sounded at the office door and in walked a middle-aged man.

"Andris?" He called as he stepped inside.

"Oh, my apologies, Miss. I was looking for Dr. Gunn."

My chest heaved from my mad dash to the couch. He looked at me strangely and a hint of panic began to engulf me. Did he know? Could he have any awareness that I was only seconds ago doing something completely immoral and illegal?

"He had to go to reception to help one of the other doctors with a patient. He should return any moment."

"Ah, I see. You wouldn't be Nicola by chance, would you?" He asked as he walked closer to me. I hugged my bag to my side, being sure that he couldn't peek through the top to see the contents inside. When I arched my brow at him slightly, his face softened and it instantly put me at ease.

"I'm Dr. Bradley Chambers. I will be taking over your care in place of Dr. Gunn."

"Oh, yes, of course," I replied as I stood up and extended my hand to him. He accepted my hand shake as a way of introduction. Except for the few brief moments when he first walked into the office, I felt a sense of ease around him. Comforted in a strange way. Normally, I never reacted to people upon introduction, just stood there stoically as they sized me up and down.

"If the patient in the lobby is who I think it is, you can rest assure that Dr. Gunn will be away for a while. We can go ahead and venture down to my office for your appointment if you wish."

"Um, yes. Okay. Let me grab my things."

I reached for my bag and my jacket, draping the coat over top of the opening to my bag, trying to hide my indiscretion as we left Andris's office and walked down the hall to Dr. Chambers' office. The atmosphere inside his office was different than Andris's. Where his was clean and masculine, Dr. Chambers' was warm and welcoming. There were pictures of his family on the walls as well as drawings from what looked like his child clients. *'I love you Dr. Chambers'* was written in messy crayon on the majority of them.

"Have a seat wherever feels comfortable, Miss Forbes."

"Thank you, Dr. Chambers."

"Call me Bradley."

"As long as you call me Nicola."

"Deal."

I took a seat in one of the plush chairs in front of his desk, needing the space of his desk between us. I could tell this man was morally strong and I felt the need to keep my sins from corrupting him. His smile made me feel relaxed, and the tone of his voice made me feel at ease.

"Please know, Nicola, that anything we discuss here in my office stays between you and me. That includes Dr. Gunn. He has informed me of your relationship and I have no intentions of discussing anything that you and I talk about, okay?"

"Okay."

"This is the point of the appointment where any normal psychiatrist would ask you 'how you feel' or 'what do you think about this or that', but I'm not going to. I've read your file. I know you have been coming here for quite some time, so I won't bore you with semantics. What I do want, though, is your honesty."

I nodded my head even though it was a lie. How could I be honest with him? How could I tell him that a fucking mob boss was blackmailing me into doing something I never wanted to do, in order to protect the two men I loved? My once steady and uneventful life had become a soap opera overnight. I had more money in the bank than I have had in years. I had deep feelings for not only one man, but two. I had one who fed my bodily cravings, and the other who fed my soul as well as my body. I felt connected to both of them, like there was some unknown force linking us together.

"Obviously you have had a breakthrough in the last several weeks. I'm to understand that your relationship with Dr. Gunn is your first. Sometimes patients with your condition can feel overwhelmed once their trigger hits, or enters their life. Is this the case with you? Am I to assume that Dr. Gunn has been your trigger?"

"Yes," I replied as my voice cracked from the acknowledgement. It wasn't that I was embarrassed or scared to admit it, it was just so new to me to admit it to someone else.

"Before Andris, it was like nothing meant anything to me. My only true distinguishable emotions were extreme happiness or sadness, and that was only due to recognizing the same reactions in people over and over. Subtler emotions never even crossed my radar. I had no empathy, I couldn't care less that I was hurting people."

"Yes, with your profession, no?"

Wow. EVERYTHING must be in my file.

"Yes. I've had very high profile clients. Some with wives, children. Men of God. It doesn't matter. When it comes to sex,

I think people have elective alexithymia. The want to shut off the feelings, only, I never had that luxury. I was cursed with the inability to feel."

"You weren't cursed. Your light was never switched on. In order to feel or experience emotions, sometimes those emotions must be exposed to you. From your file, I read that your parents were never around. You were left in the care of nannies and even sent to boarding school at an extremely early age. You must have felt abandoned, alone, angry."

"I felt nothing for those people. They left me with nothing. I lost the only home I knew. I had no friends. I was completely unsociable as a child. People thought I was weird. People thought I was crazy. I was turned on to pleasure when I was approached by a stranger in a dark alley. He paid me money to do things to him. I was hungry, so I did it. That is how I became an escort."

"I see. Although you may not have noticed it at the time, or even now, Nicola, but I think that by the way you were treated as a child, you shut off the emotions within so that you couldn't allow anyone else inside. The people who were supposed to love and nourish you gave you nothing. They were just as void of emotion as you yourself felt. That has a huge impact on a child."

"The doctors said it was from infancy. I never cried or fussed."

"So your parents claimed. Even as infants, we have instincts. You probably cried, yet it didn't help you, so eventually you stopped crying because you knew it led to nowhere."

Years of therapy. Years and years of vacant talks and half-hearted discussions with doctors about why I was the way I was and Dr. Chambers was the first person to ever insinuate that my parents could have been responsible for the vacancy inside me. Throughout my life, I always thought I was the fucked up one. I thought that I was genetically made to be void, yet all it took was this one meeting with Dr. Chambers to flip the parameters into the completely opposite direction.

"I take it this is something you are considering. Dr. Gunn was the first one to recognize you for you, Nicola, not you Jericho. He was the hand that flipped on the switch that turned your emotions on."

As I felt tears begin to sting the back of my eyes, something that felt completely normal, yet still entirely foreign to me, I tried to think back to the first time I met Andris. That is when I realized that Dr. Chambers was wrong.

"No. It wasn't Andris. I mean, he ultimately is responsible, but when I first met him, I didn't know his name was Andris, nor the fact that he was a psychiatrist.

"You met him as Sinclaire."

My head snapped up.

"What?" I asked, feeling slightly panicked that he knew about Andris's alternate life outside of the clinic. To my knowledge, no one knew of the arrangement except for Andris and Link, and Cardinelli after he had Andris followed. Now to hear that one of his employees and colleagues knew about it too concerned me. He must have noticed the fright behind my eyes.

"It's okay, Nicola. Dr. Gunn knows that I know. I'm assuming you have met Link?"

Fucking hell. How many times was he going to surprise me in one session? When I hesitated, he reassured me once again that is was okay and that he knew.

"Yes and no. I've been in the presence of Link and...and I've been contracted with him for a few weeks now to offer my *services*, but I have never seen his face. The only thing I have seen is the back of him in silhouette. Our sessions require for me to wear headphones and a blindfold."

"Yes, of course. That is the general arrangement that Link makes with his conquests. So was it Link that you felt helped ignite your emotions, or Andris?"

"I—I'm not sure. Technically, I met Andris first and felt something from the very second I found him at my door, but the first *real* feelings or emotions I felt were when I was with Link for the first time."

"I see," he replied as he wrote down notes in my file.

"You have feelings for both men. That must be difficult."

"It is. I feel awful for wanting Link to feel something for me other than sexual, especially since Andris has expressed that he doesn't want to share me with Link anymore. But I don't know if I could give up either one of them.

"Even if it meant you never got to see Link's face?" He asked, arching an eyebrow at me.

"I—yeah, I guess so. I just got the ability to feel all these things that were once completely foreign to me, I'm scared of *not* having them anymore."

"That's understandable Nicola. It is natural to attach yourself to something or someone who gives you what you were deprived of as a child."

"What's that?"

"Love."

Was I just attaching myself to Link and Andris because they were the first two people on earth to actually make me feel, or was I truly in love with them?

"Go easy on him, Nicola. When, and if, you do meet Link, go easy on Andris. You are the first woman I have ever seen him step out of his comfort zone with. You must be one very special lady."

Yeah. One that will destroy everything.

CHAPTER TWENTY

ANDRIS

I'VE PACED MY OFFICE for hours. Talked with Bradley for another hour, and even went to the bathroom thinking I was going to throw up a few times. It's a good fucking thing I kept extra clothes at my office because I had completely sweated through my other dress shirt. One would think I was an addict going through withdraws. In a way, I guess I was. I had relied on Link as my substance for so long, that no longer having him in my system—no longer having him by my side to shield me from my own self-consciousness—is hard to take.

All the patients were gone for the day. Laura Lee left the office a long time ago yet, here I still was, only delaying the inevitable. I had never once wanted to introduce anyone to Link. Never thought that I would ever have to.

But I fucking *love* her. Everything, from her perfections to her imperfections. I took pride in being the man to make her feel. It gave me something that I had lacked all of my life due to my shitty father.

It gave me confidence. It gave me the ability to think that, for once, I truly was good enough for someone else. Nicola made me look past my insecurities. She made me want to be a better man by just being in the same room. She made my dick swell in ways no other woman had. I have become completely insatiable in regards to her.

That is why I am so fucking terrified that after tonight, she will not want to be with me anymore. She will take one look at Link and run in the opposite direction. If she does, I don't know what I will do.

Then there is Cardinelli, breathing down my back. Taunting me over Nicola. Telling me that he will have her and that she would rather be with a man who could not only take care of her monetary wise, but sexually. He was like my father in many ways—knowing how to play on my own insecurities to the point that I was left doubting myself all over again.

Well, I'm not letting that happen. I love Nicola enough to tell her the truth. To show her not only the real Link, but the real Andris as well.

I walked into the bathroom in my office and turned the tap on cold, cupping my hands to catch the icy water before splashing it on my face. After drying off the water, I took one last look in the mirror and conjured up as much determination as I could.

It was now or never.

NICOLA/JERICHO

"THIS IS ALL YOU GOT?" Antonio Cardinelli asked me as I handed him the notepad I found in Andris's office drawer.

"There has got to be less than twenty sheets on this pad. He writes more prescriptions than that in two days.

"It was all I could get. Another one of the doctors walked in, so I didn't have time to find more.

And I didn't want to.

"Well, then you will just have to get more."

"No fucking way, Cardinelli. You agreed. I supply the prescription pads so you can get your drugs easier, and in exchange, you leave Andris, Link, and me alone."

Anger radiated off of me to the point I felt like I was vibrating like a nervous Chihuahua. Somehow, deep in the back of my mind, I knew it wouldn't be enough to satisfy Cardinelli, and certainly not enough for him to leave us alone for good. He was right, Andris wrote quite a few prescriptions daily. The thing I was most afraid of was that the medications that Cardinelli was seeking, were monitored drugs. Meaning once he started forging Andris's signature, I knew it would set off a red flag in the system.

"Well, then the only form of payment I will accept in return, is with you," he said, wagging his bushy, caterpillar eyebrows at me.

"You are out of your ever-loving fucking mind if you think I am going to sleep with you. You disgust me. You take advantage of people. Your wife hates you, so she seeks the pleasure of other men. How does that help you sleep at night?"

He gripped my chin painfully in his grasp, his fingernails digging into my skin.

"Listen, you fucking bitch. I don't take shit from anyone, especially some fucking whore. You forget that I could end you and your boyfriend. You will get me more tablets."

He shoved me away and I stumbled backwards, nearly falling on my ass. I watched Cardinelli get into his car with his two fucking idiots that followed him around everywhere as he left me standing in the cold. I wasn't in the best of neighborhoods and could feel the stares of all the people in the area. No doubt the majority of them were on his payroll, or worse, under his thumb when it came to the drugs they wanted.

I climbed into a cab and got out of there as quickly as I could. I hated the fact that I had to steal from Andris again.

But first, I had to get home and change. I always prided myself on having nerves of steel, but right now my stomach fluttered with what felt like a million butterflies alternating with cramping knots.

It wasn't every day that a woman met the second man in her life that she loved.

ANDRIS'S HAND FELT clammy in mine as we rode together in silence. Most of the snow had melted which allowed him to drive the black car. The one *Sinclaire* used to pick me up in. It was strange riding in the front of the car that carried me to the anonymous meeting place every time I was with Link. I couldn't help but wonder what was going through the minds of both of the men in my life as we approached this pivotal moment in our relationship. The way Andris spoke about Link and the way that Dr. Chambers told me to "go easy on Andris" had my shackles raised. Did Andris think I was going to hate him if Link wasn't what I had imagined him to be? Or is he worried that I could possibly fall deeper in love with Link as soon as I laid eyes on him?

My heart was beating loudly in my chest and I wondered if Andris could hear it. I tried to distract myself by taking in the surroundings as we passed through the late New York streets.

I noticed that Andris was taking me to a part of town that was traditionally wealthy or celebrity. Was Link some celebrity singer or music star? Was he someone else entirely?

It was strange that I had only spoken to him once, but had repeatedly allowed him to control and satisfy my body on a routinely basis. Yes, I was being paid for it, but the emotions that Link brought out in me would have let me do it for free.

Andris squeezed my hand before bringing it to his lips and pressing a gentle kiss to the back. I couldn't suppress the ache that came from deep inside me, knowing that this meeting with Link was somehow going to change the relationship between Andris and me irrevocably.

There was fear in his eyes, and worry between his brows. The youthful, sexy man that I had come to love looked like he had aged in the last few hours. The breath caught in my chest when I realized something.

Andris told me he loved me, and I never said it back.

"Are you sure you want to do this, Andris?"

He looked at me and then back to the road as he weaved through traffic, never letting go of my hand.

"Yes," he managed to say, his voice slightly croaking with unease.

"I..."

"What?" He asked as the back of his thumb slid back and forth on the back of my hand. It was almost as if he was giving me comfort and in return, comforting himself.

"I love you."

Andris pulled into a parking garage and soon into a space that held a sign with *A.S. Gunn* on it. At first, I found it strange that he would have his own personal parking space at Link's place, but then when I thought about the amount of time he spent there, it really wasn't so strange after all.

Cutting off the engine, Andris turned to look at me. Leaning in, he cupped the back of my head, threading his fingers through my hair as he brought our mouths together. My scalp prickled and my lips tingled as he slowly kissed me. It was different, slow, passionate, and filled with heaps of promise.

"You have no idea how fucking happy it make me to hear you say that. God, Nicola. I've never felt about anyone the way I feel about you. My heart races every time I touch you. I've grown stronger because of you. And if it were any other person, the possibility of what is going to happen tonight would never happen. I want you to know, that no matter what happens after tonight, I want you to know that I love you. I love you more than anything or anybody I have ever had in my life."

"You act as if I'm going to run away from you," I admitted with a smile, trying to liven up his mood.

"There's a damn good possibility that you will."

"I doubt it. Why don't you let me prove you wrong?"

He took a deep breath, as if preparing himself for what was to come before turning to me.

"Just remember, okay?"

"Okay."

Andris got out from the car and walked around to my side to help me. I took in the cleanliness of the garage as we walked towards the elevators. In New York, finding anything in a public space clean was a rarity. It felt strange to come to this place without the blindfold. Even though all the smells were familiar, it felt as if I were truly visiting the building for the first time.

Andris's nervousness was more apparent than ever as he leaned back against the mirrored walls of the elevator and closed his eyes. As the door closed, I looked up at the floor numbers.

Forty-Eight.

"What floor are we going to?"

He opened his eyes and looked straight ahead, but never at me. I wanted to do something to help him ease into what was going to happen tonight. I wanted him to know that no matter what happened, my feelings for him wouldn't change. I had already confessed my feelings to him in the car, and I didn't have anything that I knew would help him relax.

Except for one thing.

"All the way to the top."

"Good."

I stood in front of him and pulled the tails of his crisply pressed dress shirt free from his pants before placing my hands on the buckle of his belt and proceeding to undo it.

"Nicola—"

"Shhh." I said as I placed my fingers on his lips to keep him from protesting. I dropped my purse to the elevator floor, allowing it to land with a thud before I dropped to my knees in front of him. Knowing I didn't have much time, I quickly unzipped his pants and pulled them down along with his boxers only enough to expose his enlarged cock to me. Cupping his balls, I placed my mouth over the head and sucked on it slowly, only once. From there I began a steady rhythm as I hollowed out my cheeks and opened my throat up to take him in deeper.

"Fucking hell, Nicola," he managed to say between panting breaths. I enjoyed the salty taste of him and the velvety smoothness of his skin. He grew even more in my mouth and my jaw ached from the intensity of my actions, but I didn't care. This wasn't for me, it was for him. This was to show him that I'd do anything for him, even take his mind off his demons, if only for a brief moment.

His hands fisted in my hair as he held onto my head and I continued my swift strokes of my mouth. Saliva dropped out of the corner of my mouth and my eyes watered as I gagged a few times. I was turned on by the red lipstick that now coated his dick from my mouth. I continued to play with his balls, feeling them start to tighten as his orgasm quickly approached.

"Oh fuck—" he repeated over and over, I glanced up briefly.

Only ten more floors to go. Thank God that the elevator car hadn't stopped to let anyone on because they would have gotten one hell of a show.

I tasted it the second it hit the back of my throat and I worked furiously to swallow the warm salty liquid, lapping up every drop before finally releasing him from my mouth and pulling his pants back up just in time for the car to arrive at the forty-eighth floor.

I didn't get off easy as Andris attacked my mouth, pulling me closer to him and squeezing me tightly against his chest. His tongue dipped inside my mouth and I knew he could taste himself on my lips.

It was fucking sexy as hell.

The doors opened and an elderly woman stared at us in disgust as she paused before stepping into the car. Andris and I quickly broke apart and I retrieved my purse off the elevator floor before exiting the car. The old lady mumbled something along the lines of "kids these days will do anything in public" just as the elevator doors closed and she was gone.

"That was fucking priceless. Old lady Foster is probably one of the most uptight people I know. Her husband died several years back, and now she takes her solace in the ten cats she keeps in her penthouse.

"Penthouse?" I asked, arching my brows.

"Yes. There are two up here. One belongs to old lady Foster, and the other belongs to m…Link and me."

"Oh. I never knew there were two up here. Of course I never knew you brought me to a Penthouse either."

"No one knew, Nicola. You are the first person to set foot in the building with me without a blindfold on."

I guess if he was aiming to make me feel special, then I guess I was. As heart wrenching as it felt to know that I wasn't the first woman to enter here, I was certainly hoping I would be the last.

The entryway to the penthouse was beautiful. Gold plated furnishings and plush carpet laid out on dark hardwood floors. As we approached the front door, the familiar smells that I had become used to, began to assault my senses, taking me back to all the times I was with both Andris and Link. It was a smell that I would never grow tired of. Rich, deep leather mixed with sandalwood and oak—an aphrodisiac that would always be a turn on for me.

I took in every sound differently. The way he inserted the key into the lock, and the way it clicked as he turned. The creak of the door as he opened it. Only this time, I got to see all of it.

Closing the door behind us, Andris flipped a switch on the wall that illuminated the room we were in. What I saw was nothing like I had imagined it, yet it was. The leather smell was more potent now, and I knew why. Various bondage apparatuses and other things were spread out in the open-plan room. Every cuff or buckle was made of the leather that smelled so wonderful to me. A huge four-poster bed with a canopy was in the center of the room and a giant stereo system was positioned not too far away.

"This is it," Andris said with a wave of his hand, so nonchalantly that it was like he were bringing me home to his personal apartment for the first time, only this place would put any BDSM club or association to shame. There were St. Andrew's crosses on the walls as well as different varieties of benches and swings. I wasn't embarrassed by the scene in the room. Many of the devices seen before me were used by other clients. Most of those clients, though, preferred to be *in* the device with me taking charge.

I wandered over to a specific bench and ran my hands across the cool leather padding.

"This was the bench I was on the other night, wasn't it?"

"Yes."

One word. His voice taking on a new octave—one lower than I had heard from his mouth before. It was vaguely familiar, but I shook it off and told myself that it was probably due to his nervousness.

"This—this is where I would come to escape. Everyone thinks that being a doctor is so easy. I get to hear about other people's problems and issues on a daily basis. Some of the shit I've heard would make you vomit. Some of the experiences that my patients have had are things no one should have to experience. Most days, it is hard to shut that shit off at the end of the day. Know what I mean?"

"I can imagine. But you help those people, Andris. You have to remember that. You are good at what you do. Look at me. Look how far I have come."

"Nicola, eventually someone or something would have brought you out of your shell. Something would have happened to trigger your emotions. There is no way to guarantee that it was me."

I walked over to him, wrapping my arms around his waist and leaning my head into his chest as his arms folded around me. I could hear the heavy beat of his heart and his labored breath slow down as we embraced each other.

"I came alive when I met you and Link. I know you don't like the idea of sharing me. It is something I have thought about as well. I won't lie when I say that I have feelings for Link. I love him, but I also love you. Both of you are different. Both of you turn me on in many different ways, not just sexually. Thank you for allowing me to meet him. Thank you for sharing that part of you with me."

I leaned up and on my toes and pressed a slow, sensual kiss upon his lips.

"I guess now is as good as ever."

"What? He's here already?" I asked in disbelief.

"Yes. He's always here. He doesn't leave often," he said, pressing a kiss to my forehead.

"Wait here and I'll go get him."

Nervous anticipation filled my stomach as I watched Andris walk out of the room. I was bathed in silence, the only thing present was the sound of my breaths. I felt a sudden pang of unease filter through me as I paced the floors waiting for Andris to return. There were so many times when all three of us have been together, but this felt completely different. Link was practically a stranger to me, yet one I had feelings for.

It seemed like hours that I was left alone in the room, waiting for Andris to return. Left alone to reminisce as I looked around the room taking in everything. I walked over to the bed and ran my hands across the satin sheets, feeling the coolness of the fabric between my fingers. I was lost in my own world for several minutes, that I didn't even hear Andris return.

"Hello, Nicola."

My back was to the door, so I didn't see the person who had called my name. The voice was so different yet so familiar at the same time.

When I turned around, my heart seized in my chest. The air rushed out of my lungs and for several moments, I swear I forgot to breathe.

Whatever I had imagined Link to look like when I met him, the man standing before me was not him.

CHAPTER
TWENTY ONE
Jericho/Nicola

"I THOUGHT YOU WERE going to get Link?" I asked with a small tremor in my voice.

He only nodded as he slowly approached me. There was something different in his gaze, a slight swagger in his steps, as if he had all the confidence in the world.

I stood up from where I was seated on the bed and walked on unsteady legs toward him, nearly tripping over my feet in the process. He was there instantly, catching me with his strong hands. Hands that I have felt on my body many, many times over, yet these hands were a strangers.

As he helped me steady myself, a strong, but gentle hand was placed on my jaw, tilting it to where I was staring directly at him. It was then that I knew I was no longer talking to the man I loved who had walked out of the room only moments before. Now, I was talking to the man I loved, who I had never met before.

"Link?" I questioned with a whisper. His only answer was a nod as he stroked my cheek back and forth with the pad of his thumb. I felt my knees tremble as if I could fall to the floor any moment if it weren't for him holding on to me.

All this time. The entire fucking time I thought I was with Link, it had been Andris all along. It had been Andris who took control of my body, invaded my thoughts and set off the nuclear reaction that had severed my old life from my new one. It was he who ignited my vacant soul and who had manipulated my body in so many ways as I submitted to him. It was also him who paid me.

It was him the whole time.

Anger grew within me, and for some odd reason, I felt betrayed. Lied to. Deceived. Stupid, and just about every other fucking negative adjective I could think of.

"I know you are angry. I see it in the sparkle of your eyes."

His own softened, and it was like he was flashing back and forth between two different personalities.

Oh, my, God, I thought as I brought my hands up to cover my gasp. And that's when it happened. I started laughing. Hysterical, uncontrollable laughter to the point that my stomach hurt. Tears were forced from my eyes and streamed down my cheeks, but no matter what happened, I couldn't stop. Then, those laughs turned to sobs and before I knew it, my eyes were burning and my chest heaved as anger once again returned.

Andris didn't say much as I backed away from him. Or was it Link I had just lost my shit in front of?

"The entire fucking time it was you?" I asked calmly. Almost so calm, that you could never tell that I was damn near in the full stages of a panic attack only seconds before. I felt the familiar mask I had worn for so long voluntarily slip back into place. I felt my emotions once again fade away, just out of my reach.

"Yes. Nicola, Link has helped me in ways I cannot describe to anyone. Like your parents ignored you, my father did also, except when he was telling me what a worthless piece of shit I was or how I didn't deserve the air I breathed. Link was the one who helped me feel like I was worthy, even if I had to pretend to be him for a while."

"So, everything is just pretend with you, is that it, Andris? You can only fuck girls who don't have the liberty of seeing you? You get to pretend to be someone else and hide behind the image of another persona? Were you pretending the whole time with me?"

"In the beginning, yes. But you changed something within me, Nicola. You gave me the strength and the confidence to step out from behind Link. You are the first and only woman that I have made love to as Andris."

He stepped closer to me, as if needing the connection between us, but I stepped away from him. I didn't want him to touch me. I wanted to be angry with him. I wanted him to feel how stupid and worthless I felt.

"So, should I get a special prize for that? You have had plenty of opportunities to tell me the truth. So is that why you always had me use the headphones?"

He nodded.

"I made the girls wear them. I picked them up at whatever destination that Lexie told me to and blindfolded them, just as I did you. The headphones were so that they couldn't hear my voice and put two and two together. I needed the anonymity of Link to be able to even have sex. My father drilled some seriously sick shit in my head, Nicola. Shit that no one should ever have to go through."

"Huh, imagine that. A psychiatrist who has mental issues.

That isn't one that I have heard before."

"It's the truth, Nicola."

I walked up to him and jammed my finger into his chest. I felt my emotions slowly beginning to shut off. I wanted to still be angry. I wanted to hate him for what he had done to me and I needed to show him that before I lost every shred of progress I had made over these last few weeks.

"You lied to me. You played me, Andris. And I'm supposed to be okay with that? I'm supposed to say 'Come here baby. Let me hold you' after the shit you just laid on me? For *weeks*, you have let me think that I was falling in love with two men. You let me believe that it was because of both of you that I could finally function as a human being. Was I some sort of experiment, *Doctor*? Was I some kind of research you thought you could do to report?"

I was damn near spitting in his face and he never flinched. Never moved a muscle, instead, he just stood there and accepted my wrath.

"I *never* knew you were a patient, Nicola. Fuck, I was supposed to meet Kiki that first night. She was supposed to be the one I fucked and let go until the next time that I needed a fix. I work in a field where people medicate to get rid of their problems. Well, this is my medication. This is the sanctuary I come to when I feel pressure or tension. This is how I unwind and get my dickhead of a father out of my head," he said as he gestured with his arms around the room.

"The arrangements with the escorts were my way of feeling normal. They were my way of feeling like I was worthy enough to be with a woman, even if I had to pretend to be someone else to do it."

"That still doesn't explain why you continued to lie to *me*!

God, I don't know what to feel right now," I said as I laid my face in my hands.

"Tell me what you feel."

"Don't. Don't you dare try to analyze me, Andris. You knew this was wrong. You knew that there was a possibility that I could get hurt from all of this. *You* of all people should have known how this would affect me. Fucking hell! I just learned how to process all of these feelings and emotions that I never had before and now they are all swarming me at once. You should have been honest. You should have told me the truth when we started our relationship! I feel so stupid!"

My voice began to rise the angrier I became.

"You don't think I wanted to? You don't think I wanted to step out from behind the wall of Link I put up between us and be the man I thought you wanted and needed? You think it was easy for me to hear that you had feelings for Link, when I was him the whole time? It tore at me every fucking day, Nicola, but I knew if I told you…"

"You knew what?" I asked impatiently. Sweat had formed a soft sheen upon my skin, and even though internally I felt the heat rise, on the outside I was cold.

"That this would happen," he said, gesturing between us with his hands. Lifting them up, he ran both of them through his hair. The motion pulled the hair that normally fell just over the top of his brows away from his face and it was then that I could see the anguish in his features. Momentarily, I softened towards him. I knew deep in my gut that it had to take him an abhorrent amount of time to get the courage to confess this to me, but dammit if I wasn't hurt.

It's strange really, how the body reacts to certain things. Some emotions can bring on the same types of physical reactions within the body. It was insane how physical pleasure could heat me from the inside out. How it could make me think irrationally, or to do or say things that I didn't mean in the heat of the moment. But at the same time, anger could do the same thing. Or like how when you are really happy, you were brought to tears, but you also cry when you were sad or depressed.

"What do you expect from me, Andris? You knew that the inevitable outcome would be something along these lines, yet you still continued to lie to me. You made me believe I was in love with someone who doesn't exist."

"I'm sorry, Nicola. I wish I could make you understand."

"Understand? That is all people have tried to get me to do my entire life. Nicola, do you understand anger? Nicola, do you understand pain? Pleasure? Sadness? I'm so sick of people trying to constantly push things on me. But when I was with you and Link, I didn't feel pushed. It felt natural—effortless. It was like my mind and my body just knew what to do. Are there some things I still don't quite understand? Yes. But you and Link made it better."

He let out a long sigh once again, running his hands through his hair before placing them in his pockets. I wondered if he did it to try and control himself. Did he want to stop himself from reaching out to me? As much as his touch would anger me even more, at the same time I craved it. I needed comfort. I needed to know that we were going to get past this. I needed to know that I could survive the torture my heart was feeling at the moment. I hated the unnatural way my heart banged within my ribcage or the staggered breaths that were being forced from my body. For the first time since my emotions were switched on, I no longer wanted to feel anything so that this awful feeling would go away.

"All I can say is I'm sorry, Niçola. I love you. That's why I told you the truth. That is why I brought you here and confessed everything. I wanted to put all of this behind us so that we could move on together. Have a normal life. I want us to not have any secrets between us or any hidden agendas. I want nothing but love, honesty and trust with you. If that means I have to face my demons head on in the process, then so be it. You are worth it to me. I've never imagined that would ever happen with anyone."

Secrets. I had a big one. Andris had no idea that I had stolen the prescription pads from his desk. Even though he was honest with me, I couldn't tell him what I had done because he would try to go after Cardinelli. As much as I hated him at the moment, that didn't mean I didn't care about him. I didn't want to see him going to jail for helping Cardinelli with drug trafficking. There was only one thing that I could do. I needed him to hate me. I needed his love to go away, then maybe, just maybe, mine would too. My emotions were turned on when I met him and Link, how hard could it be to turn them off if I put distance between us.

Sucking in a deep breath, I walked towards him and stood toe to toe. Not quite close enough to touch, but enough that we could feel the warmth from each other's bodies. What I was about to do would no doubt destroy him, but I needed to get the point across that I didn't want this anymore. I thought I could handle the stipulations that went with having a normal relationship. I thought I could easily process all the new emotional shit that I would be experiencing, but I was sorely wrong.

Looking directly into his eyes, I said, "If you were a man, you would never have had to hide behind the image of a make believe person. Did you not have the balls to give it to a woman without the help of your imaginary friend? Sucks to be you."

Then I stepped around him and walked out of the room, straight down the hallway and into the elevator without looking back. As the elevator descended, I felt the tiny breaths of air that blew against the flame of my emotions, so that by the time I had reached the bottom floor, the flame was out. All the new emotions and feelings that had begun to smolder within me were now gone and I was once again left feeling void.

CHAPTER TWENTY TWO

JERICHO/NICOLA

GETTING USED TO WORKING at the cafe was a whole new beast. No stranger to being in the *service* industry, this was customer service not on any level that I had ever been on before. People were rude, the tips were horrible, yet I chose to come back here instead of going back to work at the agency. Did I think about it? Yes. Yet, I felt almost compelled to work at the café, like it was meant to be. Plus I really took a liking to Letta.

She was hardcore, gave as good as she got. Her laugh was contagious and I was hit with the threat of getting "fattened up" nearly every day from her. If I continued to eat all the delicious bread that I fed myself with, instead of having to allow my body to feel, I would be there in no time.

If I thought trying to understand emotions was hard, trying to turn them back off was even harder. How people lived through heartache every day was beyond me. It felt as if a piece of me was lost. I wanted to feel numb. I begged my mind to once again become the vacant parking lot of emotions like it had been nearly my entire life, but when it came to Andris, I found it nearly impossible.

"Table four is ready, Nicola," the short order cook, Henry, yelled from the kitchen. I lifted my hand in acknowledgement as I jotted down another table's order. Our lunch rush was just getting underway with the café getting louder and more crowded every minute. I heard the bell above the door ring as I walked to the counter to pick up table four's food. When I turned around, I saw a dark haired girl take a seat at one of the only empty tables left in the far back corner of the café. There was a familiarity about her that I couldn't quite catch on to, yet this was New York City. Nearly everyone had two or four doppelgangers running around.

I delivered table four's order. Two business men who barely acknowledged my presence before placing the other table's order with Henry. Then, I grabbed the pad of paper from my apron and made my way back to the back table where the dark haired girl sat.

"Hi. What can I get for you today?" I asked as I poised the pen above the pad of paper, waiting for her answer.

That is when she looked up at me and recognition set in. Her normally bright eyes were dull and the luster in her skin was gone along with the glimmer of her dark hair. She looked thin. Very fragile. Her sunken, hollowed-out cheeks and the dark circles under her eyes told me she wasn't well. She had red chipped nail polish on nails that were clearly bitten down to the quick of her skin. Her lips were pale and cracked, in need of serious moisture.

"Kiki?" I asked not believing it was her.

"Well, when Lexie told me you quit the agency, I thought she was just jerking my chain," she said with a hint of disdain in her voice. "Guess not, huh?" She asked, looking me up and down, taking in my uniform.

"Yeah, well, I thought I would try a service of a different kind," I said light heartedly, trying to get a smile out of her.

Nothing. If I would have said that the Pope died, I probably wouldn't have even got as good as a reaction as I was getting right now.

"Trying to go legit or some shit, Jericho? I never took you for someone who played by the rules."

"I guess sometimes people change."

"Yeah, I guess they do. Bring me a triple expresso. I've been up all fucking night. I need a caffeine jolt," she said, reaching into her purse and producing her electronic cigarette and taking a large draw from the contraption.

"Expresso. Got it."

I walked away to place her order with the barista behind the counter and checked on a few of my other customers before returning to Kiki's table. I took a seat in the other chair and placed my elbows on the table, just looking at her.

"What?" She asked, not looking up at me and irritation in her voice.

"Don't take this the wrong way, Kiki, but you look like shit."

She looked up at me then, and I saw the redness in the white of her eyes.

"Well, I feel like shit. Thanks for pointing that out."

"Is everything okay?" I asked, continuing to prod her.

"I'm just fine and dandy. No offense, Nicola, but when the fuck did you start caring about someone other than yourself? How's *my* client working out for you? I bet you are living the high life now with the bank you made from that man."

It stung for her to bring up Andris, but I wasn't going to let it get to me. She was clearly in more need than my desperate desire to shut off any and everything when it came to him.

"That's over and done with. Obviously, I'm not living the high life, Kiki. I'm working in a fucking café for Christ's sake."

She tried to laugh and erupted into a dreadful coughing fit. I noticed a slight tremble in her hands as she tried to bring her hair more over her face as if she were trying to hide her face from the world.

"When was the last time you ate? Can I put an order in for you?"

"I don't need your fucking charity. Can you just bring me my fucking coffee and leave me the hell alone?"

I could tell she was getting irritated with me, and the café was starting to get busier so I stood up and pushed my chair in.

"If you need anything else, just let me know. I'll be right back with your expresso."

I busied myself taking new orders and delivering others. I helped one of the bus boys clear tables, all the while keeping one eye on Kiki. I watched as she stared vacantly out the window as people walked on the streets. Every once in a while I caught her gaze, but then she would just return back to looking out the window. After about thirty minutes, she stood up, threw some money down on the table and walked out, never saying another word to me.

ANDRIS

I COULDN'T FUCKING THINK straight. They only thing I could hear was the incessant voice of my father saying to me over and over how much of a failure I was. I couldn't even hang on to my first and only real girlfriend for longer than a few weeks.

I was on robot mode when it came to my patients. I nodded my head and answered them when necessary. If they could tell a change in my mood, they didn't let on. For the first time in my career—my life—my heart wasn't in it.

Why?

Because the day Nicola walked out of the apartment, she took it with her.

"I still can't seem to focus on my studies. My thoughts bounce around in my head like a kangaroo on crack, doctor. Will it ever stop?"

"It's hard to tell, Jacob. ADD is something some people find themselves being able to overcome, others aren't so lucky. I guess it is all about finding methods that work for you. If you're easily distracted by things like the TV or people, go somewhere quiet. If music is distracting, leave the iPod off. Maybe what you need is somewhere neutral where there aren't any outside influences to grab your attention while you study. How do you do when you are in class?"

"Sometimes I can do okay, if the subject is interesting to me. But when the professor starts going on about the cardiovascular system and valves and ventricles, my mind starts shifting to her appearance or I study the other students instead of the material."

"Well, take my advice, but until then, I can give you something that might help you be able to concentrate more. It is a time released capsule, so it should last about eight hours. I suggest you take it in the morning before you go to class, and not after three pm in the afternoon. Otherwise you will have a hard time going to sleep at night."

"Thank you, Dr. Gunn."

I reached into my drawer to retrieve one of my prescription pads to write out the young college student his prescription. When my hands came up empty, I thought it odd, but shrugged it off. I write so many prescriptions per week, I could have easily ran out and not even known it. I stood up from my chair after telling Jacob I would return in a moment and left the office to go to our locked closet where we kept the sample products from drug companies as well as our supply of prescription pads. After retrieving two, I returned back to my office where I wrote out the prescription and bid Jacob good luck on his studies.

Lunch time found me sitting at my desk, staring out the window at New York. I often found myself doing that during the day, wondering where in the city Nicola was.

It had been nearly three days since I saw her. Kissed her lips. Told her I loved her and held her. My body missed her like it missed oxygen when I held my breath. My heart ached in my chest when I thought about how we could have possibly had a full and happy life.

I guess now, I'll never know.

NICOLA/JERICHO

IT WAS THURSDAY at the café and I was really starting to get the hang of things. Letta had taken a real liking to me and even began to show me how she made some of her famous bread. I enjoyed spending time with her in the kitchen, kneading dough and enjoying our conversations. Strangely, I felt like I could confide in her. If I had had a grandmother, I would hope that she would have been just like Letta.

"You have had your heart broken, no?" She asked as we both worked the roll of dough between our hands. The last few mornings found me waking up early to go in before opening to help her prepare everything for the day. I enjoyed it, and keeping my hands busy helped me keep my mind off Andris.

"How do you know that, Letta?" I asked as I began to work the dough even harder.

"Because I see it in you eyes every time the café bell ring and he don't come. And in the way you working that dough hard at the mention of it."

I paused. Apparently I wasn't that great at hiding my thoughts or feelings.

"I don't know what happen. You don't have to tell Letta, but I know you still in love. There was brightness in you eyes the day you first came see me. It no longer shine as bright."

I leaned my flour covered hands against the table and hung my head. So much for trying to keep Andris off my mind, but I felt the need to talk to someone about everything that was festering inside of me.

"He hurt me really badly, Letta. He turned out to be something, or rather someone he was pretending to be. I fell in love with him. I fell in love with both of them. Now, I don't have either of them. It hurts. I've never known this feeling before."

"Did he give you reason?"

"You mean reason for why he lied?"

She nodded.

"He did."

"Was it good reason?"

I thought about it for a moment. Andris was a psychiatrist. His job was to help others who had demons or diseases, or other mental disabilities and disorders. Not once would anyone think that someone like him would be dealing with some of the same issues that his patients did. I guess even doctors themselves get sick sometimes.

"Yes. It was a good reason. He had some issues that prevented him from revealing the truth to me, but he still continued to lie to me for weeks."

"Maybe he scared."

I arched my brows at her.

"Of what?"

"Of losing you. Being where you is now. Apart, instead of together like should be."

"It's hard to explain, Letta. There are things about my, not so distance past, that you don't know. I am not a good person. I took advantage of people. I destroyed families, and I didn't care. I was a cold hearted bitch and didn't care that I was."

"Maybe that who you pretended to be. Maybe you have been pretending long time."

"I had no choice."

"Sometimes we faced with hard choices. But it is what we do with choices that determines our outcome in life. If you love him, and he love you. Don't let that pass yous by. One day you wake up old woman kneading dough in a café every day at four in morning wishing you could go back in time."

"You talk like you are speaking from experience, Letta."

"Maybe I is."

I heard my cell phone go off in my purse and walked over to the sink to wash the flour off my hands. I scrubbed at my nails to remove the remnants of the dough before going to retrieve my phone from my purse. Who the hell would be texting me at nearly four thirty in the morning?

When I pushed the button to light up the screen, I saw that I had a text message from Lexie.

Lexie: **Call me now!**

A few seconds went by as I stared at the urgent message on my screen. It wasn't out of the ordinary for Lexie to text me at this hour, nor was it strange to get one with urgency like this one, but for some reason I had a bad feeling.

"Letta, I'll be right back. I need to make a phone call."

"Okay. I put your bread in oven. Go ahead, child."

I swiped at the screen to remove the text and brought up Lexie's name and hit dial. She answered on the second ring and when I heard her voice, I knew something is wrong.

"Nic, where are you?" She asked through sniffles.

"I'm at the café. What's wrong? Is everything is okay?"

"Kiki is dead."

I nearly dropped my phone. That couldn't be possible. I saw her just a few days ago.

"What? What happened? It wasn't a client, was it?"

"No. I pulled her off the books when she started to show signs. I couldn't let her continue to work until she got help. Clients were complaining and she was starting to look really bad. I just wanted her to get help."

"What are you talking about?"

"Well, when she hurt her foot, the doctor prescribed her painkillers. Apparently, she had become addicted to them. She hid it for a while, but then when I confronted her about it, she told me to stay out of her personal life."

"I'm still not quite understanding, Lexie."

"She overdosed, Nicola. On prescription painkillers. When

the doctor wouldn't prescribe her anymore, she went to the streets to find them. She was just taking them normally for the pain, but then she started getting high from them. I caught her doing a line off the back of the toilet at the flower shop. Fuck! I should have done something!"

"I saw her a few days ago. She came into the café. She looked really bad. I knew something was wrong. If I had known, maybe I could have reached out to her. Wait a minute…did you say she went to the streets to get the drugs?"

"Yeah," I heard her sniffle through the phone.

I literally felt sick to my stomach and had to help hold myself up against the wall. Dread filled me. It was only a coincidence. Wasn't it? Surely Kiki wasn't one of Cardinelli's customers? She just couldn't be. That meant that I could be responsible for her death.

"Does her family know?"

"She had no family. She was on her own. She was a troubled girl from the beginning, but never in my life did I ever think she would overdose on drugs. I've never lost a girl, Nicola."

"Lexie, you can't blame yourself. Do I need to come over?"

"Ah. No. Don't leave work. I am going to call the other girls and let them know. I just wanted to let you know."

We hung up after muttering a few small goodbyes and I stood there against the wall of the café trying to sort through my thoughts. Cardinelli was one of the largest drug traffickers in the city. Hell, probably in the whole state. With a death, that meant that there would be an investigation. With an investigation, that mean that Andris could be involved. I finished the bread that Letta and I had been working on until I knew that the clinic would be open. I needed to get to Andris.

I needed to warn him.

CHAPTER TWENTY THREE

ANDRIS

I WENT INTO THE CLINIC early on Thursday morning to try and get caught up on all the paperwork that I had neglected over the last few days. As busy as it would keep me, my only desire was to go home at the end of the day and lose myself in a bottle of Jack. It was the only thing that helped me to let go of the memories that haunted me on nearly a twenty-four hour basis. I needed to get Nicola back. I needed to find a way to make her understand why I did what I did. Not having her in my life wasn't an option—not one I was willing to accept, anyway.

I had been seated at my desk for a little over an hour when I heard the automatic bell go off on the clinic front door. I looked over at the clock and noticed it was only eight in the morning and knew that Laura Lee and the other doctors wouldn't be arriving for at least another hour. I rose from my chair and headed out towards reception to let whoever had come in know that we didn't open until nine.

I froze when I saw Nicola standing in reception. She had

on a uniform covered in flour. Her cheeks bore some of the same flour on her shirt. Her hair was pulled up into a ponytail and her face was void of makeup. She had never looked more beautiful.

"Hi," I said as I took a few tentative steps in her direction.

"Hi," she said a little meekly, not really meeting my eyes. God it felt good to see her.

"You have flour all over you, you know?" I pointed out. She looked down at her shirt and patted it a few times and the dust from the flour floated into the air.

"Yeah. Some of Letta's bread making lessons kinda stuck with me, I guess."

There was a hint of amusement in her voice and we both smiled, yet it didn't quite reach our eyes.

"What are you doing here? I mean, not that it isn't okay, I just...fuck. I'm rambling."

She smiled briefly again and it hit me square in the chest. It hurt like a mother fucker to be in the same room with her, yet not be able to touch her or hold her.

"I can't stay. I just came by to warn you about something."

"Warn me?" I asked, looking at her strangely.

"Someone I know died today. She overdosed on prescription drugs."

"I'm really sorry," I offered in sympathy, but still kept my distance even though I wanted nothing more than to fold her in my arms.

"I have a feeling that she got them from Cardinelli and that it is going to get traced back to you."

My gut couldn't have twisted any harder if she had physically punched me.

"How do you know about Cardinelli and me?"

"I—I can't say. Just know and be prepared, Andris. I have a feeling the police will be stopping by."

She stepped closer to where we were only a few feet apart. I could smell the familiar scent of honeysuckle filter through the air mixed with the smell of warm baked bread. It was a deadly combination for my senses.

"What the fuck do you mean you can't say? What do you know that I don't know, Nicola?" I asked, raising my voice, trying to not let her smell or her presence get to me.

"I just know that you need to be careful. Promise you will be careful."

"I can't if you don't tell me about what is going on, Nicola."

She turned to walk away and I chased after her and grabbed her by the arms and spun her around so that she had to face me again. Gripping both of her arms, I held her in place.

"You need to tell me what the fuck is going on. Right now. I have a clinic to keep open. Doctors and families to protect. Did Cardinelli do something to you? I'll fucking kill him if he touched you."

She yanked loose of my grip and took a few steps away from me.

"He didn't touch me. I have to go."

"No, tell me!" I yelled, but it was too late. She was already halfway out the door.

MY MIND RACED with all the possibilities of what could have happened between Nicola and Cardinelli. If I didn't have patients, I would have taken off from work and chased her down and demand that she answered me.

I had just finished with my third appointment of the day when Laura Lee rang my intercom.

"Dr. Gunn?"

"Yes, Laura Lee?"

"Uh, there are several officers from the NYPD here to see you."

Shit!

"I'll be right there, Laura Lee."

With unsteady legs, I walked out to reception to greet the two officers.

"Hello, I'm Dr. Andris Gunn. What can I do for you today?" I asked as I shook each of their hands in greeting.

"Is there some place where we could speak privately?" One of the officers asked. He was tall to where his partner was shorter. They both wore plain clothes and seemed to be in their mid to late forties.

"Of course. We can use my office. Follow me please. Laura Lee, hold all of my calls and please apologize to any patients that may come in and just tell them appointments are running behind."

"Yes, Doctor."

We all three made our way to my office. I couldn't help the unease I felt as Nicola's warning flashed freshly in my mind.

Be careful.

"Have a seat gentlemen. What can I do for you today?"

One of the officers reached for a pad of paper in the breast pocket of his jacket and a pen from the pocket in the front. They both flashed their badges to me to prove who they were.

"Dr. Gunn, do you know an Antonio Cardinelli?" The tall officer asked me as he poised his pen over the top of the pad of paper.

"Of course. Who hasn't heard of him? His wife is a patient of mine."

"Have you now, or have you ever, written any illegal prescriptions to Antonio Cardinelli?"

"What? No."

And it was the truth. I wasn't lying to the officers. I hadn't ever written any prescriptions to him per se, just his goons and his wife."

"We are led to believe that either Cardinelli himself, his wife, or someone who works for him is obtaining your prescription pads and writing out forged prescriptions under your name. Several pharmacies around the area have reported an excess amount of narcotic subscriptions as well as other controlled drugs like those used for ADD and ADHD that looked to be written by you."

"Are any of these your signatures?" The other officer asked as he handed me a stack of what looked like my prescription papers from my pad.

I sorted through the thirteen or so pieces of paper that all had my name on the header. Out of the thirteen, only three contained *my* actual signature.

"These three, yes. The others no."

"Would you be willing to sign your name in front of a notary public to authenticate your signature?"

"Yes, absolutely."

"Have you noticed any of your prescription pads missing?"

I thought back to the other day when I went to write the prescription for my patient Jacob, and I couldn't find the pad in my drawer. I could have sworn that I had more in there, but my head had been in such a fucking fog since Nicola left me, that

I couldn't remember if I had used them all or not. I told the officers as such.

"If you could meet us downtown at the courthouse around two this afternoon, we can go ahead and get your signature authenticated. Do you have any idea who might have taken your prescription pads, Dr. Gunn?"

"No clue. I don't allow patients to be in my office unattended. There is always myself, or another doctor present at all times. This goes for any of the other doctors as well. It is just a practice we have always stuck to. We have people who suffer from serious mental health issues. Leaving them unsupervised wouldn't be a good thing."

"Understood, Dr. Gunn. Here is my card. If you can think of anything, give us a call. We'll see you downtown in a few hours."

"Thank you," I replied as I showed the officers out of the door to my office.

When I returned to my desk, I tried to think about who could have snuck into my office to get those prescription pads. I've never left anyone alone in my office before. No one.

No one except Nicola.

Fuck me.

Nicola/Jericho

I OFFICIALLY HATE FUNERALS. The only one I had attended prior to Kiki's was my own parents. Then, I didn't care. Then, I was all dark and empty and didn't have a reaction as I sat stoically on the bench of that church as the preacher talked about what great friends, family, and parents they were.

Bullshit.

Kiki's was different. The church was nearly vacant except for a few homeless people who came in to try and get out of the cold, me, Lexie, and a handful of the other girls from the agency. Kiki was always known for her snarky and bitchy attitude, so a majority of the girls didn't take much of a liking to her.

Next to me Lexie was a mess, still blaming herself for Kiki's death.

The preacher said a few words about Kiki, but who really wanted to get enthusiastic about celebrating the life of a drug addicted whore? Everyone one went about their business after the funeral and I headed to the café. I had picked up a shift from one of the girls who needed the evening off, and truth be told I needed to keep my mind busy.

I had been sick with worry ever since I had seen Andris a few days ago at the clinic. I was terrified that my actions, although intended to do good and protect him, were actually going to hurt him even more in the long run. There wasn't anything I could do about Cardinelli, and I hadn't heard from or seen him since I found out about Kiki's death. I was pretty sure he was trying to lay low for all of this to blow over before he was back out on the streets, peddling to the next addict.

The café was slow for a Monday afternoon so I kept myself busy by refilling the salt and pepper shakers as well as replenishing the sugar and Splenda packets. I was mindlessly wiping off one of the tables when one of the three televisions in the café showed a breaking news report. I looked up and it caught my attention immediately, pausing me in my tracks. I couldn't believe what I was seeing.

ANTONIO CARDINELLI INDICTED ON DRUG TRAFFICING CHARGES

My heart dropped. I threw the towel down on the table, knocking over an open salt shaker in the process and walked over to be closer to the TV. Reaching up, I adjusted the volume, just so that I could be certain that I could hear what I was seeing.

> *"The overdosing death of a woman late last week, who was positively identified as thirty-one year old Kiki Chestfield of New York City, prompted the instigation leading up to Cardinelli's arrest. When investigators discovered that Chestfield had obtained the prescription pain killers in which sadly took her life, they followed a lead of information that led them to believe that Cardinelli had stolen prescription pads from his psychiatrist Dr. Andris Gunn and was then forging his signature to sell to buyers on the street. When pharmacists began receiving an influx of prescriptions from Dr. Gunn's office, it led police to the clinic where they met with Dr. Gunn. His signature was verified for several of the written prescriptions, but the vast majority of them were written either by Cardinelli himself, or someone employed by him.*
>
> *At this time, Dr. Gunn and the clinic will not receive any charges, but the investigation is still pending as to how Cardinelli obtained the prescription pads.*
>
> *We'll bring you more information as the story develops."*

My hands flew to my mouth as the breath caught in my

chest. Cardinelli was caught. He was caught!

"They finally got thata bastard," Letta said, coming up behind me as she wiped her hands with a towel.

I only nodded, shock apparently keeping me from finding my voice.

"Good. Maybe less drugs on street then. I sorry about your friend," she said, referring to Kiki. Even though Kiki seemed to hold onto a lot of anger, I think she was just looking for someone to confide in. She obviously had other troubles that kept her from allowing people in, and I only wished that I could have offered her some comfort.

Things picked up at the café not long after so I didn't have much time to dwell over the fact that Cardinelli was behind bars. My only fear now was that a full investigation would be launched against Andris and the clinic, then he could possibly go to jail as well. Even if his involvement with Cardinelli was inherited from his uncle.

Andris didn't really commit any wrong doing. Did he write prescriptions to patients that didn't need them? Yes. But how many other doctors in the world did that on a daily basis? Andris obviously was bothered by what he had to do, and if he had any say, I was sure he would have cut Cardinelli off completely.

I still struggled with the fact that Andris lied to me. I felt like I had been torn in two. I was still that one piece of paper that had been shredded down the middle, now I felt that the two pieces that were torn had now withered away. How does one get over not only one broken heart, but two?

My feet and back were aching by the time we got through our mid-afternoon rush of customers. I trudged through the pain to help the others get the diner cleaned up so that we could all take a break before the dinner rush was upon us. I was so busy sweeping up a pile of broken chips a child had spilled on the floor that I didn't even hear the bell ring on the door.

I swept the chips into a dustpan and stood back up and turned around to locate the nearest trash can.

That is when I came face to face with Andris and the dustpan fell to the floor.

CHAPTER TWENTY FOUR

ANDRIS

I HADN'T SEEN HER SINCE the day she came to the clinic to warn me. I wanted to go to Kiki's funeral, not only to pay my respects, but just so that I could see her. But I didn't want to give the police any ammunition to use not only against me, but to incriminate Nicola. I needed to lay low as much as I possibly could so that nothing could be dug up, and Cardinelli would stay behind bars for the rest of his life like he deserved.

God, she was devastatingly beautiful. My heart leaped, my chest seized, and my dick twitched just like it did every time she was in my presence. I missed her. Needed her. So I couldn't wait any longer and decided to see her at the café. I needed to let her know that I *knew*.

"You saw the news report?" I asked as I gestured toward the TV. The café was quiet with only a few people inside, yet I almost felt the need to whisper. It was as if I raised my voice, she would disappear.

"I did earlier this afternoon."

She broke out of her momentarily frozen state of shock by

seeing me and bent down to sweep up the trash she had dropped when she turned around and saw me.

"I wanted to come by and tell you thank you."

"For what?" She asked as she stood up, flipping her blonde ponytail over her shoulder and walking over to empty the dust pan into one of the trash cans.

"For the warning."

"Oh. Well, I just wanted to give you a heads up."

She began to walk away from me and I reached for her, closing my hand around her wrist. I could feel the frantic beat of her heart through her pulse point and it mirrored my own. The skin of my fingers burned where they touched her and it was unlike any fire you could possibly imagine. There was still a connection—a definite spark between us, and I wasn't about to let this slip away.

Was I angry with her for stealing the script pads from me? Hell yes. Not because she actually stole them, but the reason why she stole them. Cardinelli had threatened her with something and she was forced to take them. She never would have done it on her own. I knew she loved me. I saw it in her eyes every time she looked at me. Just like the way I see it now.

I gave her wrist a gentle tug and pulled her closer to me to where we were nearly sharing the same breath. I let go of her wrist and reached up to cup her face in my hands assertively, but with a gentle touch. I needed her to understand and *feel* what I was about to tell her. There would be no wondering of her eyes, only focus on me. I wouldn't have it any other way.

"Nicola, I *know* what you did, and I forgive you."

I leaned in and placed a firm, but gentle kiss on her lips, and then released her before turning around and walking out of the café doors.

NICOLA/JERICHO

I know what you did, and I forgive you.

Andris's words echoed in my mind as I watched him walk away. My feet felt cemented to the floor and my body heavy as the weight of his words came bearing down on me. You always hear about those cliché moments when someone has an epiphany, or the "light bulb" moment when their brain finally goes "aha!" and suddenly everything seems clear.

Well, those nine words from his mouth were my "aha" moment. I had concentrated on the fact that Andris had lied to me about Link for the last week, that I was too angry to actually see it from his side. When I took the script pad from his desk drawer, I did it to protect us. Mainly him, but me as well. If Andris were charged with drug trafficking, I could lose him. Families would be torn when it got out that I was an escort. Did I care in the beginning about all of that? No. Did I now?

Absolutely.

I became a new person the day Andris showed up on my doorstep. My mind was finally able to let go of the darkness inside and allow humanity in.

Andris did what he did to protect something too. His heart. Could I stay mad at the man I loved (yes, I still loved him) when he was only doing the same thing I did?

I made a mad dash out through the café doors, nearly trampling over Letta in the process. The cold air hit me in the face as I ran outside, looking down the sidewalk. I didn't have a jacket on and I was freezing, but I didn't want him to get away.

"Took you long enough," he said, pushing off a wall behind me and approaching me. The smile on his face ignited my insides as he came to stand in front of me. He ran his hands along my arms and chill bumps formed, not only from the cold, but from his touch.

"Excuse me?" I asked, arching my brow at him, "How in the hell did you even know I would come after you?"

He laughed and his head tilted back in the process. He reached for the scarf around his neck and secured it over mine and I was enveloped in the scent of him. I inhaled deeply, praying he didn't see me do it.

"I didn't know. I just hoped. I can't do this anymore, Nicola. I can't go on and keep pretending that I can live my life without you. I can't keep faking my way through my days only to rush home and beg my mind and body to fall asleep so I can finally be with you in my dreams. I'll do anything you want me to, to fix this. To fix us. I need you."

"How did you know it was me? I mean, how did you know I took the script pad?" I asked, lowering my voice slightly just in case there were wandering ears.

"You are the only one I have ever trusted enough to leave alone in my office. Then when you came to the clinic and warned me, I knew something was up. I didn't piece it all together until the police showed me the forged prescriptions and I realized mine were missing."

"Oh."

"Nicola, what you did was stupid, idiotic, and downright dangerous. If you were in trouble with Cardinelli, you should have told me. You should have let me take care of it."

"He was going to expose your involvement with the agency as well as with him. Not only would that affect you, the clinic, your employees, and me, but Lexie and the agency as well. I couldn't let him do that. I'm a pretty tough cookie. I was handling him."

"Promise me, next time you decide to go toe to toe with a crime boss, you tell me first?"

I laughed.

"Sure thing," I replied as I saluted him.

"Now, there's one more thing we need to discuss.

"What would that be?"

"Us. How we are going to move on from all of this shit between us."

I brought my ice-cold finger up to my lips, pretending to contemplate what he was saying.

"I think that can be arranged. I was so angry with you for lying to me, Andris. I want honesty. I want to know you completely. The good and the bad. And also if you don't mind sharing me."

"What? Hell no. There is no fucking way I am sharing you with anyone." He said sternly and with resonation in his voice.

"Not even with Link?"

He smiled.

"Maybe with Link. I hear you have a small crush on him." He said as he pulled me into his arms and enfolded me in his warmth. I breathed a sigh of relief and it felt as if my heart began to beat normally again.

"I love you, and he is a *part* of you."

I tried to move out of his arms, but they only tightened around me more.

"Where do you think you are going?"

"Inside to get warm. My pussy lips are freezing together

out here!"

He laughed and it was beautiful. Just like him. Just like us. We were beautiful together.

"I know of a much faster way to get you warm."

He kissed me fiercely on the lips and grabbed my hand and we took off in a sprint towards his car.

EPILOGUE

It's hot in here.
Too hot.

My body was smoldering and my legs trembled from where they were bound open. Luxurious silk was intricately entwined around my ankles and wrists.

I never grew tired of this. I never felt the flames of my desire diminish even the slightest bit with Andris. If anything, those flames only grew more and more until I was a racing inferno out of control.

It's amazing how within a span of a year, I went from nothing into someone who now enjoys life. I smile. I laugh. And I still get pleasure.

Only now it is from one (sometimes two) men only. Andris lets Link come out to play every so often, and I love it when he does.

Just like now, as I lie naked and completely exposed to him. I could feel his warm breath dance over my clit, enough to let me know he was there, yet not nearly enough to swell the ache that grew by the minute.

"Say it and I'll let you cum."

I smiled from behind my blindfold. He had been playing this game with me for several long minutes now. As much as I was enjoying the torture he was going through, the torture he was putting me through was nearly unbearable.

His strong hands massaged my thighs as he leaned in and took one, long luxurious swipe up my center and paused on my clit before he pulled back again.

"You don't fight fair," I said as my breathing increased. I felt like a rubber band that was being stretched to the max. All it would take would be a release of his fingers or tongue to send me spiraling through the air.

"I never promised to fight fair. I only promised to give you an orgasm every day for the rest of your life, but you have to say it first."

"Fine! Yes. I will marry you!"

"That's my girl," I felt his smile through his lips on my pussy. Andris's lips assaulted my cunt to the point I was coming in only a matter of seconds. And when he unbound me and removed my blindfold, we stared straight into each other's eyes as we made love.

They say love can move mountains. That it can power through all things. It is one of the strongest feelings in the world. It can help you overcome obstacles and it can heal. Love saved me from out of a darkness no one should ever have to experience. Love helped Andris overcome his own demons. Love brought us together. Even though I still had a hard time processing and understanding certain feelings, there was one thing I definitely knew. I was no longer VOID. I was now FILLED.

THE END

SOMETIMES ITS HARD TO MAKE THE SHIFT
FROM CONTROL TO SURRENDER.

the celtic knot series
BY CASSY ROOP

Available on Amazon.com and other book retailers

Made in the USA
Charleston, SC
26 February 2015